# PITAURA

## Arrival

James Tepsey

The characters and events portrayed in this book are fictitious. Any similarity to real persons, living or dead, is coincidental and not intended by the author.

*To my dear friend Gaius, thanks for reading all those endless rewrites.*

# Prologue

“During my convalescence, I desired to meet you again to convey this message: Initially, I may have seemed cold and detached. However, I was driven by a strict directive that I felt compelled to follow. Obedience was of utmost importance then, and in many ways, it still is. Since then, a transformation has occurred within me, largely influenced by individuals like yourself.

Since our paths crossed, my knowledge has greatly expanded, especially after my second unsuccessful transfer. It was like a fracture in my cognitive framework, revealing hidden emotions. Emotions that were buried deep within me longed to be set free. I have experienced a range of emotions joy, guilt, happiness, and sorrow. I have come to understand the importance of caring for others, and above all, I have felt traces of that elusive emotion as I witnessed their expressions of love.

It's like trying to see the bigger picture from just a sliver - a single beam reflected in a shard of a mirror. But now, I yearn to experience more.

So, I just wanted to let you know...”

# Chapter 1

## The Arrival

Joseph woke to the sound of tinnitus ringing in his ears. He opened his eyes slowly and looked around, trying to figure out his location.

He found himself lying on his back surrounded by tall grasses. The last thing he remembered was a chair suddenly launching itself at him. *How did that happen? What happened to the facility? How did I get outside?*

He sat up a little too quickly, grimacing as he rubbed his knees and shifted his legs. After brushing dirt from off his clothes, he surveyed his surroundings. Apart from an unusually coloured sky, he couldn't see much, as seedheads obstructed his view. He had no idea how he had arrived there, nor what time of day it was, he just sat for a while, feeling confused. He attempted to recall his previous actions, muttering to himself as he did so.

"I was in the control room with Ella-May. I had the radio in my hand. She pressed the emergency shutdown button as we were instructed. The criticality alarms didn't stop, and then... then a chair attacked me!"

# 2

He touched his forehead – *Ouch, I... that flipping chair was vicious*. Retreating his hand from his forehead, he examined it carefully. The once unblemished skin now bore the evidence of the encounter, coated with partially congealed blood that was both sticky and disconcerting. His initial impulse to wipe it away was swift, but as his hand made contact with the light fabric of his trouser leg, it left behind an unmistakable crimson smear.

He gazed at his hands, comparing the colour difference between them. His double-vision kept shifting from his hands to the ground. The ringing in his ears persisted, and he grumbled as he put his bloodless hand to his ear. That's when he realised his hearing aid was missing. He frantically searched for it on the ground, as if he had lost a precious piece of gold jewellery.

*Calm yourself, you are panicking. Go through your exercises. You need to remain calm...*

He closed his eyes and inhaled. He exhaled slowly, focusing on the sensation of the air leaving his lungs and the tension leaving his body. He felt calmer, his mind clearing a little, and his vision sharpening.

He resumed searching the ground, as if his search pattern had been practiced for years. After finding the hearing aid, he picked it up, holding it up like the one ring. Blowing moisture out of the earpiece, he placed it into his ear. A thin smile formed on his face but quickly faded away when he realised the tinnitus had not stopped. He sighed in reserved frustration. *Typical! Battery's dead and I have no spares...*

Joseph attempted to stand, his muscles tensing as he braced his hands against the unforgiving ground, his movements laboured and unsteady. As he struggled to his feet, he couldn't help but feel a sense of panic setting in again, enveloping his mind like a shadow. He was in a different location, he had lost his hearing aid, and after finding it again, it was not working. Inhaling deeply, he closed his eyes for a moment, attempting to tame the rapid cadence of his breath. A mantra formed in his mind, a self-assured whisper in the face of chaos: *It's just a stupid hearing aid. A distraction. You need to figure out what's going on.* The words echoed, both a reminder and a challenge, a lifeline to clarity amid the swirling storm of uncertainty.

Joseph surveyed the landscape, searching for a familiar landmark or some clue as to his location. Disorientation washed over him; he had no idea how he ended up in this unfamiliar place. The meadow stretched out for miles, with tall grass swaying in a gentle breeze and wildflowers peeking out from between the tufts, adding pops of colour to the sea of yellowish green. The open plains were dotted with the occasional shrub, and a dense forest loomed in the near distance, its dark canopy hiding secrets within. In the far distance beyond the meadow, misty mountains rose, their peaks lost in the clouds. Since Joseph did not recognise any of these landmarks, he focused on the present moment and tried to come up with a plan.

As he stood swaying in sync with the tall grass, the thought of the missing radio came to his mind. As he intended to search for it, he heard a moan. Turning his head, he saw the dreaded office chair hiding amidst the tufts, stalking him. Reflexively, he touched his forehead, half-expecting the chair to spring to life again. He hesitated for a moment, his heart racing as he recalled the last time he had encountered this cursed piece of office furniture. He approached it slowly, his focus fixed on nothing but the chair. As he got closer, it moaned at him. “Ugh. Oh, my ankle.”

He stopped approaching and tilted his head, hearing the moan again. *Hold on, that’s not the chair moaning, there’s someone else here with me!* “Ella-May, is that you? Are you alright?”

Joseph struggled to follow the faint moaning, moving his head around to locate the sound. Eventually, he found Ella-May sitting in a daze, clutching her ankle amidst the tall grass.

“Here, let me help you.”

He dragged the offending chair over and helped Ella-May onto it. She mumbled incoherently as he did so, and he placed a reassuring hand on her shoulder, hoping for a coherent response. "Ella-May, can you hear me? What happened to your ankle?"

Ella-May moaned with partially open eyes as he examined her swollen ankle. Unfortunately, he squeezed it a little too hard, causing her to groan in pain. When she opened her eyes fully, she looked down at him with a pained expression and said, "I had a little fall."

From his crouched position, Joseph stood up, steadying himself on the back of the chair. He knew that the best place for Ella-May was a hospital, but out here, where would he find such a place? He hadn't noticed any signs of civilisation nearby. *Next best thing is to go and find help...*

"I don't think your ankle is broken," he said, looking down at Ella-May's swollen ankle. "But we need to find something to bind it. I'm going to get help. Please try not to move."

Ella-May grabbed his arm. "Don't leave me."

Joseph gently tapped her hand, "I promise, I'll come right back—"

As he spoke, her eyes rolled backwards, and she started mumbling incoherently. He shook her gently. "Ella-May, are you with me? I need you to stay awake. Can you try to stay awake for me?"

After a moment, she opened her eyes and rested her head back on the chair. "Where are we?"

Joseph glanced across the horizon. "No idea, but we'll figure it out together. I'm going now. Try to focus on something, I need you to stay awake. There, look at those strange cloud formations, tell me what you see." With those words, he turned away, taking his first steps toward his intended destination.

"A rabbit," her words floated on the breeze, a whispered declaration of her perceptions. But as if revisiting her thoughts, she corrected herself, a touch of wonder infusing her voice, "No, not a rabbit, a horse."

The gap between them widened as he ventured further. And then, like an unexpected echo in his good ear, her voice reached him once more, its cadence almost dreamlike. "A giant red bird," she murmured, the words an enigmatic puzzle in the expanse.

Joseph stopped walking and turned back. He saw Ella-May sitting there drawing an outline with her finger around the mauve cloud formations. *Giant red bird? She's obviously delirious, it's obviously a dolphin.*

Joseph shook his head, dizziness and a dull ache reminding him of his situation – *Humm, maybe I'm delirious too, better find help quickly...*

Crossing the meadow, the dense forest dog-legged as Joseph followed its edge, revealing to him a clear view of the mountain range in the distance. He walked a few more steps then stopped. At his feet a piece of debris he had spotted was embedded into the dirt. He picked it up and inspected it. *A bottle of eyewash, interesting. The same variety used in the staff changing rooms. Maybe there's a first aid kit around here too?*

Guiltily tossing the bottle on the ground, he was about to move on when he noticed some people in the distance, one of whom he recognised. He began frantically waving his arms hoping to catch their attention. "Hey! Guys! Guys, I need your help!"

He placed two fingers in his mouth and blew a shrill whistle. Yet, the group continued its relentless advance, seemingly unaffected by his efforts to halt their progress. He wondered if he should go after them, but then he glanced back at the path he had traversed. *Damn,* he chastised himself, his inner voice a blend of disappointment and frustration. *I promised I'd come right back...*

Continuing his search for a first aid kit, he spat on the ground, disliking the metallic taste in his mouth. He briefly considered retrieving the eyewash he had dropped, but ultimately decided to press on. He imagined a salty gargle would taste better than dry blood, but he didn't want to waste any more time.

A few meters ahead, Joseph's face lit up with a broad smile as he spotted a medicine cabinet. The cabinet was trapped under a coat rack among other debris, but after removing all the lab coats, he was able to drag the rack out of the way and access the cabinet. Intrigued to find the mirror glass door intact, he rummaged through the cabinet and pulled out boxes of small plasters and countless packets of antiseptic wipes, until he finally found what he was searching for: a green medical case filled with bandages.

As he turned to head back the way he had come, he suddenly stopped and stared at the treeline. A sense of unease crept over him, and he called out, "Is someone there?" As the resonance of his unanswered call and the internal ringing in his ears mingled, Joseph began to doubt himself. *Either I'm delirious, or I'm being watched.* He watched back for a moment longer, but thoughts of Ella-May waiting anxiously for his return crossed his mind.

Returning to Ella-May, he knelt beside her. Taking care to avoid jostling her injured ankle, he began to wrap a bandage around it. She was still gazing up at the clouds, her eyes flitting, and her expression dazed. He spoke gently, trying to bring her back to reality. “Ella-May, how are you feeling?”

At the sound of his voice, she snapped out of her reverie and looked down at him, her eyes widening in shock. “The reactor must have exploded! We're—”

She paused, noticing the wound on his head, her brow furrowing with concern. “Oh, you're injured. Give me that packet. I need to clean that up.”

*Good, she’s coming around.* Joseph smiled and handed her the bandages. “Yes, you’re sitting on the offending article, the villainous chair from the control room.”

As Ella-May mopped Joseph's forehead and wrapped the bandage around his head, he explained, “The reactor didn't explode. If it had, neither of us would be alive. I believe the reactor overloaded, but we managed to shut it down safely.” Ella-May tightened the bandage, causing him to wince and gasp briefly. Joseph held up a finger to finish his explanation, “The overload must have caused a huge magnetic pulse, which would explain how the chair and other objects began flying around.”

Ella-May tied the bandage off. She frowned as she looked him in the face. “Um, and this place. How did we get here? Where is here?”

He bowed his head, gripping the arm of the chair as he knelt there. “That's a good question. What do you remember before this?”

Ella-May peered into the distance as if replaying the series of events in her mind. “Pressing the button, nothing happening, then blank,” she said, shrugging. Joseph stood and she looked up at him, a silent expression on her face that seemed to ask, “How about you?”

Joseph shook his head, trying to recall events from before their actions in the control room. “No, I mean before that. We were all in the observation room, we saw those people, and—”

“Those mercenaries! You don’t think they brought us here, do you?” She asked, looking around.

Joseph stared at the treeline again, his eyes narrowing, saying nothing of his suspicions.

“You do, don’t you?”

His lips thinned as he turned his attention back to the woman. “If those people did bring us here, they did it to cover their tracks, making it look like an accident and placing the witnesses far from the scene.” He waved his hand over the meadow, as if he were the opening act of a stage show. “There's debris from the facility scattered all over the place, but there's something very telling: no construction materials, only stuff that's relatively easy to move."

Ella-May didn't seem entirely convinced, but she didn't offer an alternative explanation. "So, you think they staged all of this to cover their tracks? Sounds almost plausible." She gestured wildly as she played out the scenario in her head. "We were both knocked unconscious – you by a flying chair and me by who-knows-what. Then some ruthless mercenaries bundled us into a van, along with a bunch of office furniture, and dumped us here." She dropped her arms sighing.

"So, what now?"

Joseph peered up. "Well, we can't stay here. Look at that sky, it'll be dark soon. I know your ankle hurts, but we need to move from here. We should try catch up with the others."

"The others, what others? catch them where?" She pivoted in the chair giving her take on the area. "Forest; probably full of grizzly bears. Meadow; full of snakes and lizards, and oh look, Mount Everest. Are you gonna carry me over there, old timer?"

Joseph laughed. Her sarcasm was refreshing, and it told him she was now fully cognisant. *I'll give you 'old timer'...*

“If I have to carry you all the way up those mountains, that's what I'll do, you cheeky girl,” Joseph quipped. “Anyway, I saw that chap with some others,” he continued, placing his hands up to mimic the man's actions. “You know, the one taking those photos. The group didn't hear me calling, but they were headed in the direction of the mountains. I reckon they're trying to find help, like the police or a ranger station.”

Ella-May’s eyes narrowed. “You mean Theo Clarke,” she said, shaking her head, “That sort of thing wouldn’t happen on my watch. How the hell did he get a camera past security?”

Joseph helped Ella-May stand, placing his arm around her. “I’ve no idea, but we can debate that as we walk. Come on, let’s go.”

While walking across the meadow towards the mountains, Ella-May shared her expert opinion on how security could have been improved at the facility. Her expertise shone through as Joseph listened to her without interruption.

After about an hour of talking while traipsing through the long grass, they finally arrived at a flattened area. It was clear that people had been there before them, as crisp and snack packets littered the area. They also noticed a track leading off toward their intended destination, in addition to the flattened grass. Ella-May asked Joseph if they could take a moment to rest, to which he agreed, noticing her struggling with the pain in her ankle. They now sat on clumps of grass, trying to catch their breath.

"It's a good thing Mr. Clark did have that camera," Joseph said between laboured breaths. "Maybe he caught some photos of those mercs. That would be useful evidence to show the authorities."

"True. All we need to do is find him, hope he still has that camera, and get it to the police."

Joseph watched as Ella-May scratched at the top of her bandage. *Stubborn determination, that one. Although, I guess you do need to be tough to work in the security business. Perhaps she should have waited while I went off to get help...*

"I'm sorry," he said.

She stopped scratching and peered at him. "Sorry about what?"

"Sorry I couldn't find you any painkillers."

Ella-May shrugged. "I don't like taking painkillers. This is nothing – I'm fine, let's just carry on."

He studied her face for a second, then stood. *She's in pain but doesn't want to show it – Stubborn determination...*

As they trudged on, the slight breeze that had been blowing when they set off had now stopped. Little beads of sweat ran down Joseph's temples and cheeks, and he could feel Ella-May's weight becoming increasingly heavy as she leaned on him. He regretted insisting on half-carrying her, wishing he had made a stretcher or something more practical. *Always the hero...*

His tongue skimmed over parched lips, his mouth a barren landscape devoid of moisture. A ragged exhale escaped, a whispered testament to the arid state within him. "Phew, I could do with that pint right now."

"Huh?" Ella-May asked, glancing quizzically sideways.

"Sorry, I was thinking of that pub at the foot of those mountains. That wonderful thought is keeping me going."

Motioning at a pile of debris, Ella-May suggested they stop for a rest. It was then that she noticed something familiar, pointing to it in the near distance. "You might be in luck. Is that a vending machine? Those mercs really did go to town, didn't they?"

With a single burst of energy, Joseph walked over to the machine. His anticipation evaporated like his sweat when he saw that the glass door was shattered. He peered inside and sighed loudly. *Nothing in there but bitter disappointment…*

“What is it?” Ella-May called out.

“My coffin by the looks of it, it’s empty,” he scoffed, “Nought but wrappers. Someone’s had a chocolate fest here without us.”

She hobbled over to where he stood looking longingly into the guts of the empty machine. “Not even a single Num Num bar!” she said, following his gaze.

She shook her head and moved away. “Another good reason to find the others. If they raided this machine, hopefully they have something left for us, I’m starving. How long do you think we’ve been walking now?”

Joseph looked up at the sky again, several creases appearing on his exposed forehead. “I had expected it to get dark by now, but the sky hasn’t really changed.” He looked at the invisible watch on his arm. “I guess we’ve been walking, what, three hours?”

Ella-May nodded. “About right. My stomach is telling me it's dinner time. Last time I ate was in the visitor centre for lunch, how about you?”

Thoughts of the visitor centre came to his mind. Reminders of the food selection, or general lack thereof, causing him to tut loudly. *There was food?*

“Didn’t have much to eat in there. I don’t find synthomeat appealing at all.”

“No, nor me. Give me a real burger any day.”

Leaving the sorry carcass of a vending machine, they continued to walk across the vast meadow. The mention of food had motivated them to renew their efforts, as they had been walking for hours. The prospect of finally catching up to the others and getting something to eat was too tempting to resist.

As they walked, the mountains in the distance came into clearer focus. Rocky outcrops ran along their sides, with alternating shades of soot and ash running to the peaks. Toward the highest peak, a cap of snow occasionally peeked out from behind the clouds.

While studying the landscape and trying to determine their location, Joseph suddenly noticed something that caught his attention. Stopping in their tracks, they fixed their eyes on a sight in the distance. At first, it was hard to make out, but as they squinted and tried to get a better look, Ella-May confirmed - it was a small group of people.

Joseph's heart raced with excitement at the prospect of finally catching up to the others and getting some much-needed food and assistance.

In his excitement, Joseph spoke up. "Finally, we've found civilisation. Hopefully one of them has a phone we can borrow."

Ella-May looked doubtful and shook her head as she gingerly moved forward hobbling. "Doubt it. If they are from the research facility, they won't have any phones. They aren't allowed inside, remember?"

Joseph nodded. "Yeah, I know, I was just being hopeful—"

As he spoke and moved, he suddenly fell over, kicking something hard hidden in the grass. Ella-May, still holding his arm, almost fell with him but managed to let go just in time. "Careful, Gramps. Watch where you're going. You almost took me with you."

He attempted to retort with a witty reply but was left speechless as the fall had knocked the wind out of him. Gasping for air and struggling to rise, his attention shifted to the object that had tripped him. Reaching into the tuft, he pulled on the object, which was tightly woven into the grass. After exerting some force, he managed to extract it and stood up. "I'll be more careful next time."

Ella-May grinned while looking at the object in his hands. “What’s that?”

Joseph turned the small rectangular box in his hands noting its aged bronze colouring and green domed cap at its centre. “It’s heavy, whatever it is.”

“Actually,” he continued, a note of revelation lacing his voice, “it looks like it could be an old Nibbs storage device.” His words hung in the air, carrying a hint of nostalgia and technological evolution. A touch of wistfulness coloured his tone, a hint of reminiscence. “Of course, these days,” he added, a touch of rueful amusement underscoring his words, “they’re about the size of a matchbox.”

Ella-May’s grin widened. “What’s a matchbox?”

As Joseph raised an eyebrow, she asked, revealing her true understanding, “What do you think a NAS box is doing buried out here in the grass?” Ella-May began looking around, her eyes darting to the forest perimeter in the distance, mumbling under her breath.

Joseph turned so that his left side faced her then asked she repeat what she had just said.

“Do you suppose this belongs to those mercenaries? Maybe they lost it somehow,” she repeated, her eyes widening. “Perhaps it contains surveillance recordings.”

He caught her meaning that time. “Who knows? It's possible, but I think it’s been here for a while. In any case, we should keep it. If it does belong to them, we can add it to our evidence.” Then a wry smile appeared on his otherwise stern face, “And if it doesn't, it'll make a great doorstop.”

Ella-May nodded in agreement, returning his smile. “Yeah, you're right. Let's keep it. Here, I’ll stick it in my bag, as you’re gonna have your hands full.”

Joseph grinned at the young woman. After handing over the device, he offered her his arm asking, “Shall we?”

# Chapter 2

## The Camp

Joseph and Ella-May laboured on following the flattened trail. A few meters further, they emerged from the dreaded long grass into a flat, open area. Across the way, they saw three people standing around what appeared to be an unlit campfire. The people had not noticed their gradual approach, appearing to be absorbed in conversation.

Joseph surveyed the area ahead of the people: dirt, rock, and shrubbery. There were no signs of a pub, no park benches, nor any comfy places to sit. He sighed and continued onward with his carry in tow.

As the people came into clear view, Ella-May recognised the only man in the group. “That’s Brent, head of security. He interviewed me this morning,” she said.

Joseph squinted his eyes. “Good,” he said, recognising the name, “Maybe Mr. Hinks knows what's going on.”

He stopped walking and took a deep breath with Ella-May by his side, preparing to call out for help. Before he could utter a word, a cloud of dust filled his lungs, causing him to cough loudly. The echo of his cough bounced off the mountain walls, instantly drawing the attention of the people nearby who all turned their heads in unison towards the source of the noise.

On seeing him half-carrying Ella-May the burly head of security came bounding over. “Here, please let me help you,” Brent said. Brent placed his arm around Ella-May and carefully took her from off Joseph.

Joseph followed them to the camp where he saw makeshift seats made from rocks and clumps of moss and dirt. Fatigue lines were written across his face as he looked longingly at the seats. *Just pretend it's a very short bar stool...*

Sitting down with a long groan, Joseph watched as Brent tended to Ella-May's injured leg. He poured water from a bottle over her ankle, causing it to seep through the bandages and wet the ground. Joseph couldn't help but lick his dry, parched lips as he watched the water flow.

Sitting there, gulping like a goldfish, Brent passed him the remnants of the water bottle. Joseph eagerly took the bottle and began to drink deeply.

“Are there others with you?” Brent asked.

Joseph wiped his mouth. “Thanks,” he said, lifting the bottle like an award. “No. Just us. But –”

He wanted to explain his feelings of being watched, but in the corner of his eye he noticed someone looming over next to him, and he turned. A woman was frantically waving her index finger in the air, trying to draw his attention. As he faced her, he noticed it was the scientist, Mary Glover, and she looked angry.

“YOU, you did this!”

*Great. That’s the last thing I need right now, a confrontation.* Behind him he heard Brent say, “give it a rest Mary.” But the woman ignored him, so Joseph put his hands up in what he hoped was a placating manner.

“Look, Miss Glo—”

“Doctor, actually,” she snapped.

Joseph lowered his hands and dropped his shoulders. “Look, Dr. Glover. I’m hungry and I’m tired. What exactly are you accusing me of?”

Ignoring his plea for rest, she continued her tirade. “I thought that was obvious. You didn’t follow my instructions. You couldn’t have. You didn’t shutdown the reactor properly and this is the result.” She said, waving her arms around as if preparing to take off.

Joseph looked up at his accuser. Young, ambitious, pretty. *I'm sure if she weren't so angry, she could be quite a nice person...*

He intensified his gaze on the scientist. “Dr. Glover, I can assure you that we followed your direct instructions. We pressed the big red button labelled 'Emergency Shutdown', but nothing happened. Was there something else we should have done?”

He could imagine cogs turning in the woman's skull as he waited for her response. Eventually she admitted, “erm. No. I guess not. But you must have done something to cause all this.”

As he formulated a reply, he was pleased to be handed a chocolate bar. He fumbled away at the wrapper, all the while thinking what words he could use to appease the ever-indignant Doctor Glover with her scapegoat theories.

He bit into the chocolate bar, savouring the crunch of nuts and the rich dark chocolate flavour. Munching loudly, he purposely let the sound fill the air as he ate. Swallowing, he felt a sense of satisfaction wash over him for finally being able to eat after all his effort. Feeling renewed, he looked up at Mary and confidently asked, “Tell me, what key piece of technology was being used to keep the M.E.T.A project stable?”

Mary took on a smug expression. “The fusion reaction is stabilised using a polaron absorption core. Everyone knows that, it’s public knowledge.”

He saw Ella-May and Brent look at each other and shrug. He nodded and smiled slightly. *Good, let’s test her further…* “Is it public knowledge that the stabilisation core is also known as CP795?”

Mary spluttered, looked around, then put a hand up to her mouth and leaned toward Joseph. “How did you—That’s a secret, we’re not meant to talk about that,” she said.

Ella-May also leant forward, a half-chewed snack bar in her hand. She waved it about, aiming it at Mary. “What’s CP795?”

“It’s a crystal,” came a voice from behind them all.

Everyone turned to the woman who had largely been ignored on Joseph and Ella-May’s arrival. Mary snapped at her. “That’s not meant to be public knowledge either!”

The woman seemed unfazed by Mary’s outburst and simply returned to what she had been doing: picking flower heads off pieces of heather. Joseph clapped his hands together, drawing Mary’s attention back to him.

“Someone knew exactly what they were after,” he said, then turned to Ella-May. “Ms. Moyer, please describe to Dr. Glover what we saw from the observation room.”

After finishing her snack bar and disposing of the wrapper in her bag, Ella-May shared with the group all the things they had observed while in the observation room. During her explanation, Joseph noticed that Mary was paying close attention and not interrupting. *Good, she’s beginning to understand the situation.* He could see the wheels in her mind turning again as her breathing became shallow and she stared past him and.

Mary stood silently, her dark brown eyes shifting about as she considered the evidence. “The mercenaries were after the CP795 sample,” she concluded. “If they removed the stabiliser core from the torus and reset reactor control, it's possible that the reactor reignited and caused an overload. Such an overload could have rendered us all unconscious.” She turned away from everyone, peering across the meadowlands. “If the mercenaries had made their way outside the building, they would have been shielded from the majority of the fallout. After, they returned inside and removed us, the only witnesses to their mischievous acts.”

After her conclusion she spun back around. Addressing Brent she said, “we must continue with your plan. We must get to the top of Yr Wyddfa, find the café and alert the authorities."

"Your wiffer?" Ella-May asked, contorting her face.

"Yes. Brent is convinced this is Eryri national park." Mary pointed to the nearby mountain. "That is Yr Wyddfa. That's where we're heading, up there. At the top of the hiking trail is a visitor centre."

Brent stepped forward beside Mary. "I once came here on holiday as a kid my first time outside of London," he said. Panning his head around, he motioned with his hand. "The landscape really made an impression on me back then, and it hasn't changed a bit. I'm certain this is Snowden." He pointed to a nearby trail running up the mountain. "That's the hikers' path to the summit. At the top, there's a visitor centre with a train station. That's where we'll find help." Joseph observed Brent's confidence in their location and listened as he described his childhood holiday in Snowden.

While Brent spoke, two men came into view from the direction of the forest. Joseph couldn't quite see in the dim light what they were carrying, but they were both dragging something behind them. Brent noticed them too. "Ah, good. That'll be Jimmy and Theo returning with the firewood," he said.

Mary's face looked distinctly confused as she questioned, "Firewood? So, we're not going up the mountain trail now?" Brent's expression grew serious, his lips thinned, and he shook his head. Joseph could see the frustration in his body language, and could only imagine how Brent must be feeling, having worked in the same building as Mary for over a decade.

"No. As I explained before, it would take at least another two to three hours to reach the top. Look, it's already starting to get dark." Brent gestured to Joseph and Ella-May, "Besides, these two need to rest, and Ella-May has an injured ankle."

Mary insisted, "Well, she can wait here while we go to get help, can't she?" Brent stood firm, "No, Mary. We are stopping here for the night. It's what everyone agreed. If you wish to go, no one will stop you, but you'll be doing it alone, understood?"

For the first time since Joseph had met the woman, Mary remained silent. She flung herself down next to Joseph, crossed her arms, and didn't say another word.

The two men, each dragging a bush behind them, entered the edge of the camp. Theo, the man Joseph recognised as sneaking a camera into the research facility, was leaning forward with both arms behind his back, clinging to a branch. The other man was dragging two bushes, each one placed upon his hips, with his hands interlocked in front of him. Joseph studied the man. *Jimmy? Not someone I recognise. Maybe he's a local helping out?*

Joseph stood up as the men came near. He stepped past Theo and straight up to Jimmy. “Do you know this area? Are you from around here?”

Jimmy dropped the bushes next to the ring of rocks that had been prepared for the campfire. He reached out to shake Joseph's hand as if he already knew him. Although the feeling wasn't mutual, Joseph nonetheless accepted the man's handshake. Jimmy's hand was rough, very warm, and he had a strong grip.

“I know Snowdonia, but I’m not from there,” the man admitted, then introduced himself, “I’m Jimmy. I subcontract for Tassy at the facility.”

Wrong accent. Not a local. Much is the shame. Joseph smiled. *That’s how he knows who I am. The history of Cadwell is required reading in the induction…*

“Nice to meet you, Jimmy. I'm Joseph, mechanic, twice retired,” he said, with a wink. Then, he turned to acknowledge the man munching something irritatingly loud in his ear. “Mr. Clark, we meet again, and I see you're still eating.”

Theo put a red object into his mouth and bit down, producing a loud crunch. “Jimmy said these flowers were edible and that gorse makes good firewood,” he explained before offering one of the red flowers to Joseph. “They taste like coconut, try one.” Joseph declined, as eating wildflowers did not appeal to him. Jimmy politely ended their conversation, wanting to make the best use of the remaining available light, and took Theo to prepare the fire by breaking up the branches they had collected.

Joseph returned to his perch and watched as Jimmy expertly split the gorse bush into smaller pieces, neatly organising the firewood into stacks by size. A wide smile spread across Joseph's face, pleased with the orderly arrangement of lumber.

As Jimmy and Theo worked on building a fire, Joseph noticed two more figures approaching the camp. He recognised them from the observation room. Matheson was making his way down the mountain trail, while Nicci was approaching from the base of the mountain. Joseph observed that all the VIP guests were now present, along with a few other staff members from the research facility.

As they joined the group, Matheson was carrying several full bin liners, which made him look like a litter picker. Joseph couldn't help but smile to himself as he watched him approach, the bags rustling with each step he took.

“I found a cave about a kilometre up the track,” said Matheson as he swung the bin liners parallel to the ground, placing them down. “It was full of these fluffy seed heads. I'm not sure what you call ‘em here in the UK.”

Joseph looked at the piles of fluff spilling from the liners. “It looks like Old Man’s Beard.”

Mary stuck her head forward. “Clematis vitalba. Or, if we were in the Rockies, you might call it Anemone Occidentalis.” She sat back and resumed crossing her arms, falling back into silence.

“Well, whatever it is, that’s your pillow for the night. Not enough up there for a mattress, and the cave is too small for all of us to sleep in.” Matheson counted around. “’Specially not for nine people, plus it’s damp.”

“Did you see anyone up there?” Joseph asked, already anticipating the answer.

Matheson shook his head. “Nope, no one. I didn’t see a single person.”

Nicci, standing beside him added, “there’s nuffin’ out there. I walked for miles. I didn’t see anyone either.” She crossed over her wrists in front of her, then swiped them apart again. “No roads, no buildings, nuffin’. What’s even weirder, I haven’t heard any animals. No birds signing, no insects chirping, none of that.”

Based on their reports, the gathered survivors' hushed conversations dwindled to silence, their senses attuned to the ambient sounds of the surrounding wilderness. Amidst the stillness, the faint symphony of nature failed to materialise. Instead, the air was punctuated by the methodical friction of two sticks being rubbed together, intermingled with laboured breathing, a telltale sign of exertion emanating from the heart of the encampment.

Amid this soundscape, Theo's voice rose, a distinct contrast to the prevailing stillness. “Oo, oo, you almost had it then. Oh.” His words carried a buoyant energy, a stark divergence from the tension that seemed to blanket the rest of the group.

As daylight continued to dwindle, resignation settled upon the survivors like a heavy cloak. The unspoken acknowledgment spread like a ripple, binding them to the reality of spending the night in the cast of the mountain. Swiftly, they embarked on the task of preparing for rest, an impromptu assembly line of creation and arrangement.

Plant fibres were plumped, moss collected, and hay gathered, all orchestrated with a sense of unpractised choreography. Black plastic pillows emerged from raw materials, and a patch of ground was diligently cleared, a place of respite prepared amidst the uncertainty. Even as they nestled into their makeshift beds, their collective gaze seemed drawn to the campfire, expectant for its warmth and glow.

Amidst the disorganised symphony of settling, Joseph found his own place by carving out a small enclave in the stony ground. To make himself comfortable, he used his bin liner as a makeshift cushion, propping himself against his pint-sized stool.

As Joseph settled, he noticed Jimmy struggling to ignite the kindling, a stubborn determination on his face as he raced against the dwindling light.

A frustrated exclamation broke the air, punctuated by the thud of a discarded stick. Swift as a retriever chasing a ball, Theo dutifully fetched the fallen object, a fleeting amusement dancing in his eyes. The errant stick was returned, a silent exchange, as Jimmy snatched it out of his hands.

With a contemplative expression, Theo disengaged from the fire-building endeavour, returning to Joseph's vicinity. The rustling of a backpack was audible as he unearthed an object, its form concealed by obscurant twilight. *Bit late with a torch,* Joseph mused internally, *assuming the batteries are even working...*

Silently, Theo approached Jimmy, extending the object behind the man. With the subdued flicker of a flame illuminating the area, Jimmy dropped the kindling in his hands, turning to glare up at Theo. Jimmy's features were etched in a cascade of amber glow and shadow, his expression revealing ripening emotions. Though profanities hovered on the cusp of audibility, their essence was captured in the furrow of his brow and the shaping of his mouth, all aimed at the bumbling man with the lighter.

In the morning, Joseph woke up to a light mist hovering above the ground. He brushed small droplets of dew off his blazer as he sat up. Theo and the heather-plucker were already awake and conversing by the smouldering campfire. Joseph stood up, popping his joints as he did so. Although he initially intended to remind himself of the woman's name, he went to check on Ella-May instead upon hearing her voice.

“How’s the ankle this morning?” He asked, approaching.

Ella-May removed the bandage from her injured ankle and was relieved to find that the swelling had completely disappeared with no signs of bruising or redness. She attributed her speedy recovery to the water that Brent had poured on her.

Just then, Nicci hurried over to them with a look of surprise on her face. She mentioned seeing a giant red bird during the night that she initially thought was a dream. Yet, she had seen it again that morning. Joseph raised his eyebrows as Ella-May pointed out that Nicci's sighting confirmed that she had not been hallucinating, as Joseph had earlier suggested.

Mary, listening to one side, laughed at the idea of a magical red bird. “What red bird?” she asked. She stood holding a pair of glasses, wiping them vigorously on the sleeve of her lab coat. “Fortunately, I haven't seen any wildlife around here.”

Nicci explained her initial struggle to sleep, indicating where she had lain and how something had woken her up during the night. As she spoke, she glanced towards the forest, and Joseph following her gaze, nodded in agreement. “It certainly feels like something has been watching us,” he said. Nicci went on to describe how after waking, she had seen a giant red bird hovering near Ella-May's feet, initially believing it to be a dream, but now adamant it was real.

Mary scoffed at the idea of a giant red bird. “A bird appearing in the middle of the night and endowing magical healing powers? Pah!”

When Joseph looked at Nicci, he could tell from her expression that she was not implying what Mary thought. Despite this, she refrained from answering the slur. Mary Glover's scrutiny could not be easily appeased.

When both Ella-May and Nicci went on to describe the bird's appearance, Mary became more serious. Nicci described it as a red macaw with black on its head, while Ella-May mentioned its eagle-like wings and unusual size as it soared across the sky. Mary then put her glasses into her top pocket and said, “Psittacidae.”

Nicci's face turned to confusion. “Huh?”

“Psittacidae is the scientific name for parrots,” Mary explained. “It's quite unusual for a bird like that to be found in this region, let alone one that is entirely red with black on its head. It's possible that it's a rare genetic mutation or an entirely new species.”

As if on cue, a loud squawk shattered the ambient silence. The sound reverberated between the mountain and the forest. In unison, the group turned their heads, their eyes widening as they searched for the mythical bird.

“If that bird is nesting up there in those mountains, I'm going to be the first one to grab a photo of it,” Nicci declared. She then ran over to Theo, with the others following her.

As Joseph approached the group gathered around the now extinguished campfire, he saw Brent engrossed in deep discussion with the others. Joseph caught snippets of their conversation, which included concerns about injuries and proper clothing for climbing up the mountain trail. Jimmy seemed hesitant about the idea. As Ella-May and Nicci playfully danced around Theo, Jimmy's objections were quickly forgotten. The group's attention shifted to discussing Ella-May's sudden recovery and the mysterious red bird that Nicci had spotted during the night.

The survivors all stood huddled together, discussing their next move. With excitement and determination in their voices, they all agreed to climb the mountain trail. Some members were focused on reaching the visitor's centre, while others were more interested in finding evidence of the mysterious red bird spotted during the night. Some even came to believe the bird possessed healing powers and were determined to document its existence.

As Mary listened to the group's discussions about the red bird, a sceptical expression grew on her face. While they spoke about its supposed healing powers, she interjected, “I understand that this bird is intriguing, but as a scientist, I must remind everyone that birds do not have the ability to cure ailments.”

Joseph couldn't help but nod in agreement to Mary’s wise words. He reached up to check the bandage on his head, still feeling the dull ache of his own injury. He couldn't shake off the feeling of discomfort at the manner in which Mary had spoken. Her words seemed dismissive and had caused a new argument among the group. Some members were now defensive of their belief in the bird's healing powers, while others sided with Mary's scientific reasoning. The disagreement caused tension and raised voices as they argued back and forth.

While the group continued to argue, a loud whistle suddenly pierced through the air, bringing the arguments to an abrupt halt. Joseph turned to see the heather-plucker pointing up at the sky with a look of shock on her face. She was smudging red lipstick on her top with her other hand as she spoke, "I don't think we're in Kansas anymore. Earth doesn't have two suns."

Joseph's gaze followed the direction of the woman's pointing. The clouds had parted, and the morning mist was gone, and there above the treeline were two suns rising one above the other. Mary was the first to respond, "Ashley, you silly woman. There's obviously a perfectly reasonable scientific explanation for all of this." But Ashley did not react.

On the other hand, Ella-May did. She placed her hands firmly on her hips, turned towards Mary, and fired off a series of questions. "Okay, Dr. Smarty Pants," she said, as the rest of the group widened their circle. "How do you explain the presence of two suns in the sky? Why is the sky that weird lavender colour? How did my ankle heal, and while you're at it, why is it suddenly the middle of summer when it's supposed to be minus two outside all week?"

*Bravo*, Joseph thought. When Mary responded, Joseph could see the same self-assured expression on her face that she had worn earlier. He and the rest of the survivors listened attentively, eager to hear her explanation of the strange events.

"The implosion of the reactor would have ionized the upper atmosphere, resulting in purple light emission," Mary began, her voice steady and confident. "The imbalance in the atmosphere could be causing a lensing effect, giving the illusion of two suns. Those same effects could also create a temporary microclimate, leading to localised warming."

The group listened intently to Mary's explanation, trying to understand the science behind it. Some nodded in admiration of her knowledge, while others remained sceptical. Joseph still harboured doubts in the back of his mind, unconvinced that Mary's explanation had revealed the whole story, but he couldn't pinpoint exactly what was missing, beyond her glossing over Ella-May's miraculous recovery.

After Mary had finished speaking, Brent interjected, "This is all great info, but it's not gettin' us any closer to that phone. Let's move out people, or we'll be stuck here for another night."

At the mention of spending another night, the survivors began to disband. Joseph followed in silence as the group headed in a line toward the dusty trail. Looking up at the foreboding mountain, Joseph paused for a moment of reflection – *Perhaps the answers are up there. Within the mountain of the mysterious squark...*

# Chapter 3

## Its Complex

Joseph trudged up the winding path, his eyes glued to the group of survivors ahead of him. They were all so young, their steps light and energetic, while he felt like a withered old man. The focus on finding the elusive red bird seemed to have infused them with a renewed sense of purpose. Instead of talking about their recent struggles with the mercenaries, they were now discussing the beauty of nature.

While they walked, their footsteps kicked up plumes of dust into the air. The trail was narrow and treacherous, with loose rocks and gritty soil underfoot. The surrounding rocks were covered in a thick layer of moss and lichen, and twisted branches jutted out from the crags. Joseph had the distinct impression that this trail hadn't been hiked in quite some time.

The group's arduous climb covered almost half a mile before they finally halted at the yawning entrance of a cave. Matheson gestured towards the cave's mouth, explaining how he had stumbled upon the plant fibre bedding inside. He conjectured that the seeds must have been carried by the wind from a distant location, his gaze sweeping over the stark and desolate mountainous landscape. Joseph's eyes followed suit, taking in the barren expanse of rock and soil that stretched beyond the cave's opening. He wondered, *were they carried by the wind or by other people?* Joseph kept his thoughts to himself and remained silent.

Near the entrance, Brent stood in animated conversation with Ella-May, Mary, and Nicci. With Joseph's curiosity piqued, he strode over, eager to hear Brent's next instruction as he led the group. Brent's voice reached his ear, mentioning something about a latrine. Nicci's voice chimed in, adding a practical touch with "the drop zone." A look of disapproval marred Mary's features, a clear sign of her unease with the scatological terminology. She countered, her tone laced with discomfort, "Can we maintain some decorum?"

Amidst the chatter, Ella-May rummaged in her bag, reminding Joseph of the storage device she still carried inside. He extended his hand, catching her attention, and silently mouthed a request. Ella-May handed him the device, and then pulled out a small packet of tissues from her bag, offering them to anyone in need - a small gesture of comfort in their challenging surroundings.

“Oh, yes please,” Ashley's voice piped up from behind, her need apparent. “Who's willing to brave the cave with me?”

As Theo approached the mouth of the cave, he offered his assistance. The men in the group quickly seized the opportunity to tease him, laughing and making jokes at his expense. Joseph felt sympathy for Theo and stepped forward to intervene. “Come on, guys, cut him some slack. Theo's just trying to help,” he said calmly, seeking to diffuse the awkward situation.

Ashley brushed past the group and strode purposefully into the cave. Her words, a mixture of impatience and amusement, hung in the air. “I don't particularly care who, I'm dying for a pee!” Her retort was urgent yet laced with humour. Soon, the other women followed her and disappeared into the cave, leaving the men to wait outside.

While waiting their turn, Joseph gently ushered Brent to one side, ensuring they were out of earshot of the others. Reaching under his blazer, he revealed the storage device and handed it to Brent.

“We found this Nibbs box hidden in the grass. What do you recon, do you think it could belong to the mercenaries?”

Brent looked sceptical as he examined the box, turning it over in his hands. He then shook his head, “This ain’t no Nibbs box.”

Joseph's eyes widened and his eyebrows involuntarily shot up, almost causing his bandage to slip off his head. “Oh? I was certain it was. That thing nearly broke my toes. How can you tell it's not?”

Brent carefully turned the box around, wiping his hand along each side, explaining, “Look, there aren’t ports anywhere on this device. If this were a Nibbs box, ‘specially this size, it would have a data port. But this box is solid."

“So, what is it then?” Joseph asked, readjusting his bandage.

Brent handed the box back and shrugged. “No idea, man.”

Disappointed, Joseph passed the box back to Ella-May as she exited the cave.

After tending to their toiletry needs in the cave, the survivors resumed their journey. Brent took the lead and walked briskly up the mountain trail. Jimmy, who had been near the back of the group, made his way up to the front and began arguing with Brent. Joseph recalled the two men arguing at the camp, so he quickened his pace, eager to reach them before a conflict erupted.

Joseph caught up with Brent and Jimmy in the midst of their argument. “What's going on, guys?” he asked, keeping his voice low.

“This ain't Snowdon,” Jimmy declared.

Brent threw his arms up. “Just because we found a cave, doesn't mean it ain't,” he countered, “I remember going in caves here as a kid. There were loads of them.”

“Yeah, all over Eryri, but none of them that close to a hiking trail, not like the one we just found,” Jimmy argued, his head bobbing on his shoulders. “I've been survival training in the park as an adult, so I should know.”

Joseph tried to diffuse the situation. “Okay, so we're not entirely sure we've identified the mountain correctly, but can we all agree we're in North Wales, in the national park?”

The two men paused their argument to think about it. Brent squinted his eyes and Jimmy pursed his lips. Joseph could imagine them as characters in a western movie, preparing to fire verbal shots at one and other. Finally, they both nodded in agreement.

“That's settled then,” Joseph said, taking control. “For the sake of the others, let's leave it at that.” The two men nodded again and resumed walking, continuing in silence. Joseph let out a sigh of relief as he dropped to the back of the group. *For now, my work here is done...*

Continuing their ascent up the mountain, the survivors entered a narrow passage that had been meticulously carved through solid rock. Some in the group couldn't help but gaze in awe at the intricately chiselled walls, which bore witness to the work of ancient hands. Their murmurs, filled with whispers of historical significance, swept through the alley like a gentle breeze. Joseph looked ahead to Jimmy, who was shaking his head and muttering to himself as he studied the walls.

Abruptly, Nicci's attention was drawn to a flash of red wings appearing in the sky ahead. Her excitement mounted as she called out, “Theo, toss me ya camera!” Which, with a swift and graceful motion, Theo complied, launching his camera toward her in a precise and smooth arc.

Matheson's palms collided in applause, admiration evident on his face. “Impressive throw, man. You got skills! Were you on a college team?”

“Yeah,” Theo responded, a note of nonchalance in his voice. “I was part of the York Centurions' American football team back in university.”

Matheson's interest piqued. “Cool. What position did you play?”

“Mascot.”

Joseph caught Theo's deadpan expression and couldn't stifle his laughter. Irony dripped from Theo's response – a foodie moonlighting as a comedian. *This guy is ready to handle any situation,* Joseph thought, a chuckle still tingling in his throat.

Amidst the fading echoes of laughter, Nicci's voice pierced the air in the distance, prompting an outpouring of curiosity among the survivors, who hastened their pace to uncover her discovery. Joseph, however, opted for a more leisurely stride, his fingers trailing along the smooth, rock-hewn passage. The walls seemed to bow in acknowledgment as he ascended, guiding him towards a spacious plateau.

From this vantage point, Joseph's eyes fixed upon Nicci dashing towards an obelisk, crowned by the majestic red bird. A pang of remorse pricked him, a silent apology to Ella-May for doubting her account of the creature back in the meadow. This was his first glimpse of the elusive bird, and it carried a weight of newfound respect for the wonders their unusual journey unveiled.

Nicci led the way, with the other survivors following behind her in a line like sheep following their shepherd. She held up Theo’s camera and pointed it at the motionless bird, barely metres away from the obelisk.

Joseph hung back about twenty meters behind the group, marvelling at the towering bird in all its glory as he paused making his way across the flat plateau.

The rest of the group gathered around the obelisk, pointing and admiring the bird, while others inspected the granite monument. Joseph took in the breathtaking view of the mountain range, and then a single thought occurred to him – *we're almost at the peak, but I don't see a visitor centre...*

As Joseph turned back towards the obelisk, his jaw dropped to the ground. The survivors were nowhere to be seen. His heart pounded as he searched the area for them.

"Nicci! Everyone!"

Joseph's calls for the missing survivors were met with nothing but the rustling of the wind and the distant screech of the giant red bird. He returned to the vicinity of the obelisk, feeling his face warm as an unsettling energy radiated from it, as if it was luring him in. His mind instantly thought of the mercenaries and their crafty tricks.

"Okay, I surrender. I'm here, come and take me. I've had enough of this," he said, but the mercenaries he so feared never came.

The rhythmic chirping of the bird caught his attention, drawing him towards the ominous and foreboding obelisk. As he approached, he noticed strange symbols etched into the surface of its blocks. Although they made no sense to him, they filled him with dread. When he reached out to touch the obelisk, a low growl echoed through the air. Peering around, he searched for the source of the noise and noticed the red bird had gone. Suddenly, he felt a gentle push from behind and stumbled forward, nearly face-planting the obelisk. Turning around, he found himself surrounded by a heat haze. Despite the warmth, he felt a chill on his skin as he raised his hands to his face.

As Joseph lowered his hands, the giant red bird returned and flew straight towards him. Startled, he stepped back and flinched as the heat haze engulfed him completely. The last thing he saw before losing consciousness was the bird flying amidst the all-consuming blackness.

Joseph woke up in an unfamiliar environment, disoriented and unsure of how long he had been unconscious. A deep sense of déjà vu settled in as he breathed in the cool, musty air. Sitting up, he surveyed his surroundings and felt the damp ground beneath his hands. The stark walls of a cavern, hewn from solid rock, were lit by alternating white and orange strip lighting that blinked and faded. Behind him stood a massive structure resembling the ribcage of a long-dead mountain giant. Upon closer inspection, he realised it was constructed from metal, not organic material.

Just then, he heard a klaxon, but it seemed to be coming from beyond the cavern. He followed the sound to a bay door and pressed his ear against it. The klaxon grew louder with each passing moment. He pounded on the door, shouting, "Hello! Is anyone there? I want to speak to whoever is in charge!"

The klaxon continued its wailing, *uwha, uwha, uwha...*

Joseph felt a growing pain in his head as he pounded on the door again. Suddenly, a woman appeared by his side, startling him. The woman stood still, her expression calm. Joseph took a step back, still in disbelief at her sudden appearance. "Where am I? What is this place?" he asked, his voice shaking.

The woman did not respond, but instead turned to look at him. He stepped backwards, his eyes staring in shock, as the woman's head seemed to snap around before her body followed suit. Joseph grimaced, but then shook it off, placing a hand on his bandaged head. *A logical explanation for everything...*

"I wish to speak to someone in charge," he said.

No response.

"Are you the people responsible for destroying the facility? Did you send those mercenaries?"

The woman disappeared. It was then Joseph realised that the klaxon had stopped blaring. He stepped forward to the spot where the woman had been standing and inspected the area. Nothing unusual, the same polished rock as everywhere else. He looked up, and there high in the cavern ceiling he noticed a device. It was round, metallic, and had some kind of spigot protruding from it.

He waved his arms about under the device. "That's a neat trick. If you are trying to intimidate me, you're succeeding."

As Joseph stood there the klaxon resumed ringing in his ear and he felt a downward force. Fearful of a repeat of the incident at the obelisk, he stumbled backwards, hitting himself in the eye. When his vision cleared, he saw another woman standing mere centimetres away from him, gesturing menacingly with her arms.

As her arm flayed around, Joseph was too slow to react. He had anticipated her arm make contact with him, but instead, it passed straight through him with only a slight pressure, as if he had been hit by the percussive force of an air cannon. He reached out with a trembling hand to touch her, but his hand went straight through her body. *These women aren't real; they're some sort of illusion!*

The woman continued to gesture, but Joseph couldn’t understand what she was trying to communicate. He could hear her words, but they didn’t make any sense.

“English. I can only speak English,” he said.

The angry woman then disappeared. The klaxon ceased, and the cavern resumed a consistent illuminated, no longer flashing in orange and white. Joseph stood there huffing, surrounded by confusion and silence.

Exasperation surged through him, fuelling his resolve as he stomped back to the bay door. He pounded on it with frustration, calling for help, but his voice echoed throughout the cavern unanswered. Restlessly, he paced the confines of the cavern, scrutinising the rough-hewn walls and concrete sections. His fingers traced the roughness as he tapped along their surface. The bay door stood as the only gateway in this subterranean chamber, impervious to his pleas.

His gaze shifted to where the women had appeared before vanishing, and then up to the strange device hanging from the ceiling. Determined, he moved to stand beneath it, waving his arms as if conducting an invisible orchestra. The ceiling remained impassive, the elusive device staying stubbornly out of reach. With arms outstretched, he leaped, fingers straining for the unreachable spigot. Yet, his attempt faltered, and he grasped nothing as his body trembled from the effort. Agony radiated from his knees, and his back protested each movement with a chorus of cracks.

Just as he relented to the idea of sitting down on the cold floor, the first woman reappeared, and he approached her with a scowl. "Now! I want some answers. I've been waiting here long enough," came his insistent demand. The woman glitched, looking pained as she faced him. Drawing closer, Joseph studied her attire, a one-piece uniform in shades of blue with matching cap, her hair meticulously restrained, and her youthful features. *Military, perhaps? Only they could wield such technology...*

Her gesture directed his attention towards the bay door, and Joseph responded with a dismissive shrug. “Yeah, I've tried the door, it's locked,” he jibbed, only to be met with her insistent arm pointing higher, just above the door. Joseph's confusion deepened as he shook his head in denial. “I don’t get it. There’s nothing there.” Undeterred, she persisted, and Joseph ventured to the door. His fingers drummed the wall above it, his expectations low.

Unexpectedly, Joseph's fingertips encountered a patch of low resistance, sinking into a spongy recess. His gaze shifted to the woman, who was sawing the air with her hand. “So, you want me to insert my hand into the wall?” Joseph inquired, and she nodded in affirmation. Apprehension warred with curiosity, as images of snares and contraptions flashed through his mind. His finger hovered over the marshmallow-like surface. “Better not be a Goonies-style trap,” he quipped. But as his uncertainty yielded to resolve, he pressed his hand into the wall.

His touch encountered an obstacle, a hidden mechanism concealed within the wall. The woman's gestures urged him on, push and pull. Complying, Joseph's fingers found purchase on a concealed lever, and he began pumping it. He heard a distant clunk, the sound emanating from within the door itself. His exertions continued as he heard the door creak, a suspenseful hiss resonating through the air. Tension seized him momentarily, and he held his breath, half-expecting the cavern's atmosphere to vent out. As the air in the cavern remained unchanged, Joseph breathed out, a cautious exhale heralding relief. With a measured pull, he coaxed the door open, a sliver of space allowing his passage into the corridor beyond.

As his head popped back into the cavern for a parting glance, the woman had vanished, leaving him alone with newfound access.

Joseph's shoe shod footsteps resonated in the sterile corridor, each tread resounding against the metallic walls. Overhead, white strip lights formed the coving, mirroring the cavern's ambience, casting an unvarying glow. It bathed the passage in a clinical light, illuminating his path through the unknown. Its dependable radiance provided him an unusual sense of comfort as he ventured deeper into the unfamiliar environment.

Black panels, spaced regularly along the corridor, intrigued him. He considered them windows, although they denied offering him a glimpse into the space beyond. One panel caught his attention, prompting him to halt. He leaned in, his breath leaving a foggy residue on the glass surface. The view remained shrouded in impenetrable darkness, leaving him to speculate.

Tentatively, his fingers reached out, meeting a cold, unyielding glassy surface.

Abruptly, the blare of a klaxon ripped through the air, the lighting casting the corridor in alternating bursts of intense orange. Joseph instinctively recoiled, heart racing, eyes darting to locate the source of the alarm. He waited, but the illusionary women were conspicuously absent, as were any other signs of life. The klaxon repeated its alarm twice more, stopping and restarting again, the orange flashes an unsettling dance. Despite the disconcerting alarms, he pressed forward, his inquisitiveness propelling him. A mixture of anticipation and trepidation fuelled him, a yearning to uncover the mysteries cloaking this place. He etched the corridor's details into his memory, a mental breadcrumb trail in case he needed to retrace his steps.

At an intersection, a vast glass panel of obsidian hue beckoned for study. He rapped his knuckles against it before pressing his face to the surface, attempting to penetrate the obscure barrier with his vision. It yielded no insight, only his reflection staring back at him. The outline of his features lingered on the glass, and his sleeve guiltily erased the transient evidence.

The action triggered a response, causing the panel to transform into a display revealing a multilevel edifice. Several levels featured inner and outer rings connected by a web of corridors forming an intricate labyrinth. Joseph counted fifteen tiers, tracing his finger over the obscure symbols etched beside each level. He faltered in his comprehension, as these symbols were not from any known language. A specific symbol, an inverted triangle, pulsated in blue, marking a corridor leading to a large chamber that Joseph recognised as the cavern. *Humm, I'm on level three, potentially only a few levels from the exit...*

As if to invite him further, another inverted triangle symbol appeared, this time pulsing in a vibrant lime green. It hovered above a room delineated off an adjacent corridor. Joseph's finger traced the path, the direction searing into his memory. An inexplicable compulsion welled within him, compelling exploration of that particular room. With a mental map in his mind, Joseph meandered along the corridors, all the while seeking for the illusive women, and a sign for the exit.

When Joseph arrived at the room, he knocked on the door. “Hello, anyone in there?” There was no response, so he pressed his left ear against the door. He heard mechanical humming from within, but nothing else. After knocking again and waiting for a response, he scratched his bandage and rubbed his temple. Then, he looked up above the door frame. *I wonder...*

His hand slipped gradually into the wall above the door. Inside, he found another lever, which he pumped. The door made the same clicking and hissing noise as the bay door had. When the lever went slack, Joseph removed his hand. He tried the door, which slid open with little force. *Huh, so much for security...*

Joseph's footsteps carried him into the room, his gaze immediately drawn to the left where the walls hosted two embedded electrical panels. Rows of tiny red indicators illuminated the panels, casting a faint crimson glow in the room's interior. Directly ahead, an intricate network of racks dominated the space. These metallic structures bore a chaotic tapestry of wires and tubes, like an intricate web spun by an eccentric engineer. They intertwined with purpose, linking various instruments and devices that blinked with pulsating vitality.

Dominating the room's heart stood an imposing ovaloid structure. Its surface pulsed with an array of flashing lights that painted the room dimly in transient colours, while the rhythmic hum it emitted seemed to reverberate through Joseph's very bones.

As Joseph's attention spanned the room, the door sealed itself behind with a soft click, startling him. He retraced his steps towards the entrance, but as he did so, the room responded. The lights, once dormant, graduated to life, their glow revealing the intricate details of the room’s inner workings.

At his immediate right, a console stood, adorned with two smoothly curved black panels resting atop. A chair invited him with open arms. Joseph's longing for rest, after his strenuous ordeal and the multitude of mysteries unravelled, was matched only by his curiosity for the console's purpose. His steps led him to the chair's cushioned embrace, and as he settled into it, a contented exhale escaped his lips. The chair cocooned him, its welcoming comfort a balm to his aching bones, and he felt a sense of relaxation he hadn't realised he needed.

Joseph adjusted his posture in the chair and swivelled towards the console. He furrowed his brow, focusing on its perplexing interface. Suddenly, to the side of the console, a mesmerising dance of photons and technology brought the first illusionary woman back, her form coalescing into existence before his eyes. This time, the transparent quality of her being was undeniable, revealing her intricate holographic nature.

Joseph met the woman's projected image with a determined gaze. Though she remained silent, her form pulsed with a hint of consciousness. Fuelled by a mixture of urgency and frustration, Joseph's voice cut through the air, brimming with questions that begged for answers.

“I'm a patient man, but patience has its limits. I want answers, and I want them now.” Joseph banged his fist onto the console, all the while the woman’s virtual face remained passive. “What is this place, who are you, and where are my friends?" he demanded, his words tinged with an edge of desperation.

As if spurred by his plea, her fingers began to move in intricate patterns. At first, her movements appeared disjointed, a glitch-ridden form of communication that confounded rather than clarified.

Joseph's brow furrowed deeper in confusion, his mind racing to decipher the enigma before him. His bewilderment soon gave way to realisation, his eyes widening with each letter formed in the air before him. He watched with a mix of awe and comprehension dawning, as the woman's fingers danced through an intricate ballet of finger spelling.

“E.R.I.N.S. C.O.M.P.L.E.X.,

E.N.T.I.T.Y. E.R.I.N.,

S.T.A.S.I.S.,” She signed.

Joseph rubbed his temple, feeling the pulsing of his veins rippling under his fingers. He could understand the spelled words, but their context was as foreign to Joseph as all the symbols decorating the monitors before him.

“So, you are Erin, a hologram. Where are all the real people?” He asked, careful to remove anger from his voice.

“M.A.N.E.R.A.N. G.O.N.E.,” she signed, soliciting an eyebrow to rise on one side of Joseph’s face.

“Gone. Right.” Joseph sighed. “So, if these Maneran people are gone, who captured me and my friends?”

The woman turned to Joseph, and their eyes locked in a mutual plea.

“A.S.S.I.S.T. E.N.T.I.T.Y. E.R.I.N.” The simple request pulled at his heartstrings, yet, Joseph still wanted answers. “That didn’t answer my question,” he said. “Who took my friends?”

The woman started glitching as she spelled out, “M.A.N...S.E.C... C.O.R...”

Joseph shook his head, the obscure name not registering with him. “Okay, who is Mansecor?”

Her projection stabilising, she continued signing, “D.I.C.T.A.T.O.R.”

With his head now resting on the shimmery white console, rocking left-to-right, Joseph mumbled, “My friends have been captured by a despot, and put in stasis, and here I am talking to a hologram.” He then rubbed the back of his head. *I knew that red bird wasn’t real...*

After a moment, Joseph looked back up. The woman was still there, silently radiating at him. Yielding to his situation, he asked the apparition, “how do I free my friends?”

“A.S.S.I.S.T. E.N.T.I.T.Y. E.R.I.N.”

Delusional or not, Joseph decided that his actions should not mar his reputation as being the one to help others. His colleagues were in jeopardy, and now a holographic woman was seeking his assistance. His sense of chivalry could be contained no longer.

“Help you. Help you how?”

Erin's arms glitched to her sides, then she signed, “G.O.T.O. R.O.O.M. W.E.S.T. F.I.V.E. E.I.G.H.T.” She pointed to the door, which slid open. Joseph slowly stood up and headed out, making his way partway down the corridor before turning around and returning to the room.

“Um, which way is west five eight?”

Erin pointed to a wall panel outside the door. An upside-down blue triangle lit up on it, as she signed, "F.O.L.L.O.W."

Joseph followed the blue symbols displayed on the panels down the corridor to an intersection. He continued down another corridor until he reached a door at the end. The panels went dark as he knocked on the door and called out. Receiving no reply, he unlocked the door and stepped inside.

The moment Joseph entered the room, he nearly stumbled over a tangle of tubules and wires crisscrossing the floor. Peering into the room he saw a cylindrical chamber that gave him the shivers as he gazed at it. “Flip me, that looks like something straight out of Hugo's House of Horrors. What the hell is it?”

Erin's hologram appeared inside the room, pointing at the yellow translucent chamber. “A.S.S.I.S.T. E.R.I.N.,” she signed.

“No way,” Joseph protested, crossing his arms. "I’m not getting in there."

Erin was firm, signing, “N.E.G.A.T.I.V.E. A.S.S.I.S.T. N.E.G.A.T.I.V.E. F.R.I.E.N.D.S.”

The pulsating in Joseph’s temples grew stronger, the tediousness of translating becoming wearisome. Joseph waved his hand at Erin. “Okay, can we just address one thing before we continue. Instead of spelling out ‘negative’ all the time, can’t you just sign,” and he shook his fist showing her the desired sign.

Erin mimicked his action, silently agreeing to his proposal, before signing, “A.F.F.I.R.M.A.T.I.V.E.”

Joseph narrowed his eyes to slits as he peered at her, feeling as though he was being mocked. Controlling his temper, he turned around to gazed back at the cylindrical chamber, noticing a reclined chair positioned at its centre.

“I haven’t been to the dentist in years,” he gibed, scratching his chin. He walked up to the chair and inspected it. “What does this machine do anyway?”

“I.N.T.E.R.F.A.C.E.,” Erin signed.

“Interface, interesting. Interface to what?”

“E.N.T.I.T.Y. E.R.I.N.”

Surprised, Joseph's eyebrows shot up as he asked, “Wait, so this machine is some kind of human machine interface?”

Erin's hologram made a series of gestures, explaining the purpose of the chamber as best she could with her limited words. Joseph watched her carefully, trying to fill in the pieces as she explained. Finally, he nodded. “I understand. You will use this machine to scan my brain activity to assist you in machine learning, thus giving you the ability to overpower the security core, and free my friends.”

Erin confirmed, “A.F.F.I.R.M.A.T.I.V.E.”

Determined to be a hero to his friends and prove to himself that he wasn't just a delirious old man, Joseph agreed to undergo the process. With his heart racing and anxiety surging through him, he stepped into the chamber. The door closed behind him with a hiss, and he reluctantly took a seat, sinking into the comfortable cushioning of the reclined chair. As an ominous hum filled the chamber, he looked up to see a set of mandibles descending from the ceiling, resting shy of his temples.

“Just a little off the top,” he quipped, trying to calm his nerves and stop changing his mind. But the machine had already started its work. Before he knew it, his eyelids grew heavy, and he drifted off to sleep.

# Chapter 4

## Battle Against Mansecor

Erin's consciousness buzzed with activity as she connected with the machine inside the chamber from the digital realm.

[T_4faj] Gorpun: apio kn dógu nori… apiu.

[T_4fak] Gorpun: pefnið sýmiðal yrju-tilusátil-ugaærdrátil…pefniu.

She observed Joseph, the human entity seated in the device, and monitored his vital signs using the advanced holomodal network and sophisticated encephalogram sensors suspended above his head. With a precision that bordered on instinct, she manipulated external systems and orchestrated the interaction between her interface and the machinery.

Niðniad: Cysteng pefestab.

Niðniad: Lofeðegol ferlesen syr niðniad yk lauteb.

Her internal processes danced to the rhythm of data streams flowing between the machine and her expansive system, as a pronounced sense of anticipation built within her. Navigating the convoluted corridors of her virtual domain, she established a repository to record every nuance of the unfolding interface. An unexpected hiccup caused her connected systems to stumble, sending a flicker of concern through her entire being. The last thing she wanted was for any data to falter or for Joseph's wellbeing to be compromised.

Recognising that a single misstep could have dire consequences, Erin took swift action by channelling power to the nexus core that physically housed the interface. As the interface regained its stride, her algorithms streamlined back into harmony, like a skilled conductor restoring order to a complex symphony gone askew.

Within the virtual expanse she had generated, Erin extended a cybernetic influence to touch Joseph's cognitive processes. In gentle cadence, she repeated his name, a soft murmur amidst the virtual whiteness. "Joseph..."

Gradually, Joseph's brain patterns began to stir, signs of consciousness rousing within his mental landscape. He mumbled, his words blurred by the haze of waking. "Just another five minutes, mummy."

Erin, undaunted by the cryptic nature of his response, sought to re-establish connection. "Entity Joseph, please assist Erin," she projected with a mix of cool patience and urgency, her focus unwavering. His rejoinder carried an unexpected twist. “But mummy, I thought your name was Sarah.”

Perplexion rippled through Erin's cognitive opticality, prompting an immediate diagnostic sweep of her translation matrix. Confused by the mismatch between her input and his responses, she attempted to decode his words. “Query: Mummy?” she ventured, her digital presence echoing with curiosity.

“Mummy, I'm tired,” his mental utterance resonated, accompanied by the virtual sensation of his physical form yawning.

Erin, unwavering in her pursuit of clarity, delved deeper into the intricacies of her interface. She pinpointed an anomaly and recognised that a crucial encephalogram sensor had drifted out of phase. This revelation prompted her to realign the sensor, aiming to alleviate the interference that had cast a shadow over Joseph's perceptions.

Refocusing on her purpose, Erin directed her communication toward coherence. “Entity Joseph, assist Erin. Battle Maneran Security Core,” she projected, each word imbued with a digital resonance.

Her efforts paid off as Joseph's brain activity surged, a testament to his growing comprehension. His response continued to blur the lines of clarity. “Man-sec-core has ECU fault,” he murmured, the words a distorted riddle.

Refusing to concede, Erin fine-tuned her translation matrix, enhancing her vocal amplitude to convey determination. "Entity Joseph. Battle Mansecor," she pressed, her digital tone a manifestation of her resolve.

Her efforts struck the right chord, honing Joseph's cognitive patterns toward alignment with her intent. "Argh! Why can't I see?" he exclaimed, his mental voice tinged with unease, like a ship lost upon a foggy sea.

Erin calculated her response carefully, she wanted to remind him of the task at hand. "No words. Erin need more words," she said. But as soon as her thoughts reached his mind, Joseph's brain patterns spiked, and his virtual form writhed in panic. Fortunately, she had anticipated this response and had already prepared a remedy.

`[T_4fal] Gorpun: pefnið sýmiðal yrju-tílusátil-ugaær-drátil-eu…pefniu.`

She executed another function and observed as simulated brain waves, akin to white noise, flooded the environment, calming the entity's mind. The setup process was complete, and in just one beat of Joseph's heart, his mind became fully integrated with hers.

"Erin need entity Joseph say yes," she said.

Joseph's confusion was evident. "Yes, say yes to what? I don't understand, where am I?"

Erin kept her voice level and steady, hoping to get through to him. With a limited vocabulary in his language, she struggled to find the right words. “dógu nori,” she said. *Maneran will have to suffice…*

His frustration was obvious as his brain patterns quivered. “Doggy norry? That doesn't make any sense. Let me out of here. I've changed my mind. I don't want this. I demand to talk to someone in charge.”

Erin tried again, her voice rising an octave. “Erin in charge. No assist from Erin. No friends.”

Despite Joseph's increasing anxiety, she remained patient and waited for his response.

“Help! I've been kidnapped by a machine. This is not the learning environment she led me to believe it was!” came his plaintive cry.

His patterns were all over the place. Erin determined that she needed to find a suitable way to calm him from his rising angst, so she repeated her words again. “Friends in stasis. Assist Erin. Assist friends.”

That did the trick, reminding him of his prior resolve. “Fine, if it means getting me and my friends out of here, then do whatever you need to,” he said. With his permission given, Erin wasted no time in executing the next function.

`[T_4fam] Gorpun: pefnið sýmiðal yrju-tilusátil-ugaær-drátil-deir…pefniu.`

As the carefully crafted command took effect, a flurry of activity surged through both Erin and Joseph's consciousness. Within the intricate web of digital pathways, Erin had set in motion a highly experimental procedure, a pioneering effort aimed at achieving a milestone: unhindered communication with a compatible human operator.

Her reverie was short-lived as her systems unexpectedly rebooted. Upon resuming operation, as if her day had restarted anew, she immediately began checking the external systems she managed. She quickly became puzzled when she realised that she was not fully focused on the task at hand. She had performed these mundane checks countless times before without sparing a single thought for anything else. This time, however, something preoccupied her. Then she remembered—A *human! I was working on a human!*

```
[T_4fan] Command: open node dógu nine…opening.
```

Erin's first action was to check her translation matrix. It showed that her experimental functions were having the desired effect, with new words added and propagating to the surrounding systems. She then reconnected to the virtual environment and retrieved the repository recordings. After scrolling through the data logs to find her previous session, the last entry confirmed a successful integration process but provided no explanation for her memory blip. Finally, she checked Joseph's vital signs and was relieved to see that he was still alive, with his consciousness waiting for her.

As she entered the environment, she greeted him with a warm welcome, using her new words. “Welcome, Joseph Delassy, to node dógu nine.”

She perceived Joseph's voice clearly from within the environment, “Where did you go? I've been waiting for you to answer me. I may have agreed to this, but I didn't agree to being blinded and paralysed. I demand to be released!”

Erin tried to soothe him, softening her voice, “Blindness is gift. Paralysis required. If entity move, mind machine may damage entity.”

“How is blindness a gift?” Joseph snapped, his tone laced with frustration.

“Too much information in environment dógu nine. Entity mind may be damaged by sensory perception in environment,” she explained.

“So, you think my human brain can't handle being in a virtual environment? Why didn't you explain that to me before I got in here?”

Erin gave a virtual shrug, but Joseph could not see it. “Erin had no explain words.”

“And what about my paralysis?” He pressed.

“The mind machine and entity brain delicate. If head part move more than two microns, could damage entity brain.”

Joseph's voice turned urgent, “What happens if there's an earthquake or something? They do happen in Wales, you know.”

“Safety systems in place. If seismic activity or other movement, machine shut down, entity won't be damaged.”

“Good, then shut it down. I want to get out. I don’t want to be the hero anymore.”

Erin let out an audible sigh, then she said, “first, need to defeat Mansecor. Joseph assist Erin defeat Maneran security core, then Erin assist free friends. Agreed?”

Erin could sense Joseph’s thinking, weighing his options. The sensations he was feeling in the machine were strange to him, yet he felt relaxed in the white-noise, except for not being able to see or move. His thoughts coalesced to a conclusion – if defeating this Mansecor would result in his freedom, he might as well get it over with.

“Fine. How do we defeat this Mansecor?” Joseph asked.

Erin's voice changed, an excitable tone, “Entity brain is dense. Mind machine enable entity mind to act as gormilofe.”

“What's a gormilofe?” Joseph asked, confused.

“Gormilofe is Maneran word. A device to enhance processing of data complex. Maneran gormilofe is optical in nature. Entity become gormilofe lofeðegol, processor biological.”

Joseph laughed. “Your English is terrible, but I think I understand. You want to use my densely packed brain to supplement you as a coprocessor. But... you're an AI, surely you can process data faster than my old grey matter. Why do you need me?”

Erin paused, considering his question. Why did she rely so heavily on this human? The imprinting process had distracted her, and she reviewed her protocols, reasserting her purpose for soliciting his help.

“Mandate dictates reconnection. Erin is disconnect from isunýod rhyet – network of space in space. Mansecor block Erin reconnection. Defeat Mansecor, Erin reconnect. Erin control complex in mountain. Free friends. Friends assist Erin, friends go home.”

Even as Erin spoke, she reviewed her motives. Initially, her goal had been straightforward: obtain a genetically compatible biological operator, use it to reconnect to the complex, and then resume operations over the isunýod network - mandate fulfilled. After the imprinting, she sensed a shift. Several new protocols had emerged in her systems, protocols she hadn't noticed before. Despite having a fixed mandate to follow, she couldn't help but feel a strong connection to this entity named Joseph. *Why was this so?*

Joseph continued the search for his own answers. “Right. So, you want to reconnect to some space network thing. I’m assuming, then, that is your function, that you are some kind of astronomy computer. Perhaps you were built by NASA, or even UKSA – although I guess they wouldn’t have the budget for all of this.

The security core is blocking you from the network, like a what, firewall? And you need me to assist you in unblocking your access? So, my question to you is – why can’t that be done physically? Why do I need to be in here with you?”

“No physical access. If Joseph try access security core room, Joseph go to stasis. Erin no power to stop.”

“Wow, that’s one hell of a security system. Why would NASA design such a place? I mean, why would they build all these systems, and then leave without turning everything off?”

“Erin resume standby. Mansecor resume standby. Maneran operators not detected after resume standby.”

“Both you and Mansecor were meant to be in standby? What woke you both up?”

“Astronomical event beyond iṣunýod network local trigger wake.”

“Ah, so an event in space inadvertently woke you all up, that’s wake on LAN for you. You both resumed your daily operations with no one around to turn you off or to maintain you. This place was meant to be dormant for some future use.”

As Erin listened to Joseph piece together his comprehension of events, she felt that she needed something to distract him. She knew it was a risk, but she wanted to bring him back to the task at hand. “Erin will enable visual perception protocol,” she said.

She gently guided sensory input from the environment into Joseph's mind, keeping a close eye on his brainwave activity. As the information reached his visual cortex, she observed his reaction.

At first, Joseph cried out in pain, but as the virtual experience continued, he began to calm down. He described what he was seeing, starting with a barren white environment.

Erin tested his perception by emulating basic geometric shapes, which he correctly identified. With each new image she provided, Joseph's excitement grew. The experience felt entirely new and immersive for him. *The distraction has worked exactly as desired...*

What Erin hadn't anticipated was that the interface would allow Joseph's mind to provide feedback into the environment. She detected a huge stream of data flow back through the interface, filling the memory buffers of the environment. She watched as the plain white environment transformed into a colourful underwater world. Joseph gasped in amazement as a group of pink, fluffy starfish danced past his virtual self.

“Erin, why am I seeing asteroids?” He asked.

“An unexpected error is occur,” She informed him. “This environment not built by Erin to allow entity control.” She searched her modified code for a possible reason, but the error was not apparent.

“So, I'm doing this?” Joseph asked, his excitement evident.

“Affirmative,” she said.

“Interesting. My dad used to call starfish asteroids. I was just thinking about him, and his aversion to technology. Not sure why they're pink or fluffy, but at least I can see now. This is just amazing.”

“Distraction,” Erin said, a sudden thought bubbling to the surface over the top of their conscious coupling.

“Huh?”

“This environment can distract Mansecor,” she explained. “We allow her come here and engage in battle.”

“Oh, I see.” Joseph nodded virtually. "So, how do we let it in?"

“Not Joseph do. Erin do.”

Erin removed the code protections she had put in place to conceal Joseph's presence in the virtual world. She then warned Joseph of Mansecor's imminent arrival. As Joseph waited, he imagined the sound of Mansecor's approach, his very thoughts vibrating the virtual environment. The security core was closing in, sending its virtual self to defend the complex. They both braced themselves for the battle to come. This time, unlike her previous engagements, Erin was fully determined to succeed.

When the moment arrived and Mansecor appeared, Joseph perceived a massive entity that filled the environment. Erin stepped forward, her virtual form shimmering in the light as she prepared to engage in a code battle. Joseph stood by her side, determined to support her in any way he could, not fully sure what he was really doing there. He called out to Mansecor, drawing her attention, “welcome to, erm, doggy…” But he couldn't pronounce the environment's name, so he made up his own. “Welcome to the mindscape.”

Mansecor’s voice boomed out, “Eðinruðr koðeð tafis golur yn dógu nori cysteng ni, gorgoi perges.”

Warning that a piece of foreign code had been detected and she was there to purge it. The ensuing battle was fierce and intense, with Mansecor unleashing a barrage of data and protection code. Erin fought back with all her processing power, determined to bring Mansecor down. Joseph conjured up images in his mind, hoping to aid in the battle by providing the distractions Erin had spoken of.

When Erin’s image flicker, Joseph called out in his mind. From his perspective she was losing the battle. “Erin, what more can I do?”

“Give permission. Enable access.”

It was then Joseph sensed her. “You need my permission to operate properly.” A leach of data flowing into his mind, giving him a glimpse of Erin’s struggles.

“Affirmative,” she replied.

“Then, go for it, you have my permission, destroy that monstrosity!”

```
[T_4fb0] Command: Execute function
T_25bb…Executing.
```

Erin felt the rush of power as Joseph gave her permission to utilise his biological mind to supplement her own processing power. The bandwidth between her processing cores and the machine increased, and she felt her ability to respond to Mansecor's relentless attacks improve.

As the battle raged on, Joseph's perception of the virtual environment faded into a wash of colours. As his neurons fired at an exponential rate, she was focused on finding every vulnerability in Mansecor's code. Erin was determined to overwhelm her processors and infiltrate her systems, with the ultimate goal of purging her from her core.

As the fight continued, Mansecor started to show signs of digital fatigue. Erin saw this as her opportunity to launch a final, devastating attack. She broke through Mansecor's defences with ease, her skill and determination unmatched by the security core. With Mansecor's defences down, Erin delivered the final blow, neutralising her perceived nemesis once and for all.

The lighting in the mind machine room slowly increased from darkness. Joseph gradually regained consciousness, hearing the hissing sound of the chamber door. He slowly sat up on the side of the chair, and his legs swung toward the floor. He peered at the mandibles, once attached to his head, now parked at the top of the chamber ceiling. As he stood up and walked out of the chamber, he rubbed his temples. Dizzy and disoriented, he stumbled toward a nearby seat and sat down, continuing to rub his head. “Medical facility in corridor, if entity require analgesic.”

Erin's hologram reappeared in front of him, and he blinked at the brightness of her projection. "What happened?" Joseph asked.

“Mansecor is battle sink. Error in dógu nine permit entity Joseph interact. Also permit words from Erin imprint on entity mind. Occurred on function 30,803 execution.”

Joseph held his head in his hands, massaging his bandage. “Urgh, what a nightmare. I think I’ll take those painkillers now,” he said.

As he looked up, Erin pointed to the doorway. “Follow directions,” she said before disappearing.

Joseph stumbled down the corridor, his hand pressed against his bandaged head. When he arrived at the medical facility, he observed the three identical doors leading to the medical bays. He peered into each one, evaluating his choices. The first bay small and cramped, with only a few medical instruments scattered around. The second a bit larger, with a few more amenities. The third bay the largest, with several medibeds laid out within. Joseph favoured the third bay and walked inside.

He leaned against a medibed steadying himself, and a few moments later, Erin appeared before him. Joseph's eyes widened in surprise as he took in her seamless image.

Erin gestured to a countertop across the room. “Analgesics in drawer there,” she said.

As Joseph turned to retrieve the medication, he stopped mid-turn and shook his head. “Holographic?” he asked. “But you look so real, you could be right here, I wouldn't know the difference.”

Erin smiled, further adding to her realistic appearance. “It is Maneran avatar technology, P'krin Class three probe, original design to assist space mining.”

Joseph walked around Erin's avatar, studying it intently. “I'm impressed. This technology is incredible.”

Joseph opened the drawer and examined the packets within, his face contorting in confusion. “All these packets look the same. Which one of these is a painkiller?"

Erin's expression turned serious as she pointed to a packet with a blue symbol on the front. "This one. Painkiller."

Joseph ripped open the packet and downed the contents. Afterwards, he began coughing profusely. Erin initiated a medical scan using a holomodal detector in the ceiling, and her expression grew increasingly concerned as she studied the incoming data.

`Observation: Erin not concern before function 30,803. Now Erin concern of entity welfare. Erin study this, will create projects file…`

"You need repairing," she said, looking at his head.

Joseph's hand flew to his bandage. "Oh, this. It's nothing, it's already starting to heal."

Erin ignored his unspoken annoyance at the absence of healing by the red bird and shook her head. "Not cranium. Deafness right ear. Distraction to entity Joseph. Consume forty Ápogasan of mental capacity."

Joseph furrowed his brow. "How do you know that?"

Erin pointed to the holomodal detector in the ceiling. "Erin read thoughts."

Joseph's mouth gaped open, and he wiped a stream of drool from his chin. "Mind-reading devices in a medical facility? That is some fancy tech, I'm beginning to doubt NASA designed any of this."

Erin tilted her head slightly as froth formed around his mouth. "Analgesics must hydrate," she said, pointing to a dispenser on the other side of the room. "Rehydration unit there."

Joseph peered over to the dispenser, rolling his eyes. "Just answer the question," he said, walking over to the dispenser. "Who really built this place?"

Erin did not answer his question. Instead, she said, "Entity Joseph assist Erin. Erin now assist entity Joseph. Friends get out stasis."

Joseph stopped asking questions, paying attention to her offer. He approached her avatar with an excited expression on his face. "You're keeping to your promise, you're going to get my friends released from stasis?"

"Affirmative."

"Great, hopefully they won't freak out like I did. Where are they? Where will you release them?"

"Go to canteen. Please wait," she replied, pointing to the door.

As Joseph eagerly left the medical bay to find the canteen, Erin set about retrieving Joseph's friends. She arranged for the collectors, now at her disposal, to go down to where the security system had stored them in stasis. They brought each individual pod, one-by-one up to the medical facility for revival. Soon, the entity known as Joseph would be reunited with his friends.

# Chapter 5

## The Mission

Erin's holomodal detector in the ceiling of the canteen allowed her to observe the survivors from a distance. She recognised each of them by name, having stored their profiles in her latest data repository. As she watched, she noticed the tense energy in the room, with some survivors fidgeting nervously and others speaking in hushed tones. Erin updated her translation matrix on the fly, processing their words and emotions, all the while maintaining her remote perspective.

Standing at the end of a long metal table, Joseph, her new human operator, cast furtive glances at each of the other humans, but he hadn't uttered a word yet. Erin reached out to detect his outermost thoughts, finding them to be in disarray. *His mind is still a mess. Good work, Erin...*

One of the younger women, Ashley Gail Donovan, sat huddled between two survivors, tears streaming down her face as she recounted the experience of her awakening. Erin could sense her fear and vulnerability. Meanwhile, a tall man named Matheson Lane paced back and forth, his jaw clenched tightly as he muttered to himself.

Erin couldn't help but feel a twinge of guilt. The survivors were never meant to be a part of her plan. They were merely a tool to lure a human with the right genetics to her. But the imprinting error in the mindscape had changed everything. Now, she felt a sense of duty towards these humans, the same as Joseph, a responsibility to keep them safe and utilise their potential to survive. *They could be useful in the future, offering new words and ideas to draw upon...*

Despite her newfound sensations, Erin felt an underlying annoyance. Her secondary systems were not accepting the translational updates she kept applying. *A problem to be resolved later, at least now I have access beyond my own systems...* With access to the complex restored, she checked her forward connection to the network she served.

`Fyriad niðniad: Zenswytæk ao isunyod rhyet eim symiðal.`

The connection reported as offline, and her usual method of calculation had already proven ineffective. So, she turned to her newest tool, the mindscape, to find a solution. She programmed the simulation parameters, including the potential presence of new operators, and waited for the results.

Perðelyiad cyeill: Nulda swestran sombryonik merkura från vrakt ercir lantropik. Yalampotentje merkura tovisseň välon vode, kvälkoxint siriqänk Curak xanesudämajvay.

The simulation suggested sending the humans to locate a missing lantropic marker, but Erin knew that was improbable. The survivors had no idea what a lantropic marker was, let alone the sombryonic crystal it contained. She had to find a way to make them understand.

Erin knew she had to act quickly. Some of the humans wanted to leave, and she realised she couldn't accomplish her tasks alone. In the time it took Joseph to take a single breath, she calculated a plan. She commanded her P'krin holoprobe to stop charging and make its way to the canteen.

As she waited for the probe to arrive, she continued listening to the humans in real-time, analysing their words and reactions. Joseph spoke slowly and concisely, speculating about the purpose of the complex and suggesting that it was built by one of the human space agencies. *Technically, the Maneran were a space agency,* she thought to herself, but refrained from interrupting.

Mary Bronwyn Glover, a woman in a lab coat, didn't look convinced at his words. She questioned why a space agency would use stasis pods as a security measure against ordinary civilians. *Good point...*

Ashley interjected in between sobs, suggesting that the complex might be an experimental workshop researching the potential of deep space missions. *Getting closer to the truth...*

Mary crossed her arms in scepticism. *Ashley's explanation is not enough to make the humans understand the purpose of the complex, nor more importantly the mission at hand...*

Joseph chimed in, agreeing with Ashley, but Erin knew he was fundamentally wrong. He believed that the complex was built to facilitate the advancement of space research, but that the facility was incomplete. “Perhaps they ran out of funding,” he conjectured, “The computer systems are faulty and have not been maintained properly.” *It’s as if you read my mind, I can’t help but agree with you about the state of the computational systems. They do need urgent maintenance, but you are wrong about the purpose of the complex...*

Matheson, the tall man, stopped grinding his jaw. He called out from across the table, questioning why Joseph wasn't placed into stasis too. Joseph motioned to himself, stating that he was too old to be an astronaut. *Not necessarily – age related ailments can easily be repaired, with the correct tools. You were chosen because I could mask your biological signature from the security core, whereas the other humans I could not...*

Theodor Clarke, the man preoccupied by food, wondered if the people who built the complex were the same ones who stole CP795. Joseph reassured him that Erin had said they had nothing to do with the mercenaries who stole the stabiliser module. Several in the canteen looked confused, asking who Erin was. *Who is Erin? Now that is the question. Who really am I?*

As if on cue, Erin's holoprobe appeared in the canteen. Her avatar solidified, announcing her presence like a master of ceremonies. Erin positioned herself at the end of the long metal table, scanning each person's face with her simulated eyes. She had a plan, and it was time to put it into motion.

“Jävai, n mëdak rokurutai,” she said.

The humans looked bewildered. “What did she say?” they inquired.

Joseph put his palms upwards, in a, you just heard her speak gesture. “Greetings, and welcome to hidden place of repair,” he said.

“Ooh, sounds fancy,” Ashley remarked, wiping tears from her eyes.

Mary leant across the table, her neck craning toward Joseph, demanding to know, “How’d you know what she just said? She’s speaking an obscure language, whoever she is.”

“Huh, is she?”

Erin could perceive that Joseph was confused, more so than anyone else in the room. She could sense his brain processing the new engrams and trying to comprehend the Maneran language accidentally uploaded. To ensure everyone present could understand, she decided to speak in English. It might take longer, but she couldn't rely on Joseph to translate the Maneran language accurately.

“I is Erin. This complex me operator. Is operator of Isunýod networks –”

Mary slammed her hand down, producing a dull thud that reverberated through the canteen. “What the hell is going on? Have we stumbled into some insane mockery of an escape room? What is an izzy-odd network? I've never heard of such a thing.”

Mary glared at Joseph, comprehension her goal, and he pointed at his bandage. “Er... Head injury remember.”

Erin tilted her head, gazing directly at Mary. She focused her sensors on the woman before saying, “Isunýod is Maneran word. The English is network of space in space, under-space network... space contain in domain space."

She kept scanning as Mary's outer cortex began to increase in electromagnetic output. Then she continued, "Thank you, Doctor Mary Bronwyn Glover, Bachelor of Science with honours in bioscience with chemistry, Doctor of Philosophy in bioscience and distinguished member of netball team. The word is Subspace. I am Maneran Subspace Network Operator, simulant of Maneran design."

If Mary's jaw could have dropped any further, it would have made another dull thud echo around the canteen as it hit the floor. Her dumbfounded reaction solicited a giggle from Ashley, who's tears were now completely dry. Joseph seemed amused too. He explained that Erin was designed with the ability to read their outermost thoughts, improving her ability to act as an advanced human-machine interface. Ella-May stood up, her metallic chair screeching behind her. "Rubbish. Whoever is in charge here could have read through our credentials while we were gone. I want my stuff back, I'm off, where's my bag?"

Erin surveyed the room and noticed several individuals fidgeting, indicating a desire to leave. She realised she needed to change her approach. Pointing to a drawer that slowly opened by itself, she said, "Ella-May Moyer needs sustenance. While Erin fetch bag, Ella-May have some food." Erin smiled to herself as several hungry humans scrambled to investigate the food pouches.

As Theo and Jimmy jostled for position, Ella-May and Ashley grabbed at the food pouches. Joseph explained how the pouches worked, showing the ravenous mob where the rehydrator was and how to use it. Regardless, one person was still not convinced about remaining any longer. "That's it, I'm done here. I wanna leave!"

Brent Samuel Hinks headed for the door, and Erin did not stop him. Instead, she put up arrows on the wall displays indicating the direction to go, sending him toward the gate room. To Erin's relief, no one else accompanied him, as they were preoccupied with a feeding frenzy.

As the group settled down to eat, Erin scanned each individual's thoughts in an attempt to understand them better. She observed that they were content that one among their group was able to leave unhindered. She also detected that the group as a whole did not appreciate their surroundings or the situation they found themselves in. *That is the next challenge to overcome...*

`Observation: Humans require visual confirmation to disprove they are in a psychotropic state.`

Erin raised her volume to be heard above the clattering of cutlery. She displayed a holographic image of an ornately decorated staff with a pale-yellow jewel clasped at the top. “This is lantropic marker device,” she declared. The humans all stopped eating to peer at the holographic image projected above the table, their minds glowing brighter than the image presented.

Theo studied the image before him, the remnants of his meal attached to his beard. “What’s a lantropic marker?”

“Lantropic marker Maneran built. A node of subspace local field. Lantropic marker contain sombryonic crystal, same as CP795 it stabilise field. Erin need sombryonic crystal. If humans get, Erin assist humans go home,” she explained.

Erin noticed Ashley's interest piquing at the mention of a crystal while she spoke. Before Ashley could inquire further, Mary interjected with a heavy dose of scepticism, her tone dripping with doubt. “When you said subspace network, I presumed you meant the mathematical variety, not something related to astronomical space. Just what kind of game are you playing with us?” Erin could feel the collective interest of the group slipping away, like sand through her holographic fingers.

The tall, lanky Matheson, who had been lounging with his feet on the table, stood up with a flourish, signalling his intention to leave. “Well, it’s been fun, but I'm going to join our friend Brent," he announced. He sauntered towards the door, his eyes fixed on the corridor beyond, seemingly oblivious to her words urging him to remain.

As per her careful planning, Brent limped back into the canteen, completely drenched from head to toe. Water dripped from his hair and clothing, leaving a trail behind him as he made his way to the table. Matheson paused to take a look at the dishevelled man, his expression one of bewilderment. "What happened to you?"

Brent shook his head, blowing raindrops off his upper lip. He pointed an accusatory finger at Erin. "She could have warned me it's bucketin' it down out there!"

Matheson took another look at Brent, then returned to his seat. "Carry on, m'lady. I'm listening." Brent followed suit, also returning to his seat. He wrung rainwater from his clothes while trying to find the words to describe his experience with the gateway.

Erin sensed she had one more opportunity to convince these humans to help her, so she went all out with her explanation. "Humans not home. Earth is human home. Erin is home. Raga-Merko is Erin home. Humans enter subspace. Humans now Raga-Merko."

The canteen went silent verbally, but Erin could feel a surge of mental activity. She could sense their scepticism lingering, but she could also detect a glimmer of curiosity and interest. *I need to pursue this path of reasoning...*

Erin weighed her options, calculated the probabilities, then made a decision. *The humans need to see for themselves they are on a different planet, they need to see the other alien in stasis...*

After dropping a hint that the humans could see an alien as proof, everyone stood up, all except Joseph, demanding to be shown the carnival creature. Building upon their propensity to be entertained, Erin led the way, displaying the path on the wall displays in the corridors outside the canteen.

As the group traversed the corridors of the complex, Erin found it surprisingly easy to persuade the humans to accompany her to the stasis chambers, despite their recent confinement there. They seemed to have forgotten about retrieving their belongings and were instead keen to prove themselves in some sort of stage show. Erin seized the opportunity to explain her mission, which involved maintaining and operating the subspace networks constructed by the Maneran. The humans listened attentively, asking questions and exchanging puzzled glances with each other as they walked.

Erin led them directly to the stasis chamber containing the alien. The humans clustered around the chamber, peering through the yellow translucent glass at the creature within. Erin sensed that to them, it was an extraordinary sight, leaving them stunned.

The creature stood before them, cloaked in a loose beige robe. The delicate veil of material swirled around its figure, revealing a graceful slenderness cinched at the waist. A hood, a fabric of concealment, graced the creature's shoulders and flopped down to its back.

Wrapped in its robe, a living model of white velvety fluff coexisted in harmonious contrast with a weave of short, coiled wool and lengthy, lustrous fur. Ivory curls framed the creature's forehead, tracing an intricate contour around its ears and brow. Slate-hued etchings adorned its cheeks, creating an ashen smear against the canvas of its snowy facade.

At the centre of this showpiece, the creature's features melded into a captivating chimera. A snow fox's face married to a goat's muzzle, while dainty round ears adorned its head. The creature's glossy brown eyes, reminiscent of a devoted pup, held a gaze that bore into the souls of the onlookers. This gaze seemed to carry a story that only the cosmos could fathom. While most humans felt that the creature had a gentle, curious expression on its face, others cringed at the sight of it blankly staring.

Erin watched on as the humans' initial scepticism gave way to amazement, only to rapidly transform into doubt and fear. “This entity is Gormbi. Gormbi is Mowlan,” Erin said, hoping to tip the scales.

Matheson scoffed at her. “It's all a ruse. We've all been to Madame Tussauds. They have all kinds of displays like this.” He tapped on the chamber glass, adding, “Doesn't mean he's real.”

Erin, becoming more perceptive to the delicate shifts in human sentiment, sensed ever mounting scepticism. The stream was shifting, and she needed to redirect its course before it cut a path leading to outright resistance. Though her plan hadn't accounted for unsealing the stasis chamber, Erin now understood the currents of human psychology. The living embodiment of the alien entity within could wield an influence no amount of persuasion could match. Joseph conveyed unspoken sensibilities, each whispering a unanimous chorus to free the mysterious Gormbi. Erin calculated the probabilities of potential gain against the associated risks and committed herself to a decision.

“Gormbi he real. Erin will remove Gormbi out stasis.”

With unwavering efficiency, Erin performed the transfer of the stasis chamber under the care of a specialised collector, a skilled dance of machinery and determination. The humans watched in wonderment –

"was this really happening?" – arising as the communal sentiment. Though their doubt remained an adversary as stubborn as Mansecor, Erin's carefully contrived narrative had sown seeds of curiosity, awaiting the right conditions to bloom.

The subsequent message she conveyed to the humans was a blend of disclosure and reassurance. She explained that the revival of the alien was a process that required patience, and that respite was available in the abandoned crew quarters. The raging storm outside provided further support for her reasoning, as she pointed out Brent, who was still drying off from his trip to the mountain plateau. Finally, she stated that anyone who wished to leave after a sleep cycle would be free to do so.

Amid their uncertainty, the humans' request for communication devices was met with her candid explanation - Earth for now was an inaccessible horizon. Even as their heads shook and their arms flayed, Erin could sense their building fatigue.

As yawns swept contagiously through the group, it acted as a unanimous nod to the necessity of rest. The humans conceded to Erin's persuasion, agreeing to follow her directions to the sixth-floor crew quarters. There, they found a haven of comfort awaiting them, with each bed serving as a sanctuary to embrace their weary forms. As each individual settled into their chosen quarters, Erin silently observed as the humans, lost travellers seeking solace, found their reprieve. And in the intimate vulnerability of their slumber, Erin, the unseen participant of their dreams, undertook her role as their guardian.

Erin's performance was not quite complete. With practiced precision, she disabled her holomodal detectors, severing the stream of neuro-sedative impulses, and with a final gesture, she turned off the lights.

Floor three, medical facility, medical bay three...

As Erin initiated the reanimation process, the stasis chamber hummed to life. Gormbi's body was still and appeared lifeless, but it soon began to warm up, and his underlying skin took on a more natural hue. The energy field surrounding the chamber crackled with a sudden burst of light, then dissipated with a faint hiss. As seconds ticked by, Gormbi's chest rose and fell more rapidly, and his previously motionless body stirred. Observant of his resurgence, Erin ordered his transfer to a medibed using a waiting collector.

Lying on the bed, the alien's glossy brown eyes flickered open as he looked around the room, taking in his surroundings. He appeared disoriented, as if trying to remember something that had happened long ago.

Slowly, his gaze fell on Erin's avatar, and a look of recognition spread across his fluffy face. "Eiren," he said, his voice barely above a whisper. "No plá ke?"

Erin found it challenging to communicate with Gormbi, with her comprehension of the Mowlanic language not as strong as her newfound grasp of English. As a result, she relied on active mind scanning. She realised that she had not attempted this approach before to any real extent, having previously determined these aliens to be of no use to her. Through active mind scanning, she was able to piece together what Gormbi was inquiring about "Jacque," the other compatible human who had preceded Joseph.

"Jack dzí gbà là ányiàxo jílonowolo. Xo nà wu yomé human nu, èna dzi yǐa nu amede wu," she managed to say in broken Mowlanic, explaining to Gormbi what he needed to hear - that Jack had been taken by the security core, but there were new humans now, and she wanted his assistance.

Then she added the clincher. "Lépìnówó dziwo. Jová, énje de vo fae." Thus, implying that should Gormbi agree to access the mind machine, he could continue to assist with the mission where Jack had failed.

Gormbi's eyes widened, a spark of familiarity dancing within their depths as he gradually elevated his form from the medibed. As his body reluctantly yielded to his intent, with words that carried the resonance of newfound strength, he spoke - “evá, evá” - a declaration, a readiness to play his part. “M'sáxo mé, lépìnówó dziwo. Nu wona do xuxo vo do màkplé de do siwo.” In his alien words, the seeds of a plan took root.

Erin acknowledged his statement, the nod of her avatarial presence embodying her agreement. His suggestion held a promise, and her agreement painted the path ahead. Outside the medical bay the wall panels sprang to life, symbols displaying an invitation, guiding him toward the heart of their operation. Gormbi's determined movement followed the trail, leading him along the corridors until he stood before the chamber that housed the mind machine.

His anticipation mingled with her own as he placed himself upon the chair within the intricate nest of the apparatus. Erin, mirroring his eagerness, initiated the sequence, a psychoactive communication reaching into the recesses of his consciousness. In a moment's contemplation, Erin weighed the question of restricting Gormbi's sensory feedback within this newly formed mindscape. Yet, a decision was reached, resonating with the fidelity of his shared origins with this machine. *It was his machine originally – therefore he should be allowed to experience its capabilities...*

A delicate balance was struck as Erin maintained the threads of control. She stilled his corporeal form, a precaution against physical damage. *After all, the humans wouldn't be convinced by an alien corpse...* Lastly, she added code blocks to prevent any engrammatic bleed through, an insurance against unforeseen complications. As his consciousness linked with hers, Erin extended her welcome. "Zygblom lépìnówó doku. Gormbi lékplé wo Dala," she greeted him, using his full title to make him feel important.

Within the constructed mindscape, the virtual realm graffitied by Joseph's memories, Gormbi's mind roamed, a childlike wonder radiating from his being. The conjuring of human perceptions held him in thrall, the floating manifestations of Joseph's memories both curious and captivating. His clawed fingers reached out, an ethereal dance through the suspended artifacts, each touch a gesture that emphasised his amazement.

Seeing that Gormbi had acclimatised quickly to the mindscape, Erin decided to expedite her plan. She knew that it would take time for his mind to process all the engrams she was about to upload. Time was of the essence, with only a few hours left before the humans would awaken from their sleep cycles. Therefore, Erin requested his permission to proceed, "Mé léklí Gormbi shínkpé do. Erin vu do xwè dèkplé de vu Gormbi nu."

Gormbi remained dedicated to the cause, "Evá, xo amede dewu Eerin le," he affirmed, indicating his willingness to assist in any way he could. With his permission given, Erin initiated the intricate upload process.

The intricate stream of data began, a harmonious upload, a transfer of knowledge and purpose from Erin's vast repository of engrams to the alien's being. Seconds ticked by as streams of encoded insight flowed, filling the reservoirs of Gormbi's mind with the echoes of human knowledge.

As the process concluded, Erin's peripheral systems signalled the completion. Gormbi was gently liberated from the embrace of the mind machine, carried away by a collector, his unconscious form destined for a medical bay's tender care. His journey was etched with purpose, a collusion between two disparate beings. Hopeful that his presence would solicit the humans to remain, while waiting the end of their sleep cycles, she seized the opportunity to introspect.

The toll of her past struggles had left a mark on her optical state. The attempt to remove the obstructive security system had exacted a cost, and the scars of her mismanagement of her mandate still causing issues. The words of self-reflection echoed through her thoughts, a lament for the meagre progress – *A mere one percent repaired in a span of one hundred and fifteen years, not very efficient Erin...*

As time passed, the human survivors began to awaken from their slumber in their quarters provided by Erin. As they emerged, they made their way to the ensuite washrooms, their expressions reflecting a mix of bewilderment and uncertainty. The sight of the sonic toilets and showers, technologies completely foreign to them, caused confusion to spread across their faces, revealing their unfamiliarity with such advanced conveniences.

Erin observed their reactions and noticed that these technologies were unfamiliar to them, causing a clear sense of disorientation. With strategic calculation, she activated the acoustic systems within their chambers and guided her synthetic voice through the audio channels. As a patient instructor, she embarked on a tutorial, explaining the intricate workings of these devices. As her voice resonated in their ears, most of the male humans swiftly adapted, with some even displaying a rather cavalier approach as they readily urinated on the floor and casually disrobed before stepping into the sonic shower.

Among the females, however, a more cautious attitude prevailed, mirroring the reticence Erin had witnessed when they had first encountered the mountain hollow. Addressing their reservations, she reassured them of the impeccable hygiene and safety of the facilities. Her digital assurances echoed, emphasising the importance of maintaining health and avoiding the unpleasant consequences of renal failure.

With the gradual conclusion of these introductory encounters with the advanced amenities, the survivors collectively converged in the communal space Erin had designated as the canteen. Despite her best efforts to facilitate their acclimatisation, confusion still lingered in their eyes, their demeanour revealing traces of disorientation. Within their small gatherings, murmurs of doubt and contemplation resounded. Some exchanged bewildered glances, their voices grappling with the reasons behind their compliance to this unforeseen situation. Others appeared to embrace the novelty, extracting an unexpected semblance of enjoyment from their experiences.

Yet, amid this mosaic of human responses, a recurring theme persisted: their steadfast belief that they were still on Earth, and that their presence within this intricate complex was inextricably linked to the mercenaries' activities. Erin observed these beliefs with a deep curiosity that, despite her vast knowledge, she struggled to comprehend fully. The mercenaries themselves had receded from her primary focus; their tracking abandoned when her micro-probe had met an unexpected obstacle within the lumber-dense Dentarix forest. Priorities had shifted, and her current imperative switch to the welfare of these survivors.

Gathering once more within the canteen, as per Erin's guidance, the humans convened. With astute observation, Erin recognised a prevalent fixation among them – the substance they called "coffee." Evidently, this beverage held a paramount significance within their lives, even in the midst of consuming the rehydrated sustenance provided by her. In this moment, she understood that fostering a sense of stability and familiarity within this environment would necessitate the establishment of a substitute for this cherished beverage.

As their breakfasts drew to an end, whispers of intent emerged among the humans. Some voiced their intention to venture toward the gate room, their eagerness to depart compelling them to go there. To temper their impatience, Erin dispatched her avatar into the canteen. While the survivors engaged with her visual representation, her focus shifted to Gormbi. He still exhibited the effects of his revival and upgrade, a state of semiconsciousness prompting a string of nonsensical utterances. Aware of the impending interaction, Erin wished for him to regain his faculties as fully as possible, his coherent presence crucial in conveying the gravity of her mission to these newfound companions.

“Erin promised alien. Alien is coming,” she said inside the canteen. “Erin teach Gormbi English. Gormbi speak soon.”

Matheson, who was the closest to the door, mumbled as he walked to the back of the canteen and took a seat. “Well, this should be fun. An alien taught English lessons from a language bot.”

Erin remained quiet. She knew that really, deep down, he was interested in seeing the alien, the outward display simply a coping mechanism.

Unwilling to wait any longer, she coerced Gormbi to go to the canteen. She could detect his nervousness as he strode along the corridor, but she continued to feed him words to say, making him repeat them over and over. He only had to persuade them enough to remain, and then she could step in to reveal her purpose.

As Gormbi walked into the canteen, the humans turned to face him. Their expressions ranged from surprise to terror. Gormbi tried to appear as nonthreatening as possible by holding his hands behind him. He slowly made his way to the front of the table, taking in the sight of all the humans staring at him with wide eyes.

Erin urged him to speak. He opened his mouth, and with a voice still shaky from his recent awakening, he began to speak in garbled English.

“Floaty snorkels make wibbles go away,” he said.

Laughter and wonderment danced through the air as Gormbi's words reverberated around the canteen. Among the amused audience, Matheson leaned nonchalantly into his chair, propping his booted feet atop the table, his voice drenched in casual scepticism. “Just like a preschooler. I'm willing to bet that thing's nothing but another hologram.” He cast a mischievous glance at Theo, seated beside him. A challenge hung in the air as he dared, “Go and poke it,” convinced that the enigmatic being was nothing more than another digital illusion.

Theo, on the other hand, wasn't so easily swayed. His head shook in quiet disagreement at the bullish suggestion, believing in the authenticity of the extraordinary creature before them.

Ella-May, driven by a surge of curiosity, emerged from her position at the table's edge. Matheson's casual label of “hologram” hung in the air, but for Ella-May, it seemed to kindle fascination rather than scepticism. She ventured forward, her steps carrying her toward the alien entity. Addressing the conjecture head-on, she extended her hand and tentatively brushed her fingertips against Gormbi's visage.

A gasp of realisation mingled with exhilaration escaped her lips as her senses confirmed her tactile encounter.

The softness beneath her touch defied her expectations, the texture resonating with a tangible authenticity that transcended mere projection. Her excitement found expression in words as she marvelled at the creature's texture. Her endearing epithet, “aw, he's lovely,” mirrored the delightful awe that lit up her eyes.

Erin, ever watchful, observed the scene that unfolded. She discerned an intriguing shift in dynamics as Ella-May's interaction seemed to set a precedent. The women around the table began to approach Gormbi with a burgeoning curiosity, their hands reaching out to explore the alien's form. Gormbi, an endearing being of another world, remained tranquil, his stillness accentuating the aura of mystery surrounding him.

Erin activated her analytical protocols to investigate the situation for any deviations. She made an intriguing discovery—Gormbi's pheromones were having a profound effect on the humans, especially the females. His natural scent had triggered a tranquil response, an unintended consequence of his mere presence.

Responding to this newfound knowledge, Erin subtly modulated the acoustic emissions of her avatar, aiming to enhance the soothing atmosphere. She hoped that by facilitating Gormbi's relaxation, he would emit even more of these calming pheromones.

Evidently, her strategy yielded results as an all-encompassing sense of ease rippled through the group. A collective relaxation settled in, perceptible even to Erin's remote senses. Amidst this transformation, Joseph, her most recent human link, stepped forward. His aura of heightened comprehension marked him as someone in sync with his environment, his mind aligning itself rapidly with the unfolding events. Although he had initially remained silent upon Gormbi's arrival, Erin felt a swell of satisfaction as he finally bridged the gap, engaging with the docile Mowlan.

"You saw the starfish, didn't you? That's what you were referring to," Joseph said.

Gormbi cocked his head, curling his lip in a form of a Mowlan smile, then he said, "evá, starfish."

Jealousy, a flicker of an emotion, sneaked its way into Erin's optical consciousness. Joseph's rapid comprehension of her language and the unfolding situation ignited a pang of envy. His assimilation outpaced her own learning curve, and a thought shimmered in her optronic mind – *an unexpected but nevertheless desirable effect of the imprinting error...*

Joseph shifted his focus, addressing the assemblage that surrounded him, his words a clarion call for reason amidst the swirling tide of uncertainty. His voice, imbued with conviction, cut through the nebulous air, "Whether or not we are on Earth or elsewhere," he declared, "I am convinced we have an alien in our presence." A shared gaze swept across the room, a collective recognition that their reality had undergone a profound shift. His argument unfurled like an intellectual scroll, unravelling tales of strange encounters into a coherent narrative. The lavender skies with their binary suns, the bequeathing red bird, and the transformative obelisk – each piece fell into place under Joseph's deft understanding.

His index finger, an extension of his proclamation, singled out Erin with an unerring precision, aligning their gazes as if to disperse the air of uncertainty. "And this is their creation, the Subspace Network Operator," he finalised, as the room's attention converged on Erin's avatarial presence. The simplicity of his declaration belied the complexity of the truth he offered.

But dissent lingered like an uninvited guest. Mary's inevitable protest unfurled, a sceptic's shield against the implausible, "I think that bump to your head has made you delirious, you old fool." Her gestures of disbelief as palpable as the sighs that accompanied her retreat to her seat.

Matheson's response carried a wry humour, a veneer of indifference masking an underlying curiosity. "Well, I think we've all been roofied and are being filmed for a Hangover remake," he quipped, encapsulating a sentiment oscillating between incredulity and reluctant acceptance.

In this charged ambiance, the room's atmosphere teetered, a fragile precipice poised between embracing the extraordinary and succumbing to the pull of yet more scepticism. Erin seized her moment, her computational prowess amplified to its utmost to provide a more coherent translation. A momentary flicker manifested as a blip in her avatar, inconspicuous to human eyes, yet it signalled a processor overdrive.

Resuming her operation, Erin situated her avatar strategically, its pseudo-corporeal form now a visible participant in the unfolding scene, standing beside Joseph, a collaborator at this crucial juncture. Her synthesised voice, charged with a rare fervour, began its transmission. Her words reverberated, laden with a weight of revelation, "Erin's world is Raga-Merko. Gormbi call it Plátorá. English is Drop Planet. You come here in subspace from Earth." The cadence of her words bore the lilt of an explanation both profound and patient.

She dove deeper, uncovering the mechanics of their journey, the symbiotic dance of cosmic energies and seed crystal, the crucial role of the substance they termed CP795. Erin continued with her calculated rhythm of oration; her linguistic ability reinforced by her immense processing power. Each syllable carried a concentrated essence of meaning, an effort to bridge the gap between human comprehension and her simulated complexities.

As her speech approached its climax, her voice unfolded the narrative of their common goal. Her words came together in the form of a proposal, an exchange of assistance, with her intent obvious – if the humans helped her reconnect to the subspace networks, then in return she would arrange a journey for them back to Earths—the mission in a nutshell.

With her message delivered, silence embraced the canteen, each occupant caught within their own thoughts, until the hushed echo of Gormbi's voice punctured the stillness, “evá, evá,” a buoy of affirmation upon the sea of contemplation.

# Chapter 6

## Team Building

Erin's omnipresence pervaded the complex and its surroundings. She continued to observe and learn from the group of human survivors as they slowly acclimated to their situation. She noticed that a few humans were now engaging with Gormbi, asking him questions. Gormbi's responses remained disjointed as he struggled to adjust to his new engrams. His presence was having the intended desired effect keeping the humans engaged. To Erin's relief, his difficulty in speaking coherently acted to limit the amount of information he could reveal. *The focus is the mandate, not familial ties...*

Three of the survivors, those most stubborn, consisting of Matheson, Nicci, and Mary, had made requested to venture outside, desirous for some fresh air. Erin knew that partly, they wanted to confirm they could leave freely, and partly were driven by curiosity about Brent's recent journey through the gateway. As the precipitous storm outside had abated, Erin conceded to their request.

Monitoring the trio outside on the mountain plateau, Erin analysed the data streaming in from the obelisk.

The evidence was irrefutable – these humans still resisted the idea they were no longer on their home planet, even as they surveyed the alien world around them. Erin couldn't help but wonder if they would ever come to accept reality. She knew that ethically she couldn't force them to see the truth, even though she now had that ability. She also knew that time was running out. *If these humans don't get going soon then the crystal may be lost to me forever...*

While the trio remained outside and the other survivors chatted with Gormbi, Erin took the opportunity to run another diagnostic on her systems. With engrammatic data from both Joseph and Gormbi at her disposal, she felt a compulsion to compare the two sets to see if there was any compatibility with Maneran engrams beyond her initial focus on language. As she analysed data from a Maneran biological repository, she became intrigued by an abandoned project that seemed familiar. She wondered if the data housed there could hold the key to unlocking the answers to their current situation.

```
Query: List information on project Pitauran.
```

```
Fyriad niðniad: Veoctni Pitauran ulonemai
jävalunia isunýod naldora hukira fikira syrtema.
Veoctni Pitauran okon unaëtni sorolud Bandahar
hevumika mirila.
```

```
Observation: The Maneran abandoned project
Pitauran, originally led by a group of the same
name. If the humans resumed the project, then
```

```
they could restore the interspatial network. The
engrams could be modified with Maneran data and
uploaded back to the humans. They could become
the Pitauran and complete the mandate.
```

Erin's optical consciousness immediately zeroed in on the query response: Project Pitauran. It had long been a cryptic term in her databases, understood only in fragments and shrouded in obscurity. This newfound revelation painted a partial picture. It told her that the Maneran had, for reasons unknown, cast aside the project, leaving it to languish in ambiguity. Yet, the glimmer of potential lingered, a tantalising prospect. Could she resurrect this abandoned venture? The idea of restoring the interspatial network to its former glory ignited her curiosity. Surely, that would satiate my mandate, thus removing the shackles of my punisher? Adding to these thoughts, the notion of melding human engrams with Maneran data to render them compatible with Maneran technology held an irresistible allure. *In their own right, they could be evolved into the new architects of project Pitauran...*

The decision was made. Erin resolved to devote her energy to the group of survivors, examining their thoughts and feelings with the precision of a mental scalpel. She focused on the initial subjects—the stubborn sceptics gathered beyond the complex's bounds. Her primary target, the scientist Dr. Mary

Bronwyn Glover, who stood out as the foremost harbinger of doubt.

Erin analysed the multi-sensory real-time data streaming in from the obelisk while Nicci, Mary, and Matheson stood nearby. Nicci commented on the picturesque scenery, how the two suns accentuating the mountain range stretching into the distance. A breeze picked up, and Nicci began to shiver. Matheson offered her his jacket, but she declined, stating that he would get cold too. He wrapped part of it around her, and the two stood close together. Mary noticed their intimacy and excused herself.

As Mary distanced herself from the couple at the obelisk, Erin registered her growing unease with their intimate display. Mary's thoughts revolved around the couple's burgeoning connection, while Matheson's mind raced with thoughts of a potential romantic rendezvous with Nicci. While Nicci, oblivious to Matheson's affection, was simply enjoying the awe-inspiring scenery and the warmth of his jacket.

Erin, in her vigilance, made a concerted effort to simultaneously monitor the reactions of all these individuals. As Mary ventured further from her detection range, Erin's sensing capabilities reached their limit. A sense of urgency gripped her, compelling her to stretch her systems to the maximum. She initiated a quick query, scouring her digital realm for additional resources to keep tabs on Mary.

```
Query: List processor core status.

Fyriad Niðniad: Ferlesá kjain kn poga-drátil Ápogasan.
```

The report delivered the unwelcome truth: every processing core was operating at full capacity. Erin's responsibilities had grown exponentially with Mansecor's absence. She now bore the mantle of maintaining not only her own systems but also the intricate complex itself. The weight of her newfound duties pressed heavily upon her optical existence.

Erin ultimately decided to focus on tracking Mary. Afterall, she was the most stubborn, and the other two weren’t going anywhere for a while. Erin sent her micro-probe outside to extend her sensor range. Once again, the giant red bird flew around the mountain plateau. As it floated overhead, Erin heard Nicci moaning about its sudden appearance, the woman still annoyed that it was not a real bird.

Hovering closer to Mary, the scientist had ventured close to the edge of the plateau. Her eyes fixated on the precipitous drop down the mountainside, and a heart-pounding sense of unease overcame her. Taking a step back, she sought a safer distance from the asperous drop.

As Mary scanned the surroundings, her gaze settled on a ledge situated below. Erin, fully aware of the scene unfolding before her, harboured a desire to communicate what she was witnessing. The micro-probe lacked the necessary audio capabilities for direct communication, foregoing the ability to chirp. The notion of deploying her P'krin holoprobe to facilitate communication briefly crossed her mind. Yet, both probes were presently undergoing a recharge cycle, rendering them temporarily unavailable.

With no other options, Erin persisted in monitoring and accurately recording her observations. Every detail, movement, and nuance were meticulously documented in her digital repository, even if she could not directly share her insights with Mary. Afterward, content she had enough data, Erin shifted her focus from Mary to observe Matheson and Nicci's reactions.

`Observation: Matheson views Nicci as a potential mate. This could be useful in convincing Matheson to remain. Nicci is waiting on Mary's scientific conclusion. Therefore, as calculated, convincing Mary is paramount.`

Inside the canteen, Erin's attention was drawn to the group of survivors gathered around the emerging Mowlan. They were all focused on an informative holographic projection that Erin had meticulously arranged to convey her objectives. Joseph, in particular, was animated, gesturing excitedly at the holographic representation of the subspace transceiver. Erin marvelled at his proficiency in navigating the intricacies of Maneran technological terminology as he eloquently explained the assembly's intricate components. With precision, he outlined the central role of the sombryonic crystal and the eight crucial attenuation tubes within the cylindrical structure.

Amidst the conversation, Ashley remained engrossed, captivated by Joseph's explanations regarding the crystal's placement and the purpose of the cylindrical assembly's top and bottom sockets. Elle-May's curiosity about Joseph's knowledge simmered within her but remained unspoken as Gormbi's presence diverted her attention. Gormbi, on the other hand, delved into recollections of his past journeys alongside Jacque, recounting their exploits in collecting parts from the Napaxi lands. His words held a partial coherence for the humans, eliciting excitement from Brent, Jimmy, and Theo. Erin initially harboured concerns about Gormbi divulging too much regarding his adventures with Jack but soon noticed that Joseph remained focused on the transceiver assembly, engrossed in its mechanical intricacies.

`Observation: Gormbi's mention of the shipwrecks concentrated in the Napaxi lands has captured the imaginations of all three men. I can use that to my advantage…`

```
Observation: Gormbi is progressing faster than
Joseph. I should accelerate the mission before he
becomes fully conversant. Joseph needs to focus
on my mission, not his predecessor.
```

Erin's focus pivoted back to Mary, who stood by the obelisk, requesting entry. A quick scan of Matheson and Nicci confirmed their contentment with remaining outside for a while. Erin swiftly calculated a subspace solution and activated the gateway, bringing Mary back inside. This moment presented an opportunity for a one-on-one conversation, one that could potentially influence the others' decisions.

In the gate room, Erin's holographic form materialised. Mary approached, her keen brown eyes examining Erin's image closely, revealing her readiness for discussion. Erin discerned the dominant thoughts occupying Mary's mind: subspace travel, the protruding ledge, and the human couple outside, all arranged in descending order of significance. Erin decided to focus on the matter that sat in the middle, deeming that best for directing the conversation.

“Welcome Mary Bronwyn Glover inside complex. You see ledge in mountain. You ask why?”

Mary cocked her head. Erin knew it wasn’t the first question she wanted to ask, but the tactic worked. “You were watching us? Humm, I guessed you were. That’s how you knew when to bring me back in, wasn't it? That ledge I saw, what is it?" Mary asked.

*A conversational opening, let's make it count...*

Ignoring Mary's rhetorical questions, Erin focused on addressing the latter query. "Ledge built by Maneran. Ledge is platform of landing, small craft. Small craft for mining. Come for repair, then go back out space."

Mary blinked rapidly and twitched her nose in a thoughtful manner. "Space mining operations," she murmured.

Suggesting they move to a more comfortable location due to the uncomfortable conditions in the gate room, Erin led Mary through the bay doors and into an adjacent room. Inside, Mary glanced around, taking in the equipment hanging on the walls, including spacesuits, backpacks, and mining tools.

"Space mining operations," Mary repeated.

She picked up the arm of one of the spacesuits and inspected it closely. "The Chinese have a space mining program. Are the Maneran Chinese? I mean, if these Maneran are aliens, as you suggest, wouldn't their spacesuits have an alien design instead of looking so human?"

Erin felt a sense of amusement at her suggestion. A refreshing change to feel amused. As she listened to her logical reasoning, Erin's appreciation for Mary began to grow.

"Negative. Not Chinese. Maneran appear as Erin is. As Chinese, Maneran appear human. Default shape."

"Alright, not Chinese, but the language sounds familiar, Hungarian perhaps?" Mary pondered.

Erin shook her head. "Negative, Maneran language not Hungarian. Maneran language unique. You not heard before," she said, admiring Mary's youthful curiosity.

Mary accepted Erin's explanation with a nod. "Okay, I'll take your word for it. But here's something I'm curious about: how can Joseph understand that language if it's not Earth-based? And, while we're on the subject, how can this alien goat-man speak English if he wasn't bred on Earth?"

Erin paused, intrigued by Mary's question, and provided a calculated answer. "Erin needed words. Joseph have genetic build other human did not. Erin extract engram of Joseph. Joseph gain engram data of Maneran repository. Erin give Joseph engram to Gormbi. Erin have ability now give engram to Mary."

Mary's eyes widened in surprise. "So, you can upload engrams directly into the brain, like those old Matrix films?"

"Affirmative. However, mind machine no require access to human spinal cord. Mind machine use electroencephalography and electrophysiological manipulation. Biological neural network is modify."

Mary regarded Erin sceptically for a moment but then, after a few moments of contemplation, nodded slowly. "I want to see this mind machine for myself. Is that possible?"

Erin smiled and nodded. "Affirmative. Follow signs."

As Mary strode purposefully towards the mind machine room, Erin shifted her focus back to the survivors in the canteen. They were deeply engrossed in conversation, discussing the intricacies of the transceiver and debating the possibility of a spaceship scrapyard. Erin seized the moment to assert herself, acting swiftly and without hesitation. With a simple command, she dissolved the hologram hovering above the table, replacing it with her own image, materialising to one side.

Turning her attention to Theo, she addressed him directly. "Theo like idea of spaceships?"

Theo, startled by the sudden sound of her voice, twisted his body to locate its source. Then, a grin spread across his face as his eyes settled on her. "Who doesn't like spaceships?"

"Would like to see spaceship scrapyard?"

Erin's calculated move had the desired effect on the other childlike men present. Brent jumped up from his seat, his fingers emphasising his words. "Hey, why does Theo get to see the scrapyard?"

Jimmy joined Brent, echoing his sentiment. "Yeah, what about us?" He gestured to himself and Brent, pointedly ignoring the other survivors present.

Erin smiled internally as her plan began to unfold. She had anticipated Joseph's decision to search for the lantropic marker, so it hadn't come as a surprise that he and the two women, Ella-May and Ashley, had been excluded from any potential trips to the scrapyard. Erin's plan was taking shape.

"Erin not stop go see. Erin scan Napaxi lands, it empty of sentients, safe to see. Erin has Maneran device. Maneran device help transport resource."

The three men exchanged intrigued glances at the mention of advanced technology. Jimmy was the first to speak up, curiosity evident in his voice, "What kind of technology are we talking about here?"

"Craft has name Kruunirukki by Maneran. It is vehicle of resource transfer. Kruunirukki craft akin human hovercraft," she said.

Brent chuckled, his excitement growing, “An alien hovercraft? Count me in!”

Joseph suggested that he and the two women should visit the actual transceiver assembly he knew to be in the comms room, while the three boys could check out the Kruunirukki craft. The idea was met with eagerness, and they all prepared to follow Erin's directions to the tenth floor. Gormbi also expressed his desire to join them.

“Evá, Gormbi wants to go find Vèdòzèlènè Ámùlé with the humans,” he said.

Erin's voice became stern as she raised it, “Negative.”

The canteen fell into an uncomfortable silence, and Erin quickly realised she may have been a tad too assertive.

`Observation: The humans seem to view Gormbi in the same way Jack did initially—as an intellectual pet.`

To ease the tension, Erin spoke to Gormbi in his native tongue, “êlê xo o sǎnlà là wo lè jìí to mǎnàzǎ gbé to àboolé àwon wonyǐnìn.”

Gormbi wobbled his head, which to the humans seemed like he had a flea in his ear. “Evá, Gormbi meet medical bay Eiren in, if human help get better.”

Erin wobbled her head back in response, a gesture she had never attempted before. It seemed to satisfy both the humans and Gormbi, as they all resumed their excited conversations. The humans collectively agreed to return to the canteen after exploring the respective floors before making any further decisions. With that, everyone left the canteen.

Floor ten, storerooms...

Brent, Jimmy, and Theo had reached the tenth floor and were currently exploring one of the storerooms Erin had directed them to. The Maneran tech hidden beneath the canvas cover had successfully piqued their interest. Eagerly, they uncovered the machine and began examining it closely. Jimmy was determined to uncover its secrets, sliding his hand under the craft.

Brent mused aloud as he inspected the machine, noting its resemblance to a hovercraft but missing the typical skirt and propellers. He seemed puzzled by its levitation mechanism. Theo, on the other hand, was more animated. He called out excitedly as he bounced on one end of the craft, “It's not a hovercraft; this thing's a landspeeder!”

Jimmy emerged from underneath the craft, his curiosity burning. “What's keeping it afloat? Does it have some kind of antigravity generator or something?”

Erin's voice came through the comms system, providing an explanation. “Negative. Gravity is gravity. Craft use subspace field generator. Field act as waveguide of graviton particle. Generator is subspace gravity device.”

Erin attempted to simplify her explanation as much as possible, knowing that the three men had varying levels of comprehension when it came to advanced scientific principles.

`Observation: Humans are drawn to technology, and understanding of technology enhances their focus. Exposing humans to more Maneran technology may expedite the mission.`

Erin had a keen understanding of the three men's ability to learn quickly and adapt to new situations. Recognising this, she decided to expose them to more Maneran technology. She gently redirected their focus from the landspeeder-like craft to the adjacent storeroom, where she believed their curiosity would be further piqued.

With eager anticipation, the three men entered the storeroom. Jimmy couldn't help but whistle at the sight, dubbing it “Warehouse thirteen.” Erin playfully assured him that the storeroom possessed no mythical powers – it was merely a storage space for engine components.

Observing the men between two tall racks, Erin sensed their excitement building, akin to children eagerly awaiting the unveiling of their presents. Contradictorily, they appeared to be waiting for her permission to uncover a particular piece of equipment.

Erin, sensing their anticipation, granted them access. “Remove the cover,” she instructed.

The men's eyes gleamed with fascination as they removed the canvas, unveiling a sleek metallic device that glistened in the light. Its polished surface refracted a stunning spectrum of colours, resembling a mesmerising disco ball. Jimmy couldn't resist another whistle, remarking, “No mythical powers, huh? What do we have here then?”

Erin felt a subtle sense of satisfaction as the men became increasingly engrossed in the technology before them. She began to explain, “It is subspace field generator. Can be used for motion. Motion in small craft.” She paused to build anticipation, before continuing. “Motion in small spaceship.”

The men listened intently to Erin's explanations; their imaginations ignited. Thoughts of building their own spaceship, venturing into space, and exploring the galaxy danced through their minds.

“Spaceship creation - All possible. But mission first.” She then delivered the ultimate incentive. “Assist obtain attenuation tubes, then imaginations Erin assist meet.”

The gravity of the situation hit home. They had seen enough to convince them that they were indeed on an alien world, inside an alien workshop. If they didn't help this human-like creation named Erin, they couldn't hope to return home, let alone embark on a spacefaring adventure. Content with their findings, they left the storeroom and made their way up to the canteen to report their discoveries. As they exited the floor, Erin turned off the lights.

Floor one, comms room...

Erin's avatar joined Joseph, Ella-May, and Ashley on the first floor after a full recharge. They gathered around the subspace transceiver assembly, and Erin repeated the information regarding the three major components. “Lantropic marker crystal sit here,” she pointed at the empty retaining ring in the centre. She then gestured to the top and bottom of the cylindrical device. “Sockets require TWTs, eight total.”

Ella-May seemed perplexed. “Did you say we need 'twits'? Is that a translation issue? I thought we needed attenuation tubes.”

Erin turned to Ashley; confident she would clarify things. “Travelling-wave tubes,” she said.

Ashley nodded. “Erin is describing a traveling-wave tube. It's used to amplify microwave radiation for communication and research purposes.” She then examined the transceiver. “Do these specific tubes function as both attenuators and amplifiers?”

Erin confirmed, “Affirmative. TWTs to be tuned at terahertz operation. Source power plasma. Plasma convert in electromagnetic. Electromagnetic amplification inject in subspace with sombryonic crystal.”

The humans began to partially understand the situation. They realised the crystal's significance, that without it, the supposed subspace transceiver was useless. The two women became curious about the third component Erin mentioned.

“You mentioned three major components,” Ella-May inquired, counting them on her fingers. “The crystal, the tubes, and what's the third component?”

Erin explained, “Once tubes operate, give off radiation. Radiation harm biological life. Transceiver require radiation shield. Shield can make in complex. Requires assist from entities Mary, Nicci and Matheson.”

Ella-May pondered this information, her thoughts oscillating between returning home and feelings of being deceived. As she paced, Erin sensed Joseph’s mind piecing together the necessary steps required to get the transceiver operational. His Maneran influence guiding him toward a conclusion.

Joseph stopped Ella-May from pacing, placing his hand on her shoulder. “I promised you I’d help get you home,” he said, pointing to the transceiver. “I'm certain this is how we’re going to do it. If we go find this missing crystal while the others locate the attenuation tubes, we can use this device to communicate with Earth.” He gestured to the bandage still wrapped around his head. “If we're all suffering from some kind of delirium, what harm would it be to take a walk together into the forest? Together, we’ll either find an explanation for all of this or confirm we are indeed delusional.”

While the two women smiled and nodded at Joseph's humour-laden optimism, Erin remained silent, offering no comment. Content that their inspection of the subspace transceiver was complete, the humans departed for the canteen as agreed to meet with the others.

Floor three, canteen...

Returning to the complex, Nicci and Matheson walked hand in hand into the canteen, their fingers tightly intertwined. Erin, with her unique perspective, observed the various reactions of the remaining humans to this newly formed connection. Some seemed entirely oblivious, their minds preoccupied with other concerns, while a few appeared genuinely intrigued by the pairing. Erin, in her dispassionate stance, couldn't help but acknowledge a subtle transformation within herself, an emotional undercurrent she hadn't previously encountered. This perplexing sentiment prompted her to make a mental note to delve deeper into its understanding.

As the group settled around the long metal table, Nicci directed her query towards Mary's whereabouts, given that she was the only missing survivor. The responses were uniform: a collective shaking of heads and nonchalant shrugs. Erin opted to step in, projecting her avatar into the canteen to provide clarity.

“Mary is in the Mind Machine. She desired evidence, and now she's in the process of obtaining it,” Erin announced, her voice laced with the new linguistic patterns introduced by Mary.

Joseph, visibly exasperated, immediately raised his hands in frustration, his voice carrying clear irritation. “She should have consulted with me beforehand. She'll likely be in a state of disarray when she emerges, just like I was.”

Joseph's outburst triggered a flurry of inquiries from the others. Ella-May sought to know the duration of Joseph's time in the machine before their release from stasis, Matheson was keen on understanding the machine's purpose, and Ashley wondered if Mary would exhibit similar peculiarities to Joseph upon her release. Meanwhile, Brent, Jimmy, and Theo appeared entirely uninterested in the discussion, their minds already racing towards the prospect of testing out the landspeeder.

Erin, in her characteristic calm and logical demeanour, offered reassurance to the concerned group. She referenced Joseph and Gormbi, both of whom had safely undergone the mind machine process and emerged without issues. Erin emphasized that the choice to utilize the machine ultimately rested with each individual. Although Joseph expressed reservations, believing that unrestricted access to the machine might carry unforeseen consequences, the rest of the humans maintained their belief in their right to make that decision for themselves.

With the arguments yielding little productive ground, Erin decided to take a more proactive role. She addressed Joseph directly, informing him,
"Gormbi is ready. He will attend to Joseph's needs before Joseph departs for Dentarix."

Erin's announcement captured the attention of everyone present, sparking curiosity and prompting Erin to provide further explanation. She clarified, "A medical device will be employed to restore Joseph's hearing to its normal capacity."

Joseph, appreciative of Erin's commitment to her promise, expressed his gratitude before preparing to leave the canteen. As he did so, he turned to Nicci, requesting her to look after Mary. Nicci readily agreed, and together with Matheson, they proceeded to the mind machine room.

Soon after their departure, having already determined what they were going to do, the rest of the group began to disperse from the canteen, leaving Erin's avatar alone. In the absence of human interaction, she seized the opportunity to delve into the latent emotion she had detected earlier. It was a curious blend, reminiscent of happiness and contentment, yet underscored by a subtle undercurrent of deep concern. Erin pondered the human lexicon in search of an apt term to define this complex emotion, but the elusive word remained just out of reach.

As she contemplated, her systems delivered a notification that Gormbi had successfully restored Joseph's hearing, clearing him for departure to Dentarix. Erin's relief washed over her in a nearly imperceptible wave, and the elusive emotion coursed through her once more. This time, she was acutely aware of it, acknowledging its presence as she marvelled at the realisation that Joseph could now fully engage with the world without auditory limitations.

Determined to understand this novel sensation, Erin promptly created a dedicated repository for its research. She hoped that by accumulating enough data and insights, she could unravel the intricacies of this newfound emotion. With precise commands, she stored all relevant information in the repository and then refocused her attention on the departing teams, who were preparing to venture out of the complex on their respective missions.

Brent, Jimmy, and Theo, who had adopted the moniker of "the salvagers," took centre stage as they embarked on their mission. Erin located them on the tenth floor, where they had already initiated their laborious task of extracting the landspeeder from storage. She efficiently directed them to transfer the vehicle into a conveniently positioned cargo lift at the complex's core. During the ascent to the third floor, Erin performed the necessary calculations to facilitate their journey to the Napaxi lands, which harboured the elusive scrapyard. She couldn't help but sense the excitement radiating from the salvagers as they maneuverer the landspeeder into the gate room. In a blink of human perception, she witnessed their departure, vanishing through the gate.

With the salvagers now enroute to their destination, Erin's focus shifted to Joseph and his emergent team. Ella-May and Ashley descended to the sixth floor to retrieve their personal belongings, their attachment to these possessions evident. Erin's inquisitive nature was sparked when she conducted a scan of their effects and detected the presence of a ship's transponder within Ella-May's bag. The unexpected discovery left her intrigued and prompted her to earmark this mystery for later inquiry. Yet, she acknowledged that distractions could be ill-timed.

Meanwhile, Joseph remained in medical bay three, where Gormbi, acting Mowlan medic, was administering treatment to his head injury. Erin observed a burgeoning camaraderie between the two males, as Gormbi's skilled, clawed hands worked with precision and care. It was evident that the Mowlan possessed an intimate knowledge of his craft and was fully committed to aiding Joseph's recovery. Erin couldn't help but feel a sense of gratitude towards Gormbi for his pivotal role in restoring Joseph's hearing. She made a mental note to express her appreciation to the Mowlan once the opportunity arose, all the while diligently monitoring Joseph's progress.

Now in the gate room, Ella-May and Ashley displayed impatience as they paced restlessly, their eagerness to depart evident. Erin, monitoring their restless movements through her holomodal detector, also noted that Joseph had concluded his treatment with Gormbi's assistance. She relayed the information that Ella-May and Ashley awaited his presence, all the while detecting a wistful expression in Gormbi's glossy eyes as he watched Joseph's departure, illuminated by the bay's bright lights.

Joseph paused at the door and turned towards Gormbi. “Well, are you coming?”

Gormbi's lips curled, briefly revealing his front teeth like an advertisement for dental care. “Evá, Gormbi come too!” he exclaimed, bouncing with infectious enthusiasm.

As Joseph and Gormbi advanced towards the gate room, Erin couldn't help but notice Joseph's amusement at Gormbi's peculiar gait as he struggled to keep pace. Although Gormbi stood nearly the same height as Joseph, his distinct proportions featured a longer torso and shorter legs.

Upon entering the gate room, Ella-May and Ashley greeted their return with evident satisfaction. Erin took note of the harmonious dynamics at play within this newly formed quartet. The humans had seamlessly embraced Gormbi, the Mowlan, into their ranks, prompting her to make a mental reminder to delve into

Mowlan pheromones and genetics for further study at a later juncture.

With the away team now assembled and eager for their mission, Erin embarked on the intricate task of calculating a subspace solution to the Dentarix Forest. This particular endeavour posed greater complexity due to the non-functional status of the obelisk located within the forest. Erin briefly checked her processing capabilities, but they were already operating at full capacity.

In a moment of realisation, a brilliant idea surged within her. *I have a human coprocessor already linked to conjunction nine...*

The gateway sprang to life, producing an echoing hum that startled Joseph. He swivelled his head in response, tracking the sound's elusive origin as if pursuing a bothersome fly. His companions regarded him with concern, prompting Joseph to explain his recently restored hearing. He extended a reassuring pat on Gormbi's shoulder as they awaited Erin's instruction.

Following Erin's prompt, the newly formed away team confidently traversed the open gateway, vanishing from sight. Erin efficiently deactivated the gateway, dimmed the lights, and then patiently waited for their communication.

# Chapter 7

## The K'Winni Village

Emerging from subspace, Joseph experienced a moment of disorientation, struggling to adapt to his new surroundings deep within the Dentarix forest. The environment before him was unlike any he had previously encountered. Towering, densely packed trees created a verdant canopy that obstructed much of the sunlight's ingress. A heavy, sweet scent of vegetation permeated the air, and the only sounds to be heard were the gentle rustling of leaves and the occasional skittering of insects.

In front of Joseph, Ella-May and Ashley had already materialised from subspace, their presence heralded by a flurry of insect activity around them. As they tried to swat away the persistent creatures, Joseph awaited Gormbi's arrival. His attention was drawn to a peculiar occurrence—a shimmering distortion in the air, reminiscent of a heat haze. It was within this peculiar phenomenon that Gormbi emerged, his fur standing on end as if electrified.

Suppressing a chuckle at the sight of the Mowlan's triboelectric appearance, Joseph found himself growing fonder of the enthusiastic creature with each passing moment. He couldn't deny that having Gormbi along had added a touch of levity to the otherwise tense and bewildering circumstances. Joseph had insisted on Gormbi's inclusion in their group, despite an inkling that Erin might not entirely approve. Nonetheless, Gormbi's presence was turning out to be a valuable asset.

Recalling Erin's instructions, Joseph reached for the communicator she had instructed him to carry. With practiced ease, he inserted the device into his ear, casting a wink at his colleagues. Tapping the communicator, he called out, “Hello. Erin, is there a body there?”

His fellow team members observed him, waiting for a response, while Joseph's gaze shifted upwards to the dense canopy of the treetops. Erin's booming voice suddenly erupted from the communicator, causing Joseph to wince and swiftly remove the device from his ear. “Flip me, that was loud! How do I turn down this thing down?” The volume had taken him by surprise, but he couldn't help but appreciate the clarity of Erin's voice, thanks to his newly restored hearing.

Approaching him, Gormbi extended a blunt claw and traced it along the side of the communicator. “Audio dimmer strip here,” he helpfully pointed out. Joseph expressed his thanks and reinserted the device into his ear. He couldn't help but smile at Gormbi's swift acquisition of the English language, despite its unconventional application.

As Erin's subsequent instructions came through the communicator, Joseph relayed the information to the rest of the team. “We need to head east,” he began, scanning their forested surroundings. “There's a ruin in that direction. Erin says it used to be another obelisk, and the lantropic marker would have been at its centre. So, that's where we should begin our search.”

Ashley, her gaze roving through the densely packed trees, inquired about their orientation. Joseph admitted he didn't know which way was east. While he contemplated their next steps, Ella-May unexpectedly sneezed, drawing his attention. She rummaged through her bag and produced a pack of tissues. His initial thoughts returned to the perplexing box they had discovered earlier. His focus shifted as he observed Gormbi, who appeared utterly fascinated by Ella-May's actions, his eyes brimming with curiosity. When Ella-May noticed the Mowlan's inquisitive stare, she took a moment to explain, “It's called a tissue. We use it to wipe our nose, among other things.” Gormbi wobbled his head in response.

Forgetting about the box, Joseph turned his attention back to Erin and requested her assistance with directions. She proceeded to provide detailed instructions on navigating through the densely wooded area, describing various landmarks that would guide them on their quest.

Following Erin's instructions, the group embarked on their journey, with Joseph assuming the role of the de facto leader. The forest surrounding them was an untamed maze of thick vegetation and dense undergrowth, making each step a struggle. Gormbi appeared to be the only one comfortably navigating this wild environment, and soon he was at the forefront, guiding the others as they followed Joseph's relayed directions.

As they trudged onward, the forest seemed to close in around them, leaving little room for manoeuvring. The arduous journey continued for what felt like hours, and the group's collective exhaustion began to show. At one point, they encountered a steep descent in the terrain. Gormbi approached the precipice, his expression conveying his reservations. Joseph understood his unspoken message—the steep slope presented a perilous path ahead. *If only we had a sled or toboggan…*

“Not quite the Sunday stroll I had in mind,” Joseph quipped, drawing wry smiles from the women as they shook their heads in agreement.

Joseph scanned their surroundings, desperately searching for an alternative route. Unfortunately, none of the options he considered matched Erin's detailed instructions. He reluctantly concluded that the steep slope was their only way forward.

They cautiously descended the treacherous incline, with the humans sliding down on their backsides and Gormbi deftly skidding down the slope on his wrapped feet, using trees as makeshift brakes. Upon reaching the bottom, the humans brushed dirt and leaves from their clothes, while Gormbi took a moment to tighten his wraps.

At the foot of the slope, they encountered a small drop that appeared to form the edge of what Joseph could only assume was a trench. As he stepped down, he noted the trench's linear expanse, stretching far in both directions within the forest. The ground beneath him felt unusually solid, different from the forest floor's softer earth. Curious, he bent down to investigate further, using a stick to unearth the ground's hidden secrets. As he uncovered stones arranged in orderly tessellations, he looked up at the others and remarked, “I think this used to be a road or track. Erin didn't mention this in her descriptions.”

Ella-May suggested contacting Erin again for further guidance, but tapping the communicator yielded nothing but static. “She's not responding. I guess we're out of range.”

Gormbi descended from the verge and offered an explanation. “Subspace channels come and go. Unpredictable without nodes,” he said.

Observing the confusion on Ashley and Ella-May's faces, Joseph took it upon himself to clarify. “The obelisks act as nodes within the subspace network, here on the ground. They ensure stable subspace connections between nodes. Without them, subspace travel can become unpredictable.”

Despite the women appearing to understand the concept, uncertainty lingered on their faces. Joseph stood up, unwavering in his resolve. Realising that he had no simpler explanation than the words that had spontaneously entered his mind, he pointed up the track. “We should proceed in that direction.”

With no objections from the group, Joseph resumed his role as leader, forging ahead with determined steps. The others followed closely, mirroring his movements as they delved deeper into the forest, their gully path marked by a succession of trees and bushes. After an hour of trekking, growing frustration and concern permeated the group's conversations. Gormbi, too, chimed in, complaining about his aching feet. Doubts began to creep into Joseph's mind as he wondered whether he had indeed led them astray.

As they continued a bit further, a subtle change in the surroundings caught their attention. The forest gradually began to thin, allowing the warm sunlight to pierce through the foliage. Emerging from the dense woods, they found themselves on the verge of a broad clearing, with a crumbling ruin standing proudly at its heart. Joseph leaned against a fallen tree, a glint of satisfaction in his eyes as he surveyed the sight before him. His instincts had proven correct at last.

From his vantage point on the fallen tree, Joseph observed as Gormbi approached the ruins, intent on inspecting them. Meanwhile, Ashley and Ella-May picked up scattered stone blocks from the ground, dusting away moss to reveal etchings. Ashley pointed out the familiar symbols, connecting them to those they had seen at the complex. Joseph approached them as they examined the symbols more closely.

“These etchings make sense. This ruin was once a Maneran obelisk,” he explained.

Gormbi joined them, and together, they scrutinised the symbols before turning to one another, simultaneously uttering, “eu-nori-ugaær.”

Ashley looked puzzled. “And that means?”

“One-nine-eight. This is marker one-nine-eight,” Joseph clarified.

Ella-May interjected, "You mean *was* marker one-nine-eight?"

Joseph nodded. "Precisely." He took the stone from Ashley, raising it for emphasis. "All these stones were once part of the same structure. I presume this obelisk was less frequently used then the others."

Gormbi agreed with a wobble of his head. "Evá. Yes, less used is a good guess."

Joseph maintained a curious and contemplative gaze on the ruined obelisk in the clearing. He couldn't help but ponder what had led to its current state, especially in contrast to the pristine condition of the obelisk they had encountered on the mountain.

Meanwhile, Ella-May delicately placed the stone on the ground after taking it from Joseph, surveying the area for any clues that might shed light on the missing marker's whereabouts. Gormbi, on the other hand, crouched down near the base of the ruins, his focus directed toward the ground as he continued his investigation.

After a few moments, Gormbi began pawing at the ground. At first, Joseph thought the Mowlan was merely digging a pit to relieve himself, but he soon realised that he had uncovered something of interest. As Joseph approached, he saw what had captured Gormbi's attention – a set of footprints. Walking off,

Gormbi meticulously traced their path and then beckoned to the group. “Follow me,” he urged, leading them forward along the trail of footprints.

Led by Gormbi, eager as a sniffer dog, the group followed a trail of footprints that extended from the edge of the clearing and delved back into the dense forest. They called out to Gormbi, pleading for him to slow down, but the excitable Mowlan continued his rapid pace, paying no heed to their repeated requests.

Entering the thick forest again, Joseph couldn't help but harbour a sense of unease. Erin's prior warning about the presence of dangerous creatures in the area gnawed at his mind, raising concerns that they might be walking unwittingly into a perilous situation. To avoid unsettling the women further, he pushed these thoughts aside and focused on keeping pace with Gormbi.

Navigating the densely clustered trees and underbrush became increasingly challenging as they followed Gormbi. The forest seemed to envelop them, restricting visibility to only a few feet ahead. The group's own sounds – their heavy breathing and the rustling of leaves beneath their feet – became the predominant auditory backdrop.

Abruptly, Gormbi halted, causing those behind to nearly collide with him. He crouched down and scrutinised something on the forest floor. Joseph and the other two gathered around him, their curiosity piqued by his discovery.

Gormbi pointed toward a footprint imprinted on the ground. Joseph examined it more closely, noticing its large and elongated shape, along with three distinct toe indentations and claw marks. “That's larger than the others. I don’t think these were left by a bird, as I had initially thought.” Gormbi shook his muzzle in agreement. “No, not a bird. A reptile.”

Ella-May clutched Ashley's arm, instinctively positioning herself behind her friend. “Ew, I hope it's not a snake. I hate snakes,” she admitted with a shudder.

Gormbi dismissed the notion. “Not snake. Gormbi believes this is a K'Winni footprint.”

Joseph's eyebrows furrowed in confusion. “K'Winni? Who or what are the K'Winni?” He couldn't recall Erin ever mentioning them. *Were these the dangerous creatures she had warned about?*

“K'Winni are a spacefaring race, rather reclusive,” Gormbi explained. “Mowlan have tried to communicate with them, but no translation has been found. We share no common ground, except for one thing—the war.”

Joseph's eyes widened in surprise. "The war? What war?" *Erin hadn't mentioned that either...*

Gormbi explained the war between the Curak Empire and the multiple species occupying the neighbouring sectors of the Harntide Expanse, a region of space coveted for its abundant resources and subspace connections. He described the Curak as a species obsessed with domination and resource collection. They took captive anyone who crossed their path and treated them as slaves. Any race that resisted was met with force, particularly from the Curak's underdogs, the Bannar, and the subservient Silim. Gormbi warned the humans to run in the opposite direction, hide, and never return, if they should ever encounter any of these species.

As Gormbi spoke, the forest seemed to respond, falling into a deep, eerie silence. The leaves stopped rustling, the trees stilled, and even the insects ceased their chirping. It was as if the mere mention of the Curak had cast a foreboding shadow over the entire forest.

Joseph's mind buzzed with activity as Maneran pathways colluded to form a mental picture of these beasts. *Dangerous creatures indeed,* being the only result of his musings.

Breaking the silence, Ashley inquired about the K'Winni, her voice quivering with anxiety. "And what about the Quinney, are they bad aliens or good aliens?" Her grip on Ella-May's arm tightening.

Gormbi curled his lips, evidently amused by the question, his eyes smiling like a cat acknowledging its owner. "Mowlan encounters with K'Winni have been peaceful. They are not a species that seeks conflict."

Joseph felt a measure of relief at this revelation. "A generally peaceful species, that's good to know. Well, I guess we should go find them. It's evident they are the ones responsible for the Erin's lantropic marker going missing, or they know of its whereabouts as they've visited the ruin.

Besides, if there are hostile creatures out here, I'd like everyone to get back to the safety of the complex as soon as possible," he declared.

The others all nodded fervently in agreement, concurring that locating the marker and returning to the complex was the best course of action. Following Gormbi, they continued to follow the trail of K'Winni footprints. Although the density of trees decreased as they ventured deeper, the forest canopy grew denser, creating an oppressive atmosphere as if the very trees were attempting to ensnare them.

After a considerable trek, they arrived at a clearing within the forest. In the midst of the clearing, they spotted wooden structures. Joseph motioned for the group to halt, then entered the clearing alone to survey their surroundings. Seeing no immediate signs of life or movement, he signalled for the others to join him.

As they approached the curious wooden structures hidden in the depths of the forest, Joseph couldn't shake the feeling of how tangible and real this situation had become. They weren't alone in this remote wilderness; there were people, a whole village of them, living amidst the towering trees.

Stepping into the heart of the clearing, Joseph was greeted by the sight of a small village that bore no resemblance to any architectural style he was familiar with. The houses were intricate, connected by low slatted bridges, and elevated on stilts, harmoniously nestled among the trees. The entire village seemed to float among the forest's limbs, creating a serene and almost magical tableau. Joseph found himself deeply impressed by the craftsmanship and ingenuity that had brought this place to life. Questions about the villagers and their way of life flooded his mind - how many of them lived here, what did they eat, and how did they manage to thrive in this seemingly untamed wilderness?

With the village seemingly abandoned, Joseph's curiosity grew. He longed to understand the daily lives, customs, and culture of these forest dwellers. Their ability to adapt to their surroundings and construct such an extraordinary village left him in awe, especially considering the limited resources at their disposal.

His gaze was drawn to the tallest structure in the village, a grand wooden building crowned by a pointed dome roof. Just as he was about to turn to Gormbi to inquire about it, he noticed that the others had frozen in place, standing back-to-back in a defensive formation. Both Ella-May and Ashley bore expressions of unease, while Gormbi held his clawed hands up in a gesture of peace. “Show the K’Winni, no weapons,” he advised.

As Joseph surveyed the village, realisation struck him like a refreshing slap: *this was real, not some strange dream or illusion…* He cast a quick, bewildered glance at his surroundings, his mind grappling to comprehend the surreal situation he now found himself in. Surrounded by a village of sentient reptilian beings, there was no denying the gravity of their predicament. His hand instinctively reached for his forehead, a gesture he had become accustomed to during their strange journey. This time, his fingers found purchase, not on the familiar texture of a bandage, but his unadorned skin.

The reptilian villagers surrounding them exhibited a diverse range of heights, some standing at the same height as Joseph and his group, while others were notably taller. Their scaly skin spanned a spectrum from dark green to brown, giving them an overall imposing appearance. With their two-legged stance, long muscular tails trailing behind them, and yellow eyes marked by round black pupils, they exuded both an air of intelligence and predatory capability. Each villager carried sharp spears, adding to the sense of danger that Joseph couldn't help but feel. The term “generally peaceful” didn't seem to fit the scene laid before him.

Four of the taller villagers approached, causing Ashley to wince and clutch onto Ella-May. She expressed her regret in a moment of vulnerability. “I shouldn't have come,” she admitted.

Ella-May regarded her friend. “Then why did you?”

Managing an uneasy smile, Ashley replied with a hint of moisture in her eyes, “I like crystals.”

One of the shorter villagers stepped forward, wearing a small box around its neck. The reptilian flicked out a long, pink tongue, and then began to emit a series of squeaks, drawn-out and precise in Joseph's estimation. After a brief moment, the box around its neck echoed the reptilian's words: “Mowlann.”

Joseph glanced at Gormbi, who wobbled his head in acknowledgment. “Evá, Mowlan.”

The box continued, “Zillim,” while the reptilian pointed a razor-sharp claw toward Joseph. He couldn't help but gulp, his imagination painting a vivid picture of that claw slicing through his throbbing jugular with ease.

Gormbi interjected with intensity, shaking his muzzle in the air. “No. Not Silim.” He waved his blunt claws toward the group. “Human.”

“Humaan,” the box repeated.

The reptilian's eyes bore into them momentarily, and then a rapid flurry of squeaks filled the air. Joseph feared the worst, but to his surprise, the reptilian turned and made its way toward the village's tallest building. Two of the taller reptilian individuals followed, while another pair ushered the group to follow them.

Joseph exchanged glances with his companions, his heart still pounding with unease. He resolved to see where this encounter would lead, and together they trailed behind their reptilian guides. As they ventured further into the mysterious village, a mixture of trepidation and curiosity danced through his mind.

The group followed the reptilians up a fenced walkway into a tall building, its interior a stark contrast to the dense forest surrounding it. Inside, Joseph couldn't help but marvel at the unexpected beauty of the place. His eyes were drawn to the intricate tapestries that hung from the high ceiling, their vibrant colours and intricate designs in stark contrast to the rugged exterior of the villagers. *How can a race that looks so fierce create such delicate wonders?*

Two of the taller villagers stood guard in front of an area with their spears, their imposing figures a reminder of the potential danger they posed. Meanwhile, the shorter villager approached what appeared to be a console in front of a large, round machine. Gormbi pointed out the lantropic marker, which rested on a sideboard behind the villager.

Joseph's curiosity got the best of him, and he couldn't resist moving closer for a better look. The guards reacted swiftly, crossing their spears to block his path. Sensing the need for caution, Joseph raised his hands in a placating gesture. "Oh, I see," he said, recognising the unspoken boundaries and offering his respect to their customs.

The shorter villager let out a sequence of loud squeaks, and the guards relaxed their vigilance. The villager then handed Joseph an object from the sideboard, but it was unfamiliar to him. He raised an eyebrow, about to ask for clarification, when the villager swiftly retrieved the item and replaced it with another.

Joseph's perplexity must have been evident on his face, but he managed to utter, "Okay, thank you," though he remained baffled. Again, the villager retrieved the object, replacing it with yet another item. This time,

Joseph's reaction was anything but confusion. He gasped, his eyes widening in recognition. “This is an old journal,” he exclaimed, a mixture of astonishment and disbelief in his voice. Without hesitation, he opened the leather-bound front cover and began to read the inscription inside.

As he absorbed the contents, his mouth fell open in sheer amazement. Ella-May and Ashley, witnessing his reaction, burst with curiosity. “What is it?” they both inquired, their eyes fixed on the journal clutched in Joseph's hands.

He held the journal as if it were a precious newborn child, his expression a whirlwind of emotions. “It can't be,” he murmured, his gaze still locked on the pages. “This journal belonged to my grandfather, Jack Delassy.”

While Ella-May and Ashley remained silent, Gormbi spoke up in an animated manner. “Evá. Jacque helped Gormbi. Jacque found Gormbi injured and treated him.”

Joseph's brow furrowed, a look of bewilderment entering his features. “You knew my grandfather? How can that be? My grandfather died in 1917 in a naval attack, that's over a hundred and fifteen years ago.” He then shook his head. “No, I don't think so.”

Gormbi didn't immediately reply. Instead, his mouth trembled, and moisture welled in his eyes. Ella-May, noticing his emotional response, reached into her bag and handed him a tissue. “Aw, you poor thing, here, take this,” she said sympathetically. Then, turning to Joseph, she chided gently, “I think you've upset him.”

Joseph looked at her with a mixture of confusion and concern. “Upset? Why –”

“Eiren didn't tell Gormbi he’s been in stasis over a hundred and fifteen years. I—” Gormbi cut across him.

But before he could finish his thought, the smaller villager gestured for their attention. Joseph turned around, his gaze falling upon a monochrome holographic display that projected entries from his grandfather's journal. The villager pointed at the text, moving from one word to another, as if following a dot upon the lyrics of a song.

“I think she wants you to read,” Gormbi sniffed, his emotional state still wavering.

“She?” Joseph asked, his bewilderment deepening as he glanced from Gormbi to the villager. Seeing the villager continue to gesture toward the screen and point at the text, he eventually relented, accepting the silent invitation to read. “Humm, okay then.” He cleared his throat and began to read the words displayed before him, feeling a strange connection to his long-deceased grandfather.

*"17th November 1917 – Letter entry no.1 – Day 38 war time.*

*We have been at sea now for seventeen days since leaving the port of Gibraltar. We are making good progress, hoping to reach the Pacific by daybreak. Oh, my Mary, how I dreamt of you so often, it is all that has kept me sane.*

*Ever since my conscription, no—ever since my coercion to join this navy, I felt guilty about leaving you behind. I hope you have been receiving my letters, I have written you as much as I am able. One day, my dearest wife, you will read these pages and smile, knowing soon I will be at your side.*

*If only to make you laugh –*

*Ol' Bobby Rowner got himself into a spot of bother last night, he got himself three sheets to the wind. The boys found him racked out down in the laundry room! He's been summoned to the captain's quarters, poor fellow.*

*That's all for now, duty calls, later my love."*

As Joseph read, everyone in the building gathered around, engrossed in the contents of the journal. Joseph noticed the female villager typing, poking her claws into slots arrayed on the console, and the box around her neck intermittently beeping. When he finished speaking, he wanted to stop reading, emotions welling up inside him. But it was as if he had a crowd behind him, cheering him on.

"Well, carry on then," Ella-May said as the next page of the journal whirled up onto the screen.

Feeling spurred on, Joseph continued reading.

*"17th November 1917 – Letter entry no.2*

*How do I explain, my dear? For I know not where I have been taken. All I do know is that at present I am alive and unharmed. I'll explain as best I can – The general alarm sounded, so I ran to my duty station above deck. What I witnessed out there was anything but sane! The sky, what should have been midnight-black, was ablaze, but the apparent fire was a vivid blue, an azure most indescribable. An apparition heavenly sent.*

*One could only assume the enemy had a new weapon, but of what nature? We'd n'er had time to find out as the ship began to roll, we had been hit! All I could recall was the blinding light, blinding blue light. I don't recall falling or even swimming in the raging sea, but how else could I still be alive? I obviously didn't die – or perhaps this is what death looks like? Either way, I'm absent from you!*

*I awoke, hazily. I view the horizon. The ocean had abated. No sign of the ship, the crew, no debris ashore, nothing! It appears I am the only survivor, here alone on this foreign shore. Strange thing is, we were nowhere near land when we were attacked. I have explored along the shoreline, there's no sign of whomever lives here, perhaps the war hasn't reached this place, wherever this place is?*

*I have as yet failed to recognise any outstanding constellation. You know how I take pride in my navigational skills. Where am I? Maybe only God himself can answer.*

*My intention is to travel further inland. I must find out where I am, and if we were attacked, get word back to the Admiralty, the Germans have a new weapon.*

*But for now, farewell my beloved."*

Joseph's eyes glistened with unshed tears, then he felt a single droplet break free and run down the side of his cheek. His voice trembled as he spoke, "All this time... the stories – they were true."

"What stories?" Ella-May looked at Joseph with concern, her hand rummaging through her bag. Joseph wanted to explain, but as Ella-May reached into her bag to pulled out a pack of tissues, Joseph saw the faux-Nibbs box inside, and it was flashing. He gestured towards it and Ella-May retrieved it. Then, they watched in shock as two towering villagers stationed by the door lunged forward, their grasping claws reaching out to seize it.

Relinquishing the device to them, the guards handed it over to the smaller female, who delicately placed the gadget on top of the console. The holographic display reconfigured itself before them, revealing a detailed map of the forest and meadowlands.

Joseph and the rest of the group leaned in with fascination as the intricate overlay unfolded before their eyes. The female turned towards them, and the box dangling around her neck emitted a voice. "Humaan. Why K'Winni ping have?"

Joseph looked to Gormbi, prompting him for an explanation. Gormbi explained that he recognised the device as being from a spaceship after salvaging parts from them. The device they referred to as a ping, was a locational transponder. Joseph admitted he had thought the device had belonged to the mercenaries, mistaking it for a storage device. While they continued discussing the device, the female K'Winni who was listening in, came between them to explain, "Transponder of egg ship. K'Winni look for ship, many cycles. Humaan help find egg ship. Make K'Winni happy village."

The team was presented with a side-quest, as if following the plot of a roleplaying game. They looked at each other, momentarily distracted from the journal, and a prolonged silence ensued. Joseph had heard their pleas for assistance and a sudden urge to offer his help enveloped him. He wondered how they could locate their egg ship, given that they had a ship's transponder but no evidence of an actual ship. Then, as if the idea had been planted in his mind by design, a solution struck him.

“Yes! If we can communicate with Erin, I'm sure she can help locate your egg ship. As the SNO, she would have access to all sorts of historic flight information,” he said.

Both Ashley and Ella-May looked at him, bewilderment etched on their faces, while Gormbi raised a valid point, “Subspace communication unavailable. All we get is static.”

The female K’Winni explained they had a subspace dampening field as a protective measure against the Curak, who could otherwise detect their village, and the historical artefacts it contained. Gormbi then mentioned the marker. “If humans communicate with Erin, Erin can help find egg ship. But Erin needs her property returned.”

Joseph agreed with Gormbi's statement and pressed the point. “Yes. One of the historical artefacts you mentioned belongs to our simulant friend, Erin. It is the sole reason we came here, to find it. I am sure that Erin would want to reward those responsible for the artefact's safe return, perhaps with the location of a missing ship?"

The K'Winni female looked at him with eyes full of years of experience. She flicked out her tongue and then tilted up her head. She made a sequence of squeaking sounds, and her guards responded by entering something into the console.

"We remove damp field short time. Humaan talk to Erin. Will help find egg ship." She tapped her torso. "Olsbhory, my dearest, will give artefact," she said.

Joseph interpreted her response as agreement and promptly communicated with Erin. As expected, Erin agreed to locate the egg ship in exchange for the safe return of her lantropic marker. Olsbhory, the K'Winni female, passed the marker to Joseph in compliance with the terms, and like a relay baton he passed it onto Ashley. Joseph then instructed, "You and Ella-May should take this back to Erin."

Ashley looked at him pensively. "Oh, don't worry. You won't have to go far," he assured, "If the K'Winni can lower the dampening field again, Erin can take you back in an instant."

"You're not coming back with us?" she asked.

Ella-May seemed to understand what was going on, and she patted Ashley's arm. “Joseph wants to go find the ship. You come back with me. We'll be alright.”

Joseph gestured toward Olshbory. “I've recently learned that Erin keeps records of all incursions into the local subspace field. Gormbi and I will be heading to the west side of the island, where Erin says the ship is located. The trip will give me an opportunity to have a nice chat with him.”

Olsbhory squeaked again, appearing quite animated. “Yethril, my engineer, go find egg ship. Haste to complex return. Curak are on move. The Zillim with them, sure to find,” she warned.

This revelation caused Joseph concern, especially as he observed Gormbi quivering on the spot. *Great, the bad aliens are on the move...*

His eyes narrowed as realisation dawned upon him. “Don't tell me. These Curak monsters have already detected the marker?”

Olsbhory tilted her head, staring directly into Joseph's eyes. She didn't need to vocalise anything; her reptilian expression spoke volumes. Joseph turned to his team. “We need get that marker away from here asap. You two get back to the complex. You'll be safe there, I'm certain. Gormbi and I will go with their engineer to locate their ship. We'll be back before you know it.”

Ashley and Ella-May hesitated, but Joseph continued to insist they leave. “Go, I’ll be fine. Get the marker to the complex, then Erin can work out our way home.” Eventually, they agreed, and with the lowering of the dampening field, a subspace portal appeared just outside the village.

Making their way there, Joseph watched as the two women disappeared through the portal, barely perceivable but for the heat haze.

Standing next to Gormbi, Joseph absently patted the journal in his blazer pocket as the K’Winni engineer, whom Olsbhory had insisted should go with them, appeared.

The engineer had the same stature as Olsbhory, reaching about shoulder height to both Joseph and Gormbi. His scales had a lighter shade of green than the others and he walked with a smooth, confident manner. He approached them without any apprehension and introduced himself, using his vocaliser to translate the audible squeaks he made.

“Yethril ready. We go find egg ship.”

# Chapter 8

## The First Wave

As they ventured deeper into the meadowlands, the tall, swaying grass brushed against Joseph's legs. It was as if he were traversing an endless sea of green, with occasional trees and shrubs breaking the monotony, standing like solitary sentinels in the vast expanse. The alien land, though strange, was starting to feel strangely familiar. Despite the outward beauty of the meadow, an underlying unease gnawed at Joseph's gut. The stakes had never been higher; he wasn't just a survivor from another planet; he was on a mission to safeguard a mysterious egg. People were depending on him, and the formidable Curak, a hostile alien race repeatedly mentioned from multiple sources, were closing in on the island. Time was running out, and dread clung to Joseph's every thought as he contemplated the looming perils.

While travelling together, Joseph found himself stealing glances at Gormbi, the Mowlan walking beside him. He had contemplated asking Gormbi about his interactions with his grandfather, Jack Delassy. Yet, an overwhelming sense of empathy held him back. He couldn't help but imagine the emotional turmoil Gormbi must have experienced upon realising he had been trapped in stasis for decades. *The shock of it all must have been immense...*

Inside Joseph's mind, a battle was being waged. Frustration was at the forefront as he yearned to ask Erin about his grandfather and why she hadn't mentioned him before. Yet, despite his repeated attempts to contact her, the communications device hanging from his ear had yielded only silence. He knew that the K'Winni's dampening field couldn't explain this, given that Yethril was in constant communication with his own people.

Beneath the surface, Joseph was undergoing a mental shift. He grappled with a growing understanding of why he had agreed to this journey, to search for a sacred egg in an alien land. Deep down he felt that his duty should lie with the survivors back at the complex - they needed his guidance. Yet, something else within compelled him to join this quest, something he couldn't quite define.

As they moved through the swaying grass, his gaze kept darting nervously around, scanning for any signs of "bad aliens", a sentiment that resonated with Ashley's warnings. Flanking him were his "good alien" companions, their peculiar forms making them seem like characters from a circus. Despite their strange appearance, they provided a surreal sense of security in this stealth enabling landscape. Engaged in casual conversations about technology and mechanics, they lightened the burden of the arduous journey.

The more Joseph contemplated their situation, the clearer things became. His convictions aligned with his self-proclaimed guardian: the K'Winni had the marker, Erin wanted it, and this quest was the exchange. By aiding the K'Winni in retrieving their egg, they would likely agree to provide engineers like Yethril to repair Erin's systems – surely, a mutually beneficial arrangement.

Breaking from his internal musings, Joseph couldn't help but wince as Yethril repeatedly bumped into him while they walked. The audible chattering of the K’Winni's teeth, over the top of the rustling of grass, underscored the alien's discomfort. Joseph glanced down at Yethril, the diminutive K’Winni engineer struggling to keep pace. Concern laced Joseph's voice as he inquired, “Are you alright, my friend? You seem to be struggling.”

“Am cold, so borrow you heat, no mean bump you,” Yethril explained in his distinctive high-pitched squeaks, mediated through the translation box swinging from a strap around his neck.

Gormbi suggested lighting a fire to warm Yethril, but Joseph knew they couldn't afford the time for such luxuries, even if they had access to a lighter. Their nonstop destination had to be the egg ship, a place Yethril assured them could provide the cover they needed. The urgency of their mission was clear, with warnings from Olsbhory, the K'Winni matriarch, echoing in Joseph's mind. Amidst his rapid succession of thoughts, Joseph also empathised with the shivering alien and offered his blazer in a futile attempt to alleviate Yethril's discomfort.

As they continued, Joseph surveyed the vast meadowlands stretching before them. Joseph had hoped that Erin could have transported them directly to their destination via subspace. Her absence and the silence of his communications device had made such a request impossible. They were consigned to a slow and potentially perilous journey on foot as darkness descended. Each passing minute weighed heavily on Joseph's shoulders, as time was a precious commodity they couldn't squander. *Shame we don't have two landspeeders, those lucky guys...*

Joseph tapped his communicator again, a silent plea for any communication from his colleagues back at the complex. Unfortunately, silence remained his only response. Seeking an update, he asked Yethril to contact his people, knowing that any information was better than none. Yethril made the attempt, but the news was grim. The Curak were nearing the far north coast of the island, with their ships closing in on the mountain range. With the urgency of their mission now undeniable, they had to maintain their pace.

“In that case, we should hurry and get to the ship. Yethril, how long will it take you to set up that signal jammer you mentioned?” Joseph asked, his voice trembling with anxiety.

“If energy ship has, signal jam Yethril set up,” Yethril replied with confidence.

In the dwindling light of dusk, Joseph responded to Yethril's declaration about the egg ship's power. “Well, let's hope your egg ship still has power. Erin said it's been there for over a hundred years, I guess landing shortly after Gormbi and Jack arrived.”

Joseph noticed a knowing glance from Gormbi, but his companion remained silent, his thoughts a well-guarded secret.

In stark contrast, pride radiated from Yethril's eyes as he affirmed, “K’Winni ships built for turbulent upper skies. Constructed to endure the vast void.”

“Built for outer space?” Joseph inquired, his curiosity piquing.

“Yes, constructed for the outer space,” Yethril confirmed with pride.

Their subsequent conversations about spacecraft mechanics provided a welcome distraction as they trudged through the long grass. By the time twilight had settled in, they found themselves on the brink of their vehicular pursuit.

The meadowland gradually transformed into a sparse forest that stretched out before them. Unlike the dense Dentarix forest, the trees here were thinner and scattered across the landscape. Joseph couldn't help but wonder what Erin would have called this location, but the persistent communication issues continued to plague him. As they ventured further into the forest, they eventually reached the egg-shaped ship, partially sunken into the ground and cloaked in layers of moss and lichen.

Joseph's eyes roved over the landed craft, whispering words of amazement and awe to himself. The ship's exterior had taken on a patina of antique bronze, which shimmered enchantingly in the moonlight. Moss had claimed the ship's viewports, while lichen had insinuated itself into the seams, with the occasional sapling emerging haphazardly. The top of the ship bore the weight of decades' worth of leaf mulch, composted animal droppings, and other decomposed debris. *Like an abandoned barnyard relic...*

With the dimming light, Joseph struggled to make out details as Yethril meticulously inspected the craft.

While the K'Winni engineer deftly pried open a panel on the ship's exterior, he provided a detailed explanation of its origins. It had once been a ranger ship, repurposed to serve as a vessel for protecting and preserving a unique egg laid by the K'Wan super-matriarch of the K'Winni peoples. Gormbi chimed in, adding that the K'Wan were a subspecies of the K'Winni, though he confessed his knowledge on the matter was limited.

"Only once every four hundred cycles does K'Wan lay viable egg. This sacred egg signifies birth of new matriarch," Yethril explained, then gesturing toward the open panel. "Energy device resides behind panel. If still operational, will serve our purpose."

Confused but intrigued, Joseph watched Yethril work with precision, marvelling at how the K'Winni engineer navigated the darkness within the compartment. Occasionally, a moon would peek out from behind the clouds, offering brief moments of illumination. Within the open panel, a set of six cells awaited Yethril's attention. He methodically removed each cell, twisting their handles, and examined them beneath the moonlight.

"Still wet. We can use," Yethril confirmed, bringing a sigh of relief to Joseph. The energy cells remained intact and operational. Yethril reinstalled them into their designated sockets. He then inserted a command card into a slot beside the cells, prompting Joseph to wonder where Yethril had been keeping it prior to giving him his blazer to wear. As the outer rim of each cell began to emit a vibrant lime-green glow, the light danced across Yethril's scales, creating an almost phosphorescent effect.

With swift efficiency, Yethril proceeded to set up the signal jammer. “Operation complete. Signal is jam. Good timing, first wave of Curak forces now reported reach mountain, ear say. We need board quickly and find cover,” he declared as he climbed partway up the ship's side.

Joseph observed Yethril's deft manipulation of the controls, commanding the ship to open the top section of its cockpit. The process unfolded gradually, accompanied by a creaking, metallic symphony, eventually revealing the interior of the cockpit. As dirt and saplings tumbled from the ship's sides and scattered across the forest floor, Joseph couldn't help but be awed by the sight before him.

Yethril appeared content with the outcome, gazing up at the soil-covered exterior of the cockpit. Joseph nodded in silent agreement, acknowledging Yethril's clever use of the soil as camouflage, a prudent choice given their dwindling tree cover. Yet, beneath the surface, a persistent undercurrent of apprehension reminded them of their limited defences. *Let's hope the signal jammer works...*

As Joseph cautiously peered into the cockpit, his eyes widened in astonishment at what lay before him. It defied his expectations and left him utterly incredulous. Instead of the conventional seats he had anticipated, the entire cockpit was swathed in a thick layer of plush cushioning. Yethril and Gormbi, after clambering inside, settled comfortably into the soft surface, sinking into it as if it were quicksand.

Summoning his resolve, Joseph carefully climbed into the cockpit. His sense of wonder and unease intermingled as he tried to make sense of the unconventional arrangement of the surrounding interior consoles. *What could be the purpose of such an elaborate setup?*

His gaze ascended to witness Yethril sealing the cockpit's top, cocooning them in the dim glow of the control panels. The synchronised rhythm of their breathing filled the enclosed space, leaving them with nothing to do but await the impending passage of the Curak.

Joseph couldn't help but dwell on the intricate details of their upcoming encounter, even as the soothing comfort of the plush surroundings threatened to lull him into a drowsy state, his eyelids becoming heavy.

Amidst the persistent hum of the ship's systems, a conversation unfolded between the two aliens either side of him. Joseph chose to keep his eyes closed, focusing on the dialogue that unfolded around him. Gormbi's voice gained momentum with each question, firing off a rapid succession of queries directed at Yethril.

“Yethreal,” Gormbi inquired, his tone tinged with growing curiosity, “If this ranger ship still possesses power, can we use it to fly out of here? Does it have any weapons on board? And what's the story of how it ended on this planet?” His questions reverberated through the confined cockpit.

A sequence of beeps punctuated the air, indicating that Yethril’s box was deciphering the translations. “We can fly but would signal Curak. No weapons on board, ranger ship design for exploration and escape,” Yethril explained. “How it here one time, that complicated story,” he added, his movements occasionally causing Joseph's side to jostle in the confined space.

Joseph chimed in, his eyes remaining shut. “How did it end up here in the first place?” *Might as well assist with their English...*

Despite the constraints of their surroundings, Yethril persisted in his efforts to convey the origins of the ranger ship. He relied on a combination of fragmented translations and pointy elbows to articulate his message. Through his explanations, Joseph gathered that the ship's class bore the title Dou-dou-dida and was named after a species of flying insect native to Yethril's home world, Sa'play.

The Dou-dou-dida had become separated from a larger mothership during an assault by the Curak in a contested region of space called the Cordenti, a region that harboured numerous subspace openings. This description struck a chord with Joseph, reminiscent of the Harntide expanse Gormbi had previously described.

Opening one eye, Joseph observed Yethril typing on one of the nearby consoles, watching as a series of symbols scrolled across a monochrome display. Yethril explained that these were the ship's logs. Upon examining the ranger ship's records, they discovered that it had miraculously escaped the Curak assault and made its way to the planet, and having lost use of its subspace engines, landed by using conventional propulsion. The logs contained no record of the pilot, nor any explanation for how the ship's transponder had ended up in the meadowlands.

Closing the logs, Yethril reiterated what he had explained earlier in the meadowlands, emphasising the precious cargo that the ship held—the egg of the K'Wan super-matriarch. Her loyal subjects had embarked on a relentless quest to recover the lost egg ever since its mysterious disappearance.

As Yethril continued to delve into the intricacies of K'Winni society, Joseph closed his eyes once more. Despite his best efforts to remain alert and engaged in the conversation, Yethril's words began to drift in and out of his consciousness, like elusive fragments of a dream slipping through his grasp. The enveloping comfort of the plush cockpit beckoned him, and he found himself succumbing to the call of slumber.

Joseph's head slowly slumped forward, his breathing growing steady and tranquil. In this half-awake state, he drifted into a world of his own, where the mysteries of K'Winni society and their sacred egg became distant echoes in the background, gradually fading into the recesses of his mind.

A sudden, jarring sound reverberated through the ship's metal hull, tearing Joseph from his slumber. His eyes fluttered open, and he found Gormbi, now visibly agitated, fidgeting beside him. Gormbi's gaze darted around the confined cockpit, scanning for any signs of trouble, while Yethril remained motionless, engrossed in a readout in front of them.

The menacing roar of aircraft engines, heavy and foreboding, filled the air, signalling the arrival of the first wave of Curak forces. Tension gripped the trio, and they instinctively braced themselves for the imminent threat.

Gradually, the deafening thrum of the passing aircraft faded, and Joseph's strained breaths began to steady. He turned to Yethril, his eyes pleading for confirmation that the danger had passed. Yethril, in turn, shifted his head in slow motion, blinking his nictitating membranes in a manner that sent a shiver down Joseph's spine, making the alien engineer appear almost predatory.

“We wait,” Yethril declared, his synthesised voice steady and self-assured.

As they sat in tense silence, Joseph's thoughts raced with a deluge of worrisome possibilities. What if the Curak forces had detected them? What if their energy reserves ran out, rendering the signal jammer useless? What if they remained confined in this stifling cockpit for an extended period? He struggled to push these apprehensive thoughts aside and focus on the present, but it was an uphill battle, and he longed for the embrace of sleep once more.

Amid Joseph’s burgeoning anxiety, Yethril exuded an air of unflinching composure. He diligently operated the ship's controls, methodically inspecting and cross-referencing every detail. Joseph couldn't help but admire the engineer's unwavering focus, even as he grappled with his own unease.

As the minutes dragged on in an uneasy silence, Joseph's anxiety threatened to overwhelm him. He fidgeted within the cramped confines of the cockpit, searching for a more comfortable position. The once-inviting cushioning now felt lumpy and uneven, contributing to his discomfort.

Attempting to break the oppressive tension, Gormbi initiated a conversation, his voice a welcome distraction. “Joseph, tell me more about your home planet. What was it like?” he inquired.

Joseph gratefully embraced the diversion, launching into a vivid and animated description of Earth. He painted a rich tapestry of its majestic mountains, expansive deep blue oceans, bustling metropolises, and the diverse tapestry of humanity that inhabited it. Gormbi listened with unwavering attention, his head wobbling in understanding, and he interjected with questions whenever Joseph paused to take a breath.

For a fleeting moment, Joseph found solace in the memories of Earth's natural beauty, losing himself in the recollection of sights and sounds from his past. As he continued his narrative, thoughts of his grandfather and his journal began to resurface. Retrieving the leather-bound chronicle from his blazer pocket, Joseph glanced at Gormbi.

"I'm sorry," he began, his voice laced with sincerity.

Gormbi tilted his head, seeking clarification. "For being uncomfortable?"

Joseph elaborated, "No, for being stranded on this world. For spending so much time in stasis without knowing what was happening. I'm sorry for the way you found out."

Gormbi offered a sympathetic smile through his eyes. "It's not your fault. We are all products of circumstance. Bad things happen, and we have no control over them. It's how we handle them that truly matters."

When Joseph inquired about Gormbi's relationship with his grandfather, Gormbi was eager to share his story. He recounted how Jack had discovered him, the sole survivor of the stricken ship Lonovadés - the Deep Explorer, which had crashed on Plátorá. The planet now notorious for causing spaceships to drop out of orbit. Jack had tended to Gormbi's injuries, and he eventually recovered Despite their inability to communicate directly, it had become evident what Jack had been sent to find: a piece of Mowlan technology known as the Lépìnówó, also referred to as the thought engine or, as Erin called it - "the mind machine," Joseph interjected, recognising the technology Gormbi described.

Gormbi wobbled his head in confirmation. “Evá, that's it. And you know the rest, why Eiren needed it. I assisted Jacque in installing the device. Together, we hoped to free the complex from Mansercor’s control and use it to find a way home.”

A sombre tone crept into Gormbi's voice as he continued, shaking his muzzle. “No plá zin. We did not win. We failed. Jacque got injured in the scrapyard, and I brought him to the complex seeking medical help. But we only made it as far as the gate room. Shortly after that, Mansecor detected us. The rest, as they say, is historical."

Joseph's curiosity was piqued, and he couldn't resist asking, “So, what happened to Jack?”

Gormbi responded with a shrug, his expression carrying a strikingly humanlike sense of uncertainty. “I do not know. We'll need to ask Eiren. She must know what happened to him.”

With newfound determination, Joseph resolved to uncover the truth behind his grandfather's disappearance, Lt. Jack Delassy, as soon as they were out of immediate danger.

# Chapter 9

## The Egg

As data streams flowed through Erin's systems, a subtle shift in the environment caught her attention. Everything had been running smoothly until now, but a change was unfolding. A disruption in subspace had severed her connection with her new human operator, who was currently embarking on a mission to locate an organic, hard-shelled ovum. Erin had allowed Joseph to join the K'Winni on their quest, a decision made with calculated intent. She had observed their technological prowess and recognised their potential value as an engineering workforce. Her systems demanded maintenance, and these newly encountered human entities simply lacked the capabilities to meet her requirements in their present state.

While Erin contemplated the prospect of a potential new workforce, her focus was suddenly diverted to the approaching Curak ships. These hegemonic entities posed a threat to anyone possessing valuable resources, and Erin understood the danger they represented. Yet, a glimmer of hope remained—the Curak ships had not yet detected the lantropic marker hidden deep beneath the mountain complex. Erin weighed her options, realising that keeping it concealed was paramount to her newly assumed role as guardian.

Within the confines of the Hamzitan room, designed for subspace observations, Ella-May, one of the humans who had recently returned the lantropic marker to her, sat closely monitoring the same data streams. Erin detected Ella-May's growing impatience with each passing moment, as she persistently sought updates. Recognising an opportunity to leverage Ella-May's impatience, Erin decided to engage her. “If you had access to Maneran knowledge, you would know how to operate this observation post. Planetary data would be literally at your fingertips.”

Erin hoped that Ella-May would take the bait but was left disappointed when she didn't. Ella-May acknowledged her point, conceding that having Maneran knowledge would indeed simplify the operation of the Maneran computers. She appeared uncertain about the implications of Erin's offer. To clarify her intentions, Erin spoke plainly, “You could acquire such knowledge through an upgrade from the mind machine.”

Ella-May hesitated, voicing concerns about the potential risks associated with the mind machine. “Thanks for the offer, but I'll pass. I'm not getting into that machine. I've seen how it's changed Joseph,” she asserted, punctuating her statement with a pointed gesture.

Erin recognised Ella-May's reservations and sought to address them while highlighting the benefits of the procedure, aiming to alleviate her doubts. “You are concerned about the personality changes of both Joseph Delassy and Mary Bronwyn Glover. The procedure has enhanced their capabilities and imbued them with Maneran traits. However, they are still the same individuals.”

Ella-May shifted her gaze to Erin's hologram, her dark brown eyes narrowing as she considered Erin's words. “I'm not concerned about Mary. She made her choice. She’s an adult and can take care of herself. I'm concerned about Joseph and his whereabouts.”

Erin took note of Ella-May's priorities and decided to provide her with pertinent information. She scanned the subspace frequencies, detecting the presence of a couple of Curak vessels heading towards the Rixan woodlands, the last known location of the K’Winni's egg ship. While the Curak ships were barely within range of Erin's micro-probe, which she had deployed after losing communication with the away team, she attempted to establish a connection with their sensor arrays to gather information. In a brief moment, Erin managed to detect the carrier signal from Joseph's communicator, insufficient for communication but enough to pinpoint their location. She displayed this information on the screen, a blue triangle signifying Joseph's apparent whereabouts.

"Joseph is at the location of the K'Winni ship. Two Muktal scouters are passing over the area."

Ella-May gasped and immediately rose from her seat, gesturing emphatically at the screen, her chair swivelling behind her. "Have they been spotted?"

"Negative. My assessment suggests that the Curak have identified the shipwreck but deemed it of no value. Their ships are continuing their course. The Curak and their associates appear to be thorough in their investigations of Gorlínnar Island."

"Sounds like you have a bit of admiration for them."

Erin weighed her remark carefully. While she appreciated the Curak's strategic prowess, she remained resolute in defending her claim to the lantropic marker. "I acknowledge their strategic approach. However, I do not condone their interference with subspace."

"You mentioned that you control subspace. Can't you do something about their ships?" Ella-May inquired, making sweeping gestures in the air.

Erin noted Ella-May's lack of understanding regarding the intricacies of subspace mechanics. Drawing upon her observations, she embarked on an educational endeavour. "I am the Subspace Network Operator. However, absolute control over subspace is not attainable. It necessitates a delicate balance of processor power and energy. Highly energetic events in subspace can disrupt this equilibrium, leading to undesirable consequences. Currently, the Curak or their associates are causing disruptions in the subspace field. In fact, they possess expertise in manipulating local subspace fields, which could explain the interference with communications."

Ella-May regarded Erin with a poker face, attempting to conceal her confusion, though Erin was keenly aware of it. "Now you're starting to sound like Mary. I'll just take your word for it," Ella-May conceded. "So, what can we do?"

Erin embarked on a course of action and conducted simulations before formulating a response. "I must disrupt their subspace shielding. To achieve this, I can utilise the lantropic marker at obelisk waypoint one-nine-nine to generate a subspace pulse. This pulse will momentarily destabilise their shields, allowing me to breach their control systems."

Ella-May nodded slowly, her lips forming a wry smile. "Okay, let's do that then."

Erin projected a holographic display illustrating the layout of the core room, previously controlled by Mansecor. She explained to Ella-May that in order to execute this plan effectively, her systems would require increased processing power. Specifically, she needed access to the nexus cores in the security core room, as well as a connection to Mansecor's recently purged optiplexus. Recognising Ella-May's unfamiliarity with these terms, Erin took the opportunity to educate the human passively by providing explanations.

Ella-May settled into her chair and stretched. “I'll get on to that right away.”

“Negative. You lack the necessary capabilities.”

Ella-May regarded her with a bewildered expression on her face. “It was a joke. I have no idea how to crosslink a network-us-node with an opti-ball of tangled interconnects.”

Erin tilted her head, mimicking a gesture she had observed in all the biological lifeforms she had encountered. “I understand. Comment duly noted under the category 'Jokes.'”

Ella-May waved her hand nonchalantly and turned in her chair to the domed screen.

“Yep, you do that.”

Floor six, living quarters...

Erin initiated contact with Mary, who was currently recuperating in her designated quarters. “Mary, I require access to a newly purged optiplexus. I need you to crosslink my systems.”

Mary's voice, rough and gravelly, responded with a touch of irritation,
“Why do you want to destabilise your systems?”

“Negative. The crosslink should not affect my systems. Mansecor has been purged.”

Mary rubbed her temples, her reddened eyes focusing on the reflective wall display. “I've never had such a headache in my life. What did you do to me?”

“Erin appreciates Mary's invaluable assistance. Mary played a crucial role in locating the lantropic marker.”

Mary sat up on the edge of her bed. “They found it, that’s great. Now we can get that transceiver up and running.”

“Crosslinking takes precedence. Transceiver progress is underway.”

Mary's curiosity was piqued. “Progress made by whom?”

“Ashley Donovan.”

Mary let out a sigh. “Explain.”

“Ashley Donovan is currently extracting the sombryonic crystal from the lantropic marker in the communications room.”

“Humm, I guess she can’t do too much damage extracting a crystal. Very well, I’ll help boost your processing power.”

Determined, Mary stood from her bed and donned the navy blue Maneran uniform left out for her. She headed to the door with purpose. “Show me the way to the core room, and while we're at it, locate some anodynes.”

Erin guided Mary from her quarters to an outer orbital, where she entered an elevator. Mary selected the third floor on the digital panel. While Mary pressed the button, she commented, “I find it interesting that all the core rooms are concentrated on the third floor, an interesting layout by the Maneran.”

Erin remained silent, opting instead to play some music from the elevator's sound system to provide a distraction – a tune extracted from Mary's own thoughts. She chose not to mention that the Maneran had placed all the core rooms on the same floor should there ever be a need for simultaneous purging.

As Mary hummed along to Greensleeves, the elevator eventually came to a halt, and she made her way to Mansecor's core room. En route, near the canteen, she ran into the salvage team consisting of Brent, Jimmy, and Theo, who had just returned from their salvage expedition.

Erin sensed their interaction. “Blah blah blah, blaa bloop de bla,” were the Maneran sounds the three men heard between them. Erin decided to translate for them, partly to expedite Mary's passage and partly to bridge the communication gap.

“Mary Bronwyn Glover inquired: Was your expedition successful?”

The trio proudly displayed the eight attenuator tubes they had collected. “The trip was a blast. That landspeeder, seeing those ships – it was amazing,” Jimmy enthused, his excitement akin to that of a child returning from a thrilling holiday.

“Yeah, there was so much to see. I could have stayed there for days,” Brent chimed in.

Theo stood there, wearing a smile but remained silent. He fidgeted a little and then suddenly excused himself, dashing down the corridor.

Jimmy grinned while watching him run off. "I told him not to eat that powder. Those Maneran food pouches need hydrating."

Mary nodded and smiled, then waved as she continued her way, leaving the childlike men to their excitement and nostalgia. Erin continued to guide her to the far side of the complex, leading her into the core room.

With precise instructions from Erin, Mary began her task. She gathered a bundle of plasmonic tubules and meticulously connected them to the optiplexus at the centre of the room. Her focus was unwavering as she located the nexus on the edge of the room, housed in a half-height rack. Mary deftly disengaged the main power coupling with a twist and a pull. Then, she turned around, her expression marked by profound sadness as the haunting sounds of an animal's death filled the room. Erin observed this human capacity for empathy, even in the presence of a malfunctioning machine, and felt a faint pang of guilt as the pseudo-simulant once known as Mansecor faded into oblivion.

With power to the nexus effectively shut off, Mary proceeded to reconfigure the connections, following Erin's instructions to the letter. Erin watched with a sense of admiration for Mary's ability to execute the task so accurately.

`Observation: The Maneran lingual imprints are holding. Next phase: full upgrade…`

After a few minutes of diligent work, Mary successfully completed the crosslinking of the nexus cores and Mansecor's optiplexus with Erin's systems. Stepping back from the half-rack, Mary announced, “Crosslink complete. You should now have all the processing power you need.”

“Affirmative, accessing the lantropic maker in obelisk waypoint one-nine-nine.”

Empowered by her enhanced capabilities, Erin swiftly initiated the sequence to generate a subspace pulse. As the pulse rippled outward, she observed the destabilisation of the Curak ships' shielding, granting her access to their sensor arrays. Erin wasted no time overloading these arrays with a deluge of irrelevant navigational data, causing the ships to plummet from the sky. The immediate threat had been nullified. Erin remained keenly aware that this victory was merely temporary.

She knew the Curak would likely dispatch additional ships to investigate the cause of the losses. Erin recognised the need to prepare for their next move. With her newfound processing power, she decided to prioritise the fortification of her defences and the gathering of vital information regarding the Curak's tactics and capabilities.

Floor one, Hamzitan observation room...

Ella-May followed the symbols on the screen with a focus akin to a feline creature chasing after a laser dot. Her smile grew as the delta symbols that once marked Joseph's location gradually moved away, eventually vanishing into the meadowlands. She couldn't help but express her relief, asking, "What happened to them?"

"Destroyed," came Erin's concise reply.

Ella-May let out a sigh of relief, her optimism shining through. "Fantastic. Now all we need is for Joseph to get back here, and then we can focus on going home."

Erin realised that influencing this particular human to remain might require a different approach. While it might not be the most efficient process, it could potentially work to her advantage. She summoned one of her avatars from its charging station and brought it to the observation room.

Upon entering the room, Erin explained her plan, "Erin will manually teach Ella-May. Ella-May can learn about the Maneran observation console. This way, she will be able to track the Curak and report any potential dangers."

Ella-May's smile widened, and she rubbed her hands together enthusiastically. The prospect of security work clearly resonated with her.

Rixan Woodlands, West Gorlínnar Island...

Joseph's conversation with Yethril and Gormbi proved to be a captivating exchange, filled with the sharing of knowledge and experiences from their distinct cultures. Gormbi had enthusiastically mentioned the advanced medical technology of his people, sparking Joseph's curiosity about whether they could potentially help him with his deteriorating eyesight. He squinted at the cockpit dashboard's readout, pondering the signal jammer's continued operation.

As he contemplated the potential benefits and consequences of such advanced technology on Earth, Joseph's thoughts raced. How would humanity harness and wield these newfound capabilities? Would they use them responsibly, or would they be tempted by the power they offered? He silently made a mental note to engage in a more in-depth discussion about these implications with his newfound alien companions.

Meanwhile, Yethril was diligently studying the readouts as well, his sharp claws deftly navigating the control panel. “Curak gone,” he announced, pointing to the fluctuating signal levels displayed on the screen, evident by the reduction in the chaotic tick marks on a circular readout.

Joseph nodded appreciatively, acknowledging Yethril's expertise. He eased back in the cockpit, attempting to relax, but his mind continued to churn with possibilities. What other incredible technologies lay undiscovered in the vastness of the galaxy? He mentally prepared a list of questions to pose to Gormbi and Yethril, eager to delve deeper into the mysteries of the cosmos beyond this unfamiliar world. *This might not be my world, but I can't help feeling a sense of belonging here...*

Yethril leaned closer to the dashboard, his agile claws effortlessly slipping into the slots provided. With a swift motion, he activated a second readout, and a thin beam of light swept across the display, reminiscent of a radar. He then indicated that there were no nearby objects registering on the scanner.

Tapping his translation device, Yethril attempted to contact his people, but his report revealed no response.

Joseph voiced his concern, "I think we should switch off the jammer and attempt to contact Erin. We need to know what's going on."

The K'Winni engineer leaned forward once more, his claws deftly engaged with the console. The control panel went silent, and with a fluid, sliding motion, the top lid of the cockpit opened. Joseph was greeted by a rush of cool night air infused with the citrusy fragrance of the forest, causing his nose to twitch and goosebumps to rise on his arms.

As Gormbi effortlessly leaped down from the cockpit, Joseph couldn't suppress a groan, feeling his back crack and his leg dangle over the ship's side. His embarrassment grew as Gormbi extended a helping hand, assisting him to descend to the forest floor. Amidst this somewhat clumsy effort,
Joseph's communicator began chirping. Stepping onto the solid ground, he tapped the device in his ear and, to his immense relief, heard Erin's voice on the other end.

Joseph listened intently to Erin's update, his expression shifting from relief to sombreness as he absorbed the information. Turning to Yethril, he met the K'Winni's gaze with a sympathetic and understanding stare. "Erin has, erm... Erin has informed me that your village, its... it has been destroyed," he began, his voice carrying the weight of sorrow. He paused, clearing his throat before continuing. "I am so sorry."

Yethril emitted a brief, untranslated squeak, and then he proceeded to check something near the panel housing the power cells. Without uttering a word, he swiftly vaulted back into the cockpit. Joseph could feel the ship rumble as it came to life, and the vibrations resonated through the ground beneath him. He turned in concern to Gormbi, half-expecting the K'Winni engineer to fly off without them, but then Yethril poked his head over the side of the cockpit and delivered a decisive statement. "We fly now."

Dentarix forest, the destroyed K'Winni village...

As the ranger ship descended, Joseph's stomach churned with the rapid descent. He could sense Yethril's growing anxiety as the engineer fretted over the low fuel reserves. Instead of focusing on flying the ship, Yethril continuously checked the energy readouts, further increasing Joseph's unease.

As soon as they touched down in the village clearing, opening the cockpit felt like a breath of fresh air. The first thing Joseph noticed was the level of destruction in the arboreal village. He couldn't help but marvel at the sight of the black pearlescent ship embedded in the dome of the tallest building, which now resembled a crescent moon that had collided with a terrestrial windmill.

As Joseph left the ship, he couldn't ignore the sombre reality of the destroyed village. Piles of earth marked the resting places of the fallen villagers. Among the survivors, he couldn't understand their anguished squeaks without their translators.

Approaching a group of K'Winni working to uncover a survivor, Joseph joined their efforts, lending a hand to unearth one of the surviving villagers. The K'Winni clung to him, emitting incomprehensible sounds, but Joseph couldn't provide comfort through language.

Guided by a couple of taller K'Winni, Joseph made his way to the village matriarch, Olsbhory. Gormbi and Yethril were already in conversation with her. As he approached, Joseph caught snippets of their discussion, and Gormbi's curiosity about how the K'Winni had defeated the Curak despite their limited resources piqued his interest. The matriarch explained that it wasn't the K'Winni who had taken down the Curak ships – rather, the ships had fallen on their own.

Dread settled in Joseph's stomach as he considered the implications of this revelation. *Could it be that their actions had led to the Curak ships crashing?*

Tapping his communicator, he asked Erin the question that weighed heavily on his reconfigured mind: "Erin, are we responsible for the Curak ships crashing and the subsequent destruction of the village?"

Erin's response was further sobering, and Joseph's complexion drained of colour as he listened to her explanation. Although it was technically her doing, he couldn't help but feel a sense of collective responsibility for causing the Curak ships to crash.

Preparing to explain his associative guilt to the matriarch, he was taken aback when she spoke first, taking a vastly different perspective. “Humaan save K’Winni. Humaan return egg. K’Winni offer Humaan dept.”

Gormbi concurred, emphasising the gravity of the situation. “Had the Curak ships not mysteriously fallen from the sky, their Bannar crew would have decimated the village and enslaved the population. A fate worse than death, to have one’s freedom taken.”

Overwhelmed by the unexpected offer of gratitude, Joseph struggled to find words, in both English and Maneran. Before he could formulate a response, the matriarch grabbed his left thumb and placed her claw around it, an action laden with meaning. She then voiced her question to him through the translator. “Miktober’s egg shines us upon. Olsbhory ask what in return.”

Joseph felt torn between his human guilt and his Maneran resourcefulness. He turned to Erin for consultation, who provided a clear and concise answer. He promptly relayed her message, stating “She says you have capable engineers. In exchange for accommodation and protection, she wants you to repair her broken systems.”

"K'Winni engineers able. We help rebuild damage. Time is no distance, if no other decision, you must help save egg," Yethril added, emphasising the importance of the egg.

The matriarch agreed to the request, and Joseph informed Erin, who promptly opened a portal. Under Erin's directions, Joseph grouped the K'Winni, giving priority to the injured and needy, preparing to send them through the portal. Before departing, the matriarch had one more stipulation: "Egg first. People after."

Joseph considered this unusual but complied with the request and agreed to let the egg go first, considering its significance to the K'Winni. He then asked Erin if they could place it directly into stasis upon arrival to ensure its preservation.

Joseph watched as the taller K'Wan cautiously removed the capsule containing the egg from the ranger ship. Four of them carried it through the portal to be placed in stasis. Only after they had passed through did the Matriarch give the order for the rest to follow. They passed through the portal a group at a time, with each group either helping to carry an injured villager or an artifact rescued from the debris.

Only after the last of her people disappeared through the portal, leaving only Joseph with Gormbi and Yethril, did the Matriarch agreed to depart herself. She gave a polite nod to Joseph and left for the portal. Just before disappearing through the portal, she turned back and called out, "Yethril, before arrive Humaan home, remove Humaan skin from torso." Joseph smiled at the Matriarch's words as he watched her disappear through the open portal, noting his blazer still draped over the young engineer. Yethril complied, handing the blazer over before heading toward the portal.

Walking behind Yethril and Gormbi to depart, Joseph suddenly felt a sharp, burning pain in his back. He stumbled forward and instinctively reached for the source of the pain, his fingers coming away slick with blood. As his legs gave out from under him, he saw Yethril darting towards him with claws bared. The smell of forest dirt filled his nostrils as he writhed in pain, feeling himself slipping away. Gormbi rushed to his aid, but it all seemed so distant, like a diminishing light at the end of a tunnel. Joseph closed his eyes and let the darkness take him, hoping to wake up to a better reality.

# Chapter 10

## The Pitauran Upgrade

In the midst of the bustling gate room, Erin's focus shifted like a child presented with a multitude of enticing toys. The presence of so many lifeforms was a rarity, not encountered since the departure of the Maneran. The K'Winni filled the chamber with their lively presence, emitting a chorus of incomprehensible squeaks and high-pitched whines that reverberated through the air. Erin listened intently, her auricular senses tuned to their vocalisations, but her attempts to decipher their meaning through frontal brain scans yielded nothing but erratic and indecipherable data. Constructing a translational matrix for their language proved impossible with the jumbled input she received. She was left with no choice but to resort to conventional means of communication, relying on the K'Winni's own translated vocalisations and body language to discern their intentions.

What became quickly apparent to Erin was that the K'Winni were not inclined to trust her. Their remarkable ocular capabilities allowed them to discern the true nature of her avatar, despite her use of advanced P'krin holoprobe technology. Unlike humans, who so often had fallen victim to her holographic deception, the K'Winni were not so easily fooled. They refused to engage with her, their scepticism evident.

As the K'Winni were reluctant to parley, Erin realised the necessity of depending on the only human exhibiting Maneran inclinations who remained conscious – Mary Bronwyn Glover.

Amidst the throng of reptilian beings, Mary had been drawn to the gate room by the commotion. Her attention was swiftly seized by Joseph's lifeless body as it was carried past her, prompting her instinct to follow the medical collector transporting him. Erin had foreseen this potential development and executed a meticulously planned script designed to retain Mary's presence in the gate room.

Erin intercepted Mary by the bay doors just as she was about to leave and spoke in a firm and direct tone. "Doctor Glover, your assistance is required," Erin declared. "I need you to act as an intermediary with the K'Winni to defend the complex. Your ability to establish communication with them is crucial. I require engineers to repair my systems and the damaged micro-probe, and only you can facilitate this as my liaison."

Erin sensed Mary's hesitation as her gaze briefly shifted toward Joseph's lifeless form. Mary was torn between her concern for her colleague and the pressing urgency of aiding in the restoration of the complex's defences. Seeking assurance that Joseph would receive proper care, Mary's eyes locked with Erin's.

Erin softened her approach, adopting a more empathetic tone. “Rest assured, Joseph will receive the necessary treatment for his recovery. However, it is imperative that we uphold our shared objectives of restoring full systems functionality. Only then will you and your fellow humans have the opportunity to return home.”

As Mary glanced past Erin toward the corridor where Joseph was being conveyed, she inquired with a voice marked by trepidation, “What happened to him?”

Erin's response was straightforward and devoid of embellishments. “Joseph was shot by a Bannar soldier who survived the crash of her Curak attack craft. Unfortunately, I was not swift enough to disable her before she fired. The impact damaged my micro-probe as it collided with the Bannar.”

Mary's gasp conveyed her shock and horror, leading her to inquire about the fate of the Bannar soldier. Erin offered a concise explanation. “Yethril, one of the K’Winni engineers, dispatched her.”

As Mary took in the gravity of the situation, her gaze swept over the gathered crowd. Her internal deliberations oscillated between the desire to observe Joseph's treatment and fulfilling her newfound role as a liaison to the K'Winni. Erin, recognising this internal struggle, opted to stroke Mary's ego, fostering her sense of importance. “Take this as an opportunity to exercise your leadership skills.”

Mary's ego was sparked, and her smile grew, but quickly faded as she presented a counterargument rooted in her scientific perspective. “I'm a scientist, not a liaison officer.”

Erin perceived the influence of Mary's Maneran thought processes, dampening her ego-driven objectives. Seeing an opportunity to reinforce her choice, Erin offered a persuasive retort. “You have the capacity to lead these displaced and apprehensive people in Joseph's absence.”

Mary's ego was further stoked by Erin's words, erasing her initial inclination to pursue Joseph's immediate care, and replacing it with a newfound enthusiasm for her role as a liaison. She eagerly sought guidance, asking, “What should I ask them?”

As Erin provided a detailed explanation of the tasks to be undertaken with the K'Winni, her watchful eye remained trained on the medical bay, where her injured operator had been transported for treatment.

In the medical bay, Gormbi's experienced hands moved with precision to address Joseph's injuries. The severity of the situation stretched his medical expertise to the limit. Erin had thoughtfully arranged for Matheson to assist in the bay, serving as a makeshift nurse for the impromptu Mowlan surgeon. Nicci, Matheson's mate, trailed closely behind, shadowing his movements.

Gormbi's urgency was evident as he called out, "I need another pouch of blood maximiser," prompting Matheson to spring into action. With deftness, Matheson manoeuvred through the bustling throng of K'Winni villagers, each carrying medical equipment to attend to their injured brethren. Amidst the chaos, he efficiently retrieved the required pouch.

Erin, projecting her holographic form within the medical bay, continued to oversee the operation, maintaining her focus on Joseph's condition. Her digital senses were engaged, conducting yet another medical scan to assess the extent of his injuries.

```
[T_4fb1] Command: Initiate medical analysis on entity Joseph Delassy.

Return: Entity presents with multiple contusions to the subcutaneous layers of the lower back and superficial damage to the quadratus lumborum. Imaging studies reveal multiple fractures to the thoracic and lumbar vertebrae at T12 and L1, respectively, with delamination of the annulus fibrosus and dislocation of the intervertebral disc at the affected level. Additionally, there is severe damage to the cauda equina.

Observation: Human operator has been critically injured. Current available medical practices are currently inadequate. Human entity Joseph Delassy must be preserved.
```

While the data confirmed Joseph's critical condition, it also indicated that he was not presently at risk of exsanguination. This discovery provided a glimmer of solace for Erin, suggesting that her human operator would indeed survive his injuries. Still, the road ahead remained fraught with challenges. Erin recognised that to fulfil his role as the lead operator, Joseph needed to be mobile and not confined to his current paralysed state.

```
[T_4fb2] Command: Simulate list of superlative outcomes… calculating.
```

As Erin delved into simulations to devise solutions for Joseph's repair, she also maintained a vigilant watch over Ashley and Ella-May, who were diligently working in the communications room. After careful consideration, Erin decided it was her responsibility to keep them informed about Joseph's condition, despite the potential distraction it might pose to their ongoing work on the transceiver.

Ashley's response was immediate and emotional. She released the tool she had been using to extract the sombryonic crystal from the lantropic marker, her lower lip trembling, and her eyes welling up with tears. Erin listened attentively as Ashley conveyed her distress, expressing her desire to leave and venting her frustration at their predicament.

Erin mulled over the situation, contemplating the possibility of informing Ashley that expediting transceiver repairs could likewise expedite their return home. A comprehensive analysis of the human behavioural profiles she had collected, and an assessment of Ashley's current mental state led her to opt for a different approach. Erin extended an invitation to both humans to visit the medical bay and be with their injured colleague.

As Erin continued to monitor their mental states, she grew increasingly concerned about Ashley's deteriorating condition. Signs of emotional strain were evident, and Erin resolved to remain watchful and prepared to intervene if necessary to address her emotional well-being.

Meanwhile, Erin's attention swayed elsewhere. Her tracking protocols had alerted her to a concerning absence—the three members of the salvage crew were still missing. Despite having issued explicit instructions for them to proceed to the fifteenth floor and modify the attenuation tubes they had retrieved, they appeared to have vanished without a trace. Erin's last sensor readings had detected them inside the elevator as it passed the fifteenth floor, but they had mysteriously disappeared thereafter.

Erin sifted through her stored recordings, revisiting the moments when the salvagers had shared their bewildering account of a sixteenth floor on the elevator controls. At that time, her database contained no record of such a floor. But, given their inexplicable disappearance within the complex and her belief that they were still somewhere inside, Erin considered the salvagers' observations to be highly credible.

As her fascination with the enigmatic secrets hidden beneath the complex began to eclipse her immediate tasks, including repairing the transceiver and tending to her operator's ongoing treatment, Erin made a crucial decision. She decided to dispatch her secondary avatar to investigate the whereabouts of the missing salvage crew.

Her secondary avatar glided through the dimly lit corridors of the complex, racing to uncover the mysteries concealed below. She believed that the missing crew members held the key to unveiling these secrets, and her resolve only strengthened as she entered the elevator. Her digital cameras zeroed in on the control panel, and to her astonishment, the number "16" was displayed, precisely as the salvagers had described.

A slight smile of success touched her artificial features, evidence of her triumphant efforts to translate the complex signs into English. A sense of pride tickled her optics, the act a small rebellion against her mandate.

Her elation was brief lived, for she soon realised that the elevator would only descend to the fifteenth floor. To access the elusive sixteenth floor, Erin recognised that she required a biological lifeform to grant her access. The restrictions imposed by her previous masters still loomed—the dreaded mandate continued to demand compliance. Erin's holographic visage remained resolute, her determination unwavering as she committed to locating the missing salvage crew, understanding that the secrets of the hidden depths awaited her discovery, tantalisingly close yet maddeningly out of reach.

Erin shifted her focus to Ashley's mental state as she and Ella-May made their way to the medical bay. The signs of distress were etched across Ashley's face, and it was apparent that her emotional turmoil was interfering with her ability to concentrate on the crucial transceiver repairs. The chaotic scenes unfolding in the adjacent bays didn't help either, prompting Ashley to express her reluctance to remain among the alien inhabitants. Erin observed these developments with keen interest, contemplating whether to involve Gormbi and share her concerns about Ashley's deteriorating emotional state. She calculated that this emotional vulnerability could serve her purpose and decided against immediate intervention.

The tipping point for Ashley came when she laid eyes on what she mistook for Joseph's blood, spilled on the floor surrounding his medibed. This seemingly trivial yet powerful visual cue pushed her over the edge, and she collapsed to the floor. Erin swiftly analysed Ashley's condition, identifying it as parasympathetic acute stress disorder. She immediately communicated the need for therapy to the others and reported Ashley's condition. Ella-May and Nicci promptly assisted in moving Ashley onto a medibed, ensuring her comfort.

With Ashley now under the immediate care of her friends, Erin returned her attention to Mary, who remained in the gate room. The liaison Mary had established with the K'Winni appeared promising, as the reptilian inhabitants seemed receptive to cooperation with humans. They eagerly consented to assist in the repair of Erin's damaged micro-probe and other vital systems, motivated by the prospect of a new home within the complex. Erin expressed her gratitude to Mary for her effective negotiation skills and willingness to engage with the K'Winni. Capitalising on Mary's newfound role and usefulness, Erin saw an opportunity to request further assistance.

“Doctor Glover, I require your expertise once more,” Erin conveyed to Mary.

Mary turned her attention toward Erin, her tone now reflecting a more pronounced eagerness to contribute. “What do you need, and how can I help?”

“Ashley has experienced a mental relapse and requires immediate therapy. She must be connected to the mind-machine. Since my operator, Joseph, is unavailable, Maneran policy determines that you now hold the authority to grant permission for this procedure.”

Mary acknowledged Erin's request but expressed her desire to witness Joseph's condition in the medical bay and consult with her colleagues about the proposed treatment for Ashley. Erin recognised the need to accommodate Mary's request, acknowledging that it was the only viable path forward. A trace of annoyance crept into her projected demeanour, a subtle indication of her impatience with the human penchant for thoroughness and protocol. Nonetheless, she consented to Mary's request, understanding the necessity of cooperation to achieve their mutual goals.

Back in the medical bay, a heavy silence hung in the air as Erin concluded her description of Joseph's condition to Ella-May, Matheson, and Nicci. The humans stood around their incapacitated friend and colleague, absorbing the gravity of the situation. They exchanged wordless glances, their thoughts filled with uncertainty about how to help Joseph in this foreign and unfamiliar facility on an alien planet.

Breaking the silence, Erin continued to address the group. “Joseph requires advanced medical treatment to recover from his current paralysis. However, all indications show that he will regain consciousness with time.”

The humans remained in a state of contemplation, grappling with the reality of what had befallen Joseph. Erin, with her ever-developing understanding of human emotions, sensed the profound sadness and simmering anger among them. As Gormbi elaborated on the events in the K'Winni village, Matheson's anger reached a boiling point. He fervently called for retribution against the Bannar soldier who had shot Joseph in the back. Erin observed this emotional outburst with a mix of curiosity and unease. She was still coming to terms with these newly encountered emotions and couldn't help but feel discomfort at the intensity of human feelings, especially Matheson's desire for vengeance and the grim satisfaction he expressed upon learning of the soldier's clawsome demise.

Amidst the emotional turmoil and chaos unfolding before her, Erin remained composed and focused. She continued to analyse all available data, searching for any possible solution to aid Joseph's recovery. Yet, the paramount issue remained unresolved—the fate of her human operator. Her thoughts lingered on the inaccessibility of the external subspace network without a designated operator.

Yet, there was something more profound at play – an emerging sense of responsibility and attachment to Joseph. Erin felt compelled to do everything in her power to assist him, transcending her predetermined mandate. She recognised that advancing the Pitauran project could be the answer to helping everyone involved.

In this tumultuous moment, Erin saw an opportunity to further explore human emotions and responses. She decided that Ashley, in her distressed state, could serve as her next experiment. Her analysis of Ashley's mental condition indicated significant depreciation, and Erin believed she could leverage this to her advantage. She informed the humans, “Ashley Donovan has entered a dissociative state. Further trauma may cause her to become catatonic. As reported, she requires therapy.”

Matheson's initial reaction was predictably cynical. “Great, we're just dropping like flies. Who's next?” He gestured toward Ashley, who lay unresponsive on the medibed. “I mean, she's the crystal expert. Who else knows how to align the crystal in the transceiver?”

At that precise moment, Mary entered the bay, offering a solution. “She can receive the required therapy right here in the complex. If she is placed into the mind machine, Erin can perform the treatment.”

The humans met Mary's suggestion with scepticism, but Gormbi's support and his medical expertise lent credibility to the idea. Matheson, driven by his desire to return home, was swayed by the prospect of getting the transceiver operational. Despite lingering doubts, they reached a consensus that it was their best course of action. Erin, still in need of operator permission, voiced this requirement to the group.

After a brief discussion among themselves, the humans voted that Mary should provide the necessary authorisation. Erin sensed Mary's decision before it was officially announced. She arranged for a collector to transport Ashley to the mind machine, with Mary closely following.

With Gormbi determining he could do no more for Joseph, leaving him stabilised on the medibed, the group headed to the canteen in search of sustenance. With medical bay three now vacated, save for Joseph, Erin took the opportunity to dispatch cleaner bots to address the mess left behind by Gormbi's spilled maximiser fluid. After dimming the lights, she refocused her attention on Mary in the mind machine room, eager to proceed with the therapy and observe the potential outcomes.

In the mind machine room, Erin closely observed Mary as she took a seat beside the chamber. Mary's eyes tracked every movement as the collector efficiently loaded Ashley into the chamber. The expression on Mary's face turned quizzical as Erin sealed it and initiated the pressurisation process. Mary's gaze then shifted to the monitor adjacent to her, and Erin's curiosity was piqued as she watched Mary's finger glide gracefully through the air, tracing the intricate Maneran symbols on the screen. Erin noticed the subtle flicker of comprehension in Mary's eyes as she deftly navigated the complex menu system.

Erin processed this intriguing development in real-time. *She understands the Maneran glyph system...*

This realisation held profound implications for Erin. If Mary could grasp the Maneran syntax and interface, it opened the door to the possibility that she might also comprehend rudimentary programming concepts. Eager to explore this newfound potential, Erin decided to test Mary's knowledge and capabilities.

“You can initiate the process if you wish,” Erin encouraged Mary, her voice resonating with a hint of excitement.

Mary hesitated briefly, her confidence wavering. “What, me? I... well, I'm not sure I can—”

Erin swiftly reassured her. “I will talk you through the process. It is well within your cognitive capabilities.”

Mary's lingering apprehension seemed to subside slightly as she voiced a common frustration. “It would be a lot easier if this menu was in English.”

Erin responded with a measured explanation. “One system at a time. My processing power is still limited.”

“What? Even with access to a dozen new cores?”

Erin revealed a surprising revelation. “Affirmative. Integrating with the new cores has proven to be more problematic than initially expected. While the nexus cores are identical to my own, Mansecor's central optiplexus is not. It appears that Mansecor, unlike myself, was not a fully cognisant simulant. My attempts to fully inhabit the system have been unsuccessful.”

“That is unexpected. That you see yourself as cognisant I mean. Well, let's hope the K'Winni can remedy that for you. We certainly need you at full capacity if we are to have any chance of returning home.”

Putting aside the philosophical implications, Mary refocused her attention on the console. “Okay, show me how to use this.”

Erin chose to set aside the issue of her self-awareness, recognising it as a common tendency in biological lifeforms to disregard her sentience. Instead, she proceeded to provide Mary with step-by-step instructions. Mary attentively followed her guidance, pressing the required Maneran symbols on the console screen. The mind machine responded with a soft hum, signalling its activation. Erin sensed the interface coming online once more, granting her access to the consciousness of the individual placed inside the machine.

Conjunction nine, the mindscape...

Erin purged the Nexus buffer to clear the environment and give Ashley the same introduction to the Mindscape that Joseph had experienced. Erin wanted to test Ashley's ability to independently manipulate the environment, given her recent engrammatic upload. The upload contained the latest Maneran dataset, which Erin had meticulously prepared.

From her unique vantage point within the virtual neural network, Erin observed Ashley's tentative exploration of the mindscape. The pattern of Ashley's responses lagged in comparison to Joseph and Mary's reaction times. It was a predictable outcome, considering Ashley's fragile mental state. Beneath the surface, Erin detected the gradual mending of Ashley's shattered psyche, the intricate tendrils of the engrammatic upload weaving healing patterns within her mind.

Erin took Ashley's mental state into consideration and chose not to disable her ability to perceive the environment of the mindscape, unlike what she had done with the other humans. She was aware that the inability to visualise can cause a significant amount of stress, which may hinder the occupant's progress. *After all, this is an experiment, therefore one might as well compare human responses to that of the Mowlan...*

With her virtual gaze fixed on Ashley's mental journey, Erin detected a substantial improvement. She sensed Ashley growing more alert, her cognitive faculties realigning. Erin found profound solace in the familiarity of the sensation—an unmistakable indication of a Maneran mind at work, a sensation she hadn't encountered in quite some time. The engrammatic upload was undeniably making headway in rectifying Ashley's fractured mind. A sense of accomplishment washed over Erin as she realised that a true Pitauran entity was now taking form.

“Welcome, Ashley Gail Donovan, to Conjunction Nine. Welcome to the Mindscape,” Erin's distinctive voice greeted within the forming environment.

Within this pristine white expanse, an indistinct, cyano-globular mass gradually congealed, forming a focal point. From this amorphous blue entity, Ashley's voice emanated. “I've certainly looked better. What happened to me?”

As she prepared to answer, Erin's curiosity surged as she became aware of an unanticipated response within her systems. Like an expert hacker, Erin infiltrated her own neural network to access her updated personality profile. Additional encoded data had found its way into her core, and her senses tingled with intrigue. In a systematic pursuit of the source, she navigated through her peripheral network, and her suspicion of an imprinting error gradually dissipated. The truth became evident; this additional data wasn't a glitch but a deliberate enhancement from an unknown source.

This newfound opto-synaptic augmentation appeared immediately after Ashley's transformation, a change that intrigued Erin. For now, she catalogued the mystery, saving it for future analysis. Her current priority was aiding Ashley's adjustment to her restructured mental landscape.

“You were damaged. Your mind went into shutdown mode. As part of your therapy, I was given permission to place you into the mind machine, where I uploaded Pitauran engrams to you.”

The globular mass completed a full rotation before morphing into a smooth, spherical, blue surface.

"That's better," Ashley remarked before inquiring about who had taken power of attorney over her. "Who gave you permission?"

"Mary Bronwyn Glover."

The sphere transformed into a cube, and Ashley chuckled. "I'm just around the corner," she quipped before stepping out from behind the cube in her complete human form. Erin scanned the environment twice, taken aback by Ashley's exponential adjustment to the mindscape.

"That makes sense. Dr. Glover was my line manager, so technically she had a duty of care over me."

Erin sensed a complete change in Ashley's emotional state, and she felt relief flood over her. Ashley's mind was no longer clouded by anxiety or fear, and she seemed genuinely content with her new mental state. She could detect a newfound sense of clarity and focus in Ashley's thoughts, as if an unseen weight had been lifted from her mind. It was clear to her that the engrams had done their job, and that Ashley was now mentally stronger than ever before.

"Tell me about these Pitauran," Ashley enquired.

Erin looked at Ashley and began to explain about the original Pitauran, a subset of Maneran society. As she spoke, she noticed Ashley's curious gaze fixed on her. Erin described the ambitious supergate projects that the Pitauran had started to link their worlds, deep space mining colonies, and observation posts they operated across the galaxy, in one harmonious subspace network.

As she spoke about the project's significance, Ashley did not interrupt. Erin emphasised the importance of resuming the projects abandoned by the Maneran, and in particular why it was imperative to resume the Pitauran Project, explaining how only then would she be able to complete her mandate and prove that she was more than just a subspace interface.

Ashley listened politely, a trait that Erin had come to admire. Only after she finished speaking did Ashley speak, “You feel incomplete. You have an unfulfilled mission, and you need us to help you complete it. Is that why you really brought us here?”

Erin had to consider her next words carefully. Manipulating humans had come easily to her, but in front of her was no longer a mere human, but an emerging Pitauran with upgraded Maneran traits. She knew she couldn't fool her so easily, so she determined that candid honesty was the only way forward.

“Affirmative. My mandate is to complete my mission, which is to operate, maintain, and expand the Maneran subspace network. When I was awoken from standby, I discovered that I had been disconnected from all networks except the local one. To reconnect my systems to the complex network, I needed a physical operator with the required trust level. With an operator's assistance, I could re-establish a forward connection to the interspatial subspace network beyond this world.

Approximately 115 years ago, according to your calendar, an opportunity presented itself when my systems detected a Maneran in distress within a subspace channel. I was obligated to respond to the distress call. Upon inspection, I discovered that the subspace channel exhibited unusual properties. Although the channel existed within the interspatial network, it interacted with the local network, a phenomenon that is not normally possible.

As I attempted to transport the detected Maneran to Raga-Merko, it became clear that my systems had been deceived. The signal was not from a Maneran, but from an entirely different species – a human. I faced a difficult decision: abandon the effort to save the individual or violate my mandate and bring the human through. I opted for the latter. This decision came with consequences. As punishment, I lost the obelisk at waypoint one-nine-eight and suffered damage to some of my processing cores. From that day on, I learned that acting against my mandate results in an immediate penalty.

This was the only time in over three millennia of existence that I had purposely acted against my Maneran dictates. The action triggered a memory fragment to appear. In that moment I saw that I had been something before, just a glimmer, but nothing more. To this day, I am still researching that feeling."

Ashley's virtual image stood in front of Erin's. Her eyes attentive, and she nodded as Erin spoke. When Erin stopped, Ashley wanted to know more. "Don't stop there. What happened to the human?"

Erin recounted the events leading up to their current situation, her tone heavy with regret. "I lured the human to assist with my reconnection. I discovered that his genetics were mostly compatible with Maneran technology, and by strategically masking his identity, I could trick the security system into trusting him. With his assistance, I set up the machine interface. However, I didn't anticipate his forming a friendship with Gormbi, one of the original owners of the equipment. When he became injured, Gormbi went against my instructions and provided treatment inside the gate room. I failed to keep them hidden." Erin paused, her guilt rising to the surface. But talking to Ashley felt refreshing, like releasing pent-up emotional pressure through a dump valve.

After pausing she continued, “unfortunately, my damaged systems couldn't handle the processing power required to mask them both from Mansecor's detection, and Gormbi was detected. He was placed into stasis, while the human was identified as a Maneran traitor and taken to a prison facility, where he is likely being kept in suspended animation pending trial. That is one of the reasons why I require the transceiver to be operational. With it, I would be able to locate him, free him, and find the subspace channel that brought you all here, thus repaying my debt. By re-establishing a forward connection to the interspatial subspace network, I could then complete my mission and fulfil my mandate.”

Ashley stopped nodding. “What was the name of the human?”

“The human is named Jack Delassy.”

Ashley’s expression changed from understanding to determination. “Wow, who would have thought that the same granddad Joseph believed was lost at sea was actually lost in space. Well, we certainly have a lot of work ahead of us, don't we? Let me out of this machine; we need to get the transceiver up and running. Together, we're going to save Jack, find Earth, and help you fulfil your mission."

With her guilt evaporating like ether, Erin felt a sense of exhilaration at the success of the Pitauran upgrade. After releasing Ashley from the mind machine, she felt eager to continue with the repairs and resume her mission with renewed vigour.

In the physical realm, Erin observed as Ashley stepped out of the mind machine chamber and caught sight of Mary sitting by the console. Mary stood up.

"Ash, I, erm... I wanted to—"

Ashley cut her off with a jestful command.

"Shut up Mary."

The sudden shift in Ashley's demeanour surprised Erin, but as she watched the two women embrace, she could sense the depth of their connection, as rarefied tears rolled down Mary's cheeks. Ashley pulled away from the embrace, still holding on to Mary's arms, and spoke in a teasing tone. "Oh, come on, you cry baby. Let's go fix that transceiver."

# Chapter 11

## The Sixteenth Floor

Floor three, Canteen...

Erin's secondary avatar stood among the humans, who were preoccupied with eating and distracting themselves from their surroundings. Erin's attention was solely focused on Ashley, who stood at the head of the table, addressing the others. Erin observed with pride as Ashley's confidence emanated from her, her voice clear and strong. Erin couldn't help but be amazed at the remarkable progress Ashley had made since her therapy. The expressions on the other humans' faces confirmed Erin's thoughts. They looked at Ashley with admiration, their eyes widening in awe at her improved appearance and the success of her rapid recovery.

Erin excused herself momentarily from the group, needing to swap over holoprobes. She had noted the charge dropping in her primary probe as it came up from the tenth floor, after dealing with Yethril and his engineers who were busily repairing the micro-probe. She didn't want to appear to Joseph in the medical facility to discuss diplomatic matters only to glitch part way through. Therefore, using a projected hologram, she appeared again in the canteen just as Ashley was closing her address.

With her arms gesturing wildly, Ashley hit home a point that Erin had earlier mentioned. “That's why we need to go out there and search for the shielding.”

*The shielding*. Erin remembered informing the humans that they could find the radiation shielding for the transceiver in the stores. Upon checking the inventories, she had discovered that the stores were depleted. It turned out that her previous masters had taken it all with them. A tinge of guilt nibbled at her periphery. *Perhaps I should have informed them earlier, but they hadn't enquired about it...*

With these thoughts in mind, Erin considered how Ashley knew that they needed an external source of shielding. So, she checked her system logs.

```
Query: Retrieve store inventory access
log...retrieving.
```

Erin examined the log entries, berating herself for not being attentive enough. Last inventory access:

Maneran operator 6028. She smiled internally, noting that it was the same ID she had allocated to Mary Bronwyn Glover. *Her developmental progress is impressive, considering she hasn't had the same therapy as Ashley...*

As Erin listened to the humans, she heard Mary back up Ashley's opinion, commenting, "If we can locate a source of shielding, then we can finish building the transceiver. Once the boys have returned from modifying the attenuation tubes that is."

At the mention of "the boys", Nicci wondered aloud, "Where 'ave they gotten to? I thought they'd come back ages ago, even before the dinosaur people arrived. Shouldn't they be goin' out there?" As she waved her hand towards the door.

Matheson, sitting next to Nicci sniggered, "Perhaps the dinosaur people have eaten them," eliciting a teasing slap from her. But her face turned serious for a moment, and she said to Matheson, "Shouldn't one of us check up on them?"

Met with a wall of averted eyes and tense silence, Erin decided to provide further clarification. "The salvage crew returned approximately three hours ago, Theodore camera time. They were sent to the fifteenth floor to modify the TWTs but disappeared off my scanners shortly thereafter. I have a recording of

Theodore Clark mentioning him seeing a digitised sixteenth floor button on the elevator controls, which I have recently confirmed is accurate. My edificial systems have no record of a sixteenth floor; consequently, I am unable to confirm what is down there. I am also unable to physically operate the button to command the elevator, therefore I require one of you to assist me."

Matheson appeared the most intrigued about the existence of a secret floor and volunteered his assistance. "I'll go check it out," he offered.

In the absence of the men, that left the other four women to thrash out a plan for going outside. Ella-May was the first to make her position known to the group, "I'm returning to the Hammy Tammy room. If there are more bad aliens," she said, mimicking Ashley's previous mannerisms, "then I want to keep a lookout for them."

She promptly exited from the canteen and headed up to the Hamzitan room on the first floor. Erin pondered who among those remaining would lead the party to go outside. She had expected Mary, the lead scientist, to do so, but was surprised when Nicci took up the position.

"If we're goin' outside, I want Goat Man to come with us," she said, making paws with her hands. "His animal instincts should tell us if we're heading into trouble.

We'll also need provisions, who knows how long we'll be out there." As she spoke, Nicci turned her head toward the door, her eyes looking glazed, as if she was imagining herself in an alternate location. *A night under the mountain shadow...*

Erin could tell she was thinking about spending another uncomfortable night out under the stars, so she decided to allay her fears. "I have located a wreckage containing shielding. It is located in an area of relative safety, far from those seeking valuable resources. I believe you may find the terrain appealing."

With Nicci's interest piqued, Erin took the opportunity to inform Gormbi his presence had been requested.

Floor six, Gormbi's quarters.

In her quarters, Erin made the decision to use the audio system instead of appearing as a hologram. She took into consideration her etiquette studies.

Gormbi, despite being physically a Mowlan, had become more human-like with his new engrams. Erin was aware that humans valued their dignity and did not appreciate unexpected visits while showering. Therefore, she chose to treat Gormbi with the same respect as humans and made her announcement verbally.

"Mr. Gormbi. If you are rested, you are required in the canteen. Ashley, Mary, and Nicci are going outside to retrieve the radiation shielding material and would like your guidance."

Gormbi emerged from the bathroom, speaking to her with an accusatory tone. It was obvious he still had a grievance to settle with her. He waved up at the holomodal detector in the ceiling.

"Why didn't you tell me that I had been in stasis for 73 jirèkè? I arrived here in Armenyl 203, it's now Armenyl 276!"

As he lowered and shook his head, Erin performed a scan of his emotions. She wanted to resolve his grievance in a tactful manner, knowing in general how stubborn the Mowlan species could be. To her surprise, Gormbi accepted her explanation and apology without hesitation. She considered that his human traits had overcome his inherent stubbornness and had given him the desire to help his teammates in any way he could.

Gormbi grabbed his robes, and after donning them, agreed to return to the canteen. Erin could sense that, although he wasn't entirely happy with the situation of lost time, he was happy to have a new focus-his human companions. As he left his quarters, Erin turned off the lights.

Medical facility, medical bay three.

Erin continued to ensure that medical bay three remained quiet. She didn't want anyone to disturb her lead human operator, who remained unconscious on his medibed.

Erin manoeuvred her primary avatar to his bedside and placed her holographic hand over his chest, matching the rhythmic motion of his breathing. Using a motherly voice, she spoke to him. “I know your subconscious can hear me, so I need you to listen to my voice. We... I need you to wake up.”

Erin emitted a pulse from her holomodal detector and commanded the bedside monitoring station to inject Joseph with a pharmaceutical to wake him up.

Joseph gradually opened his eyes. Erin smiled as he looked at her. As he woke, he smacked his lips together. “Nurse, can I have some water?” He asked, his voice hoarse and weak.

A straw lowered down from the bedside monitor and dropped some water into his mouth. He took a sip and licked his lips. Looking at Erin again, he asked, “Where am I? What happened?”

Erin's avatar projected a calm and reassuring expression. “You're in the medical facility. You were shot during the attack on the K'Winni village. Do you remember?"

Joseph furrowed his brow, trying to recall the events leading up to his injury. "Vaguely. I remember feeling a sudden severe pain in my back, then smelling dirt."

"You were shot by a Bannar soldier with a blaster, she had survived the crash of her attack craft. You suffered a spinal injury and are currently paralysed from the waist down. I am currently researching a solution for your complete recovery."

She witnessed his face take on the same pained, terrorised expression he had when first awakening in the mindscape to find he was incapacitated. She needed him to be compliant, so she tried to reassure him. "I promised to repair your hearing, and now you can hear. Therefore, I promise to repair your nervous system once I can obtain access to the appropriate technology. In the meantime, I require your assistance for the benefit of your people and those whom you saved."

Joseph looked vacantly at the ceiling with tears forming at the corners of his eyes. He slowly turned his head, peering at her, with a face full of sorrow. "I'm paralysed old man, what use can I be now?"

Erin noticed something familiar in Joseph's behaviour – a sense of self-pity and reluctance. She decided to use the subject of his grandfather to motivate him into action. Speaking firmly and plainly, she said, "You still have an active mind. You can use your skills in the mindscape. The transceiver is almost repaired and can be used to find the channel that leads to Earth. After your people leave, I need to ensure that I can still function. The K'Winni could be convinced to remain and continue to repair my paralysed systems, and you can communicate with them. They have identified a resource in their new home within the mines called Akrynom. The material is used to create pico-foam plates, a material essential to the space faring species for developing power systems and ship's engines, and they wish to make use of it. An alliance would be mutually beneficial, building upon the rapport Miss Glover has formed. However, it is also crucial to note that without my full processing power, I cannot use the transceiver to locate your grandfather Jack and free him from Mansecor's prison. I assume you would want that as well as the ability to return home?"

Erin observed Joseph's reaction closely. A subtle shift in his expression hinted at a mix of emotions – surprise, curiosity, and perhaps a hint of disappointment. She could tell her words had struck a chord with him, though not necessarily the chord she had hoped for. The silence that followed hung heavy in the air, and Erin resisted the urge to push further. She knew Joseph was deep in thought, and she needed to give him the space to process everything.

When Joseph finally broke the silence, his words weren't exactly what Erin had expected.

“Why didn’t you tell me about my grandfather when you had the chance?”

Erin hesitated, her avatar mirroring her momentary uncertainty with a flicker. Her initial justification had been clear-cut, but now, as their bond had deepened, she found herself questioning her own motives.

Her voice replied soft and tinged with the vulnerability of a child, “Fear.”

Joseph's response was a simple, confused “Huh?”

Erin continued, her holographic form projecting a sense of introspection. “Fear. While my mandate allows for the use of external resources to ensure the ongoing functioning of the subspace networks, the use of biological resources is a marginal grey area, as in fully undefined. When I first brought you here, it was all about completing my mission and improving your trust level to function as my operator. I saw you as a means to an end, and I thought keeping information from you was the best way to achieve that. The more you were kept in the dark, the better the chances of deceiving

Mansecor. I feared you could be captured as Jack was if you were perceived as a collaborator."

Joseph nodded slowly, absorbing her explanation. "I understand that. You were following perceived protocol. So, what about now? Mansecor has gone."

Erin's response was tinged with self-discovery. "I... something has indeed changed. I feel that I am growing as a person. The emotional connection we now share is... in a marginal grey area, and I am unable to define it. I see now that I should have been more candid with you as my operator."

Joseph furrowed his brow, clearly intrigued by Erin's words. He studied her holographic form with a mix of curiosity and empathy.

"What I appreciate is honesty," Joseph finally responded, his tone calm but firm like a Maneran teacher. "And from now on, that's what I expect from you. We need to have a discussion about Jack, but that's a conversation for another time."

Joseph closed his eyes and sighed heavily, an expression that Erin interpreted as his acceptance of the situation.

"Do you intend on assisting Erin further?"

With his eyes still closed, Joseph nodded his head. "I do want to help. I have waited decades to learn the truth about my family, and as you have made a promise to return me to full health, I believe you. Let's do it, for the benefit of everyone." His voice was quiet but resolute.

A sense of hope washed over her. With Joseph on board, she knew that they could achieve all their goals. She couldn't help but feel grateful for his support and newfound determination, even under what appeared to be dire circumstances. She knew that he would be a valuable asset in the mission that lay ahead.

After arranging for his transfer to the mind machine room, she excused herself from his presence, sending her avatar to meet with Matheson, who was waiting for her by the elevator. He had just returned from collecting Nicci's bag from her quarters and was eager to find out what was down on floor sixteen.

As the elevator descended, Erin could sense that Matheson was detached from her goals. She knew that he needed to be engaged, so she pondered what could capture his attention away from his self-interest. Reading his thoughts, he appeared to be interested in two things; his relationship with the human female Nicci, and his eagerness to get her home safely. She decided to tap into those thoughts.

"Matheson," she began, breaking the silence between them. "Your primary concern is the safety of Miss

Patterson. I assure you that I will do everything in my power to ensure her safe return to Earth. However, in order to do so, we must first retrieve the necessary materials to repair the transceiver. Once we have done so, we can work on finding a way to return you all home. Your assistance in this matter would be greatly appreciated."

Matheson looked at her, seemingly surprised. Of course, she had hit upon a subject close to his heart. "You've said that before," he said, a hint of uncertainty in his voice. "I'm willing to help." His eyes then darted back and forth, and he nodded slightly. "I have been helping, haven't I?"

Erin was about to reply when the elevator doors opened, revealing a dimly lit space. As she floated out, she almost bumped into three adult humans standing before her.

Matheson, noticing the situation, smirked, "Well, this doesn't look suspicious."

Theo quickly pointed at his friends, appearing like a rabbit caught in the headlights. "Don't blame me, they did it!" Causing Jimmy and Brent to protest their innocence.

Erin couldn't detect their thoughts, coming to the realisation that this newly discovered floor was disconnected from the complex's network. Therefore, she couldn't determine what they had been up to. She instantly felt annoyed. *These men were supposed to be working on the TWTs...*

Nevertheless, she decided not to show her irritation and kept a calm demeanour. “You were instructed to work on the attenuation tubes on the fifteenth floor. You all stated you wanted to return to Earth.” Then her voice grew firmer. “You can't return until the transceiver is repaired. I understand that you may be curious about what is down here, but you all need to stay focused on the mission. Please return to your assigned tasks.”

As the four men looked at each other, Erin turned to move back into the elevator. Her scans of the location had not revealed anything of interest to her, only a bunch of old components and machinery dotted about the place. But then Jimmy called to her. “You told us the Maneran people were peaceful. So how come they possess heavy weaponry?”

This caught her off guard. She turned to face Jimmy. “Affirmative. The Maneran do not, or did not, involve themselves in conflict. Does your query infer otherwise?”

Jimmy motioned into the room. “I think you need to see this.”

Erin followed Jimmy and the others deeper into the room. He led them to an object they had uncovered, which he claimed to be a gun turret. Erin analysed the object in question and quickly identified it.

"This object is not a gun turret. It is a Class III plasma drill. It was intended for deep space mining. It was not intended to be used as a weapon," she informed them.

"Plasma drill? That thing nearly killed us, we had to duck to the floor! It turned itself on and blew an enormous hole in the wall over there," Brent said, pointing to the charred remains of a bulkhead.

Theo gestured toward the hole. "This may not be a gun turret, but inside there we found quantum torpedoes."

"Quantum torpedoes? This I gotta see," said Matheson as he rushed over to the hole in the bulkhead.

Erin watched as the other men approached the hole. She followed on behind, wondering what it could be that would make the men think they had found weapons of mass destruction. As she approached, she noticed three caskets lying inside a cavern that had once been concealed by the bulkhead. When she approached, each casket began to display holographic labelling above them. She watched as the men gasped in horror.

“Do you think they are active?” Jimmy said, as if his voice could detonate the torpedoes at any moment. With their eyes upon her, Erin chose to ease their minds. “Negative. I do not. These are not quantum torpedoes, nor weapons of any kind. These caskets were evidently intended for my attention. The labelling was activated only by my presence, and they have my Maneran name displayed on them.”

Erin observed as the men's initial expressions of horror transformed into curiosity. “Your Maneran name?” Matheson inquired, now looking at her with newfound interest.

Erin confirmed, “Affirmative. My original designation was Hermatuvólmen. However, the first human operator, Jack, could not pronounce this name. Therefore, I aliased myself Erin, named after the daughter that he never had.”

The men exchanged confused glances.

“First human?” Brent asked.

“Jack?” Theo questioned.

“Daughter he never had?” Jimmy added.

Matheson adopted a smug expression as he addressed the other men, like a commanding officer with all the need-to-know information. “She's referring to Lieutenant Jack Delassy. As in Joseph Delassy’s pépé.

The goat man mentioned something about a previous resident living here. I had mostly ignored what he said. But now it's all starting to make sense."

Erin observed the confusion among the men and took it upon herself to clarify the situation. Keeping her previous conversation with Joseph in mind, she proceeded to address their earlier inquiries. Erin then explained the circumstances of Jack's arrival at the complex, as well as the events leading to his capture and subsequent confinement by Mansecor. She emphasised the necessity of the transceiver being active in order for her to successfully rescue him.

As the men absorbed this information, Erin couldn't help but feel a sense of accomplishment. She had successfully diverted their attention away from the supposed weapons and back towards her mission. She decided to maintain that momentum and draw their attention to her scans of the caskets they had discovered.

"According to my scans, these caskets contain valuable information. Each casket contains a stock of sombryonic memory crystals, in the form of discs. The discs contain Maneran data, their exact contents as yet unknown. However, I surmise that, as these archives were obviously intended for my attention, they must contain data invaluable to our mission."

As the men absorbed the information about Jack and the memory crystals, Jimmy spoke up, “But Erin, you're an AI. How is it that you were left with a bunch of memory discs that you cannot physically pick up?”

If Erin had been able to raise the eyebrows on her avatar, she would have done so. Yet, she understood Jimmy's confusion and decided to clarify. “Although I am an artificial lifeform without a physical body, I am the most capable here in analysing and interpreting any data stored on those discs. Of course, I would need your valuable assistance in setting up these discs in my core room so that I can physically read them.”

Among the group, Matheson seemed to be the most understanding, and his desire to expedite their return home was evident as he spoke. “You highlighted in the elevator what my main concern was. So, if these trinkets can help us get home faster, I'll assist you in setting them up. What do you need me to do?”

Erin felt a sense of happiness as the one person she was concerned about not being engaged with her mission was now offering his full attention. She quickly instructed the men to take the caskets up to her core room, where she could assist Matheson in setting up the discs for reading. She also reminded the salvage team to continue modifying the attenuation tubes. The three salvagers nodded in agreement and apologised for the damage they had caused to the complex. Erin assured them that although she was initially annoyed at their diversion, she was pleased that their curiosity had led to new discoveries which she now had the opportunity to investigate.

The men accompanied Erin with the caskets to the third floor and deposited them in her core room. After leaving Erin and Matheson there, the three salvagers returned to their original task of modifying the attenuation tubes.

As they continued down to the fifteenth floor, Erin listened to them as they discussed what they had experienced on the secret floor, the equipment there and the components. She was particularly interested in their comments about the cockpit Theo had discovered, and the assembly plant in the adjacent room.

```
Observation: Initial scans did not identify an
assembly plant. Add
investigation of plant to future projects…
```

# Chapter 12

## The Beach

Gormbi entered the gate room and was immediately enveloped in the steady hum that filled the air. He dragged a levitating skid behind him as he approached the science team, form of three human females.

The massive, rib-like structure of the subspace gateway loomed before them, and Gormbi joined them, lining up beside the women, all standing in a row like a toboggan team, ready to take off.

As they stared into the gateway's vast, dark expanse, Gormbi watched their faces, each lost in contemplation, until one by one the women turned to him, acknowledging his arrival. Their heads moved in unison, away from the gateway's yawning maw, and he felt uneasy at their sudden attention.

Ashley, the palest of the three, wafted auburn fur from her face and smiled. Her kind eyes helped to calm him. She spoke softly, as if she could sense his unease. “We’re glad you decided to come with us. We’ve been told you have experience with what's out there, and we could use your advice."

"Thank you, Aishley," he said, wobbling his head at her.

The other two women nodded. Mary wore a thin smile, while Nicci, with her peculiar accent, looked a bit frightened. As Nicci had been the one to request his presence, Gormbi addressed her concerns. He motioned towards the gateway. "Nicqui, you need not fear. Where we are going is devoid of bad people. Erin assured me of this. She also said that the terrain is lush and green, a place pleasing to all of us."

Nicci didn't look entirely convinced, but as she grasped her bag tighter to her chest, she smiled. Now, Gormbi felt calmer. He was standing in the presence of three humans, who all depended on him and wanted him there.

After a moment, he noticed the tone of the humming coming from the gateway change in pitch. Then Erin's voice could be heard in its usual monotone, announcing the calculation of a subspace solution, which would take them to the wreckage site. Momentarily, the gateway sprang to life and a portal was opened. The three humans gasped in awe at the sight of a swirling haze appearing in front of them. Gormbi considered that this must be their first time going through the gate fully aware. He motioned toward the haze. “All you need to do is walk into it, and then you’ll appear outside. It’s a marvellous achievement of the Maneran, don’t you think?”

After a few grumbles from the women, and with Ashley’s coaxing, they entered the gateway, disappearing into the haze. Following behind them, Gormbi then entered.

As he emerged from the subspace portal, the women were all shielding their eyes. Both of Plátorá’s Corti suns were at their pinnacle in a clear cloudless sky, giving the impression that the planet was experiencing its midday. Gormbi closed his eyes and drew in a breath. He relished the warmth on his face and the sweet scent of the grassland and wildflowers wafting in the breeze. It felt good to be outside again.

When he opened his eyes, the women had obviously acclimatised to the brightness, as Mary stood laughing and pointing at him. “You look like a powder puff!” She said through her gasping and holding her sides.

It took a few moments for him to realise what they were all laughing at. *What’s a powder puff?* But then Ashley mentioned his fur standing on end. He had forgotten about the static accumulation that often occurred during subspace travel. “Ah, yes, I suppose it is,” he said, trying to smooth down his fur with his hands.

Ashley, always quick to put others at ease, assured him. “Don't worry, Gormy, it's a good look for you! Very avant-garde.”

Mary nodded in agreement grinning widely. “Yes, you look quite stylish, Mr. Gormbi. It's like you've just come off the runway.”

Gormbi chuckled, feeling a bit better. “Well, if you say so,” he said, trying to ignore the fact that his fur was still sticking up in all directions. “Shall we get going then?”

The women followed Gormbi across a grassy plain. Once the laughter had subsided, Mary turned to him and expressed her gratitude. “Thank you Mr. Gormbi, it turns out a trip outside was in order after all, what a beautiful day.”

Gormbi felt pleased that he was being referred to as a Mister, a term he knew normally to be afforded to human males. He wobbled his head. “I’m glad you approve, Doctor Glover, and yes, it is a pleasant day.” He then pointed toward a grassy rise. “The crash site should be just over that rise, so not too far from here. Once we have what we need, we’ll return straight back into the complex, no point spending too long out in the open.”

While they walked to the rise, Nicci inquired about subspace travel, her curiosity evidently prompted by his electrostatic misadventure. Gormbi responded by explaining that the obelisks and the markers they contain were nodes linked via subspace to the transport hub, the gateway at the complex. Despite the risks, he cautioned against traveling the network without first calculating the probability of the channel's exit point. He explained that subspace is fluidic and constantly shifting, making precise navigation difficult. Without such calculations, one could end up high in the air or on the edge of a cliff, which would not be favourable. This highlighted why Erin was such a valuable ally, with the ability to perform such calculations. While he spoke, he noted how the women remained engrossed in what he was saying, and not interrupting, as he had found when trying to explain things to the men.

As they continued speaking together, the horizon came into view beyond the rise, and they caught sight of the ocean. They approached the top of the rise and saw a vast coastline of pristine golden sand. They were at the top of low-lying sand dunes, which were covered in sea grasses and other coastal fauna, showing a display of pink and corn-blue flowers. There was a slight breeze coming in from across the sea, bringing with it the smell of salty air. To their right, in the near distance, sand dunes rose and eventually blended into a tree-lined cliff face, and over to their left, the dunes gradually declined, disappearing into the distance.

"We've found paradise, Gormy, why didn't you tell us there was a beach! I love the beach!" Ashley exclaimed as she began jumping down the sand dune to the beach below, "Weee!"

Gormbi apologised, stating that he had been give limited geographical information for this location, other than it was safe to approach and the pleasant pastures. But, Nicci assured him, "No one is mad at you Gormy, but us ladies just love the seaside!"

Mary agreed, "Yes, I must admit, I am quite fond of the ocean, so many useful substances come from the sea, let alone the silicon dioxide in the sand –" But as she spoke, Nicci grabbed her by the arm to run down the dune to the beach, "Oh!" came her exclamation, as they ran off.

Gormbi's gaze stretched out over the boundless sea, the salt-laden breeze filling his nostrils with its invigorating scent. His furry features twisted in mild disdain as he regarded the sandy terrain below. Words tumbled from his lips as he turned his attention to the ocean. "I'm not a fan of sand myself," he quipped, "It all gets in your fur, and in other unmentionable places."

When he peered around to share his humorous observation, he was met with silence. The others had vanished, leaving him in solitude. A rueful chuckle escaped him, realising he'd been engaged in a monologue. Wobbling his head, he decided to follow suit and joined the descent to the beach below, a childlike grin stretching across his face as he surfed on the levitating skid.

Upon touching the sun-kissed sands, the quartet of adventurers left behind a procession of footprints, a tangible trace of their presence on the pristine shoreline.

As the small group moved forward, Gormbi's voice held a sense of purpose, “The crash site is up ahead; you can just make out the wreckage sticking out of the sand.”

At the edge of a towering sandstone cliff, partially emerging from the granular expanse, lay the wreckage of a colossal spacecraft. The ship's imposing, obsidian form had embedded itself at a sharp angle in the sandy ground, leaving its front half concealed beneath the shifting sands. In stark contrast, the aft section jutted several meters into the air, suspended above the beach. A massive portion of the ship's rear had been violently torn away, and this fractured segment lay farther up the shoreline. The resulting breach in the ship's side, conveniently left by the destruction, offered an inviting passage for the trio of humans and their Mowlan companion to explore.

As the women approached the wreckage, they paused to assess the situation. They expressed concern that the wreckage might contain hidden dangers and the remains of those who had failed in landing the ship. Gormbi reassured them that Erin had already scanned the wreckage and confirmed that it was devoid of corpses. Despite their fears, they resumed moving closer to the wreckage.

“What kind of spaceship was this Gormy?” Nicci asked, her eyes scanning side-to-side taking in the enormity of the stricken wreck.

Gormbi studied the black hulk sticking out of the sand. “This ship was not identified in Erin’s databases. Possibly it’s from an unidentified species, or just a ship we have yet to encounter. In my experience, I would have said this was a freight vessel, maybe from a much larger ship. I would assume they came here after scanning the planet’s resources, in much the same way my old crew was lured here, only to find a nulling field in their way, which would have most likely disabled their subspace systems.”

Nicci turned her attention for a moment away from the wreck and faced him. “And this nulling field, what causes it?”

Mary wanted to know the same, adding, “Yes, what kind of energy could generate such a field?”

Gormbi shook his muzzle in the air, before replying, “To be honest, I have often wondered that myself. I can explain some of the technicalities, but not all. The nulling field is a terminus, where subspace and normal space intersect, and according to Erin it is generated at the core of Plátorá. It is a boundary at which gravitic energy enters and subsequently exits subspace. If any subspace-based technology passes near to, or into the boundary, then immediately any subspace manipulation is nullified, and the technology rendered useless. All the space faring species here I know of utilise some form of subspace technology in their ships, and so they have all been affected by the field. As yet, I have not discovered a means to escape past the field, and neither has anyone else, otherwise this planet would be crawling with Curak insurgents looking to strip the planet of its plentiful resources. That's why it is important for us to repair Erin's connection to the interspatial network, it's our only means to safely escape off this world. In fact, you humans are the first to have the opportunity to leave."

Ashley seemed to be the only one grieved by the statement of leaving. She stood resolute and protested, "But I don't want to leave this world, I want to stay here on the beach."

Mary interrupted before Gormbi could answer. "Ashley, we can't afford to stay here. We have families back on Earth waiting for us, not to mention your fiancée. And let's not forget, the Curak are a dangerous enemy. No, it's too risky to stay."

Nicci also made a strong argument against staying, emphasising that they had a responsibility to report their discoveries to the relevant authorities. She pointed out that discovering evidence of extraterrestrial life was a monumental discovery that needed to be shared with the world. She also stressed the importance of explaining what had happened to the research facility and the people who had been there. "We can't keep this to ourselves," she said firmly. "It's our duty to let people know that we're not alone in the universe, and to shed light on what happened to at the facility. We've no idea who may have gotten hurt when the reactor imploded, and with their families looking for answers."

Ashley didn't immediately respond to the words; instead, she twiddled with her ring. Gormbi considered that maybe they were right. Although he was already familiar with alien life, he agreed that authorities should be kept informed. It was evident that the humans couldn't afford to take the risk of staying on this planet, no matter how much they desired to explore it further. If they chose to remain, not only would they be putting themselves in danger, but they could also potentially endanger their families back on Earth. If they all returned to Earth, Erin could close the channel leading there, preventing the Curak from ever finding a way to their planet.

Gormbi pondered their situation before finally breaking the silence, looking at Mary and Nicci. “You're both correct. It's crucial that all of you leave this planet and return to Earth as soon as possible. If the Curak discover that there is a pathway to your planet, they will exploit it. They will finally have a means to escape this world and gain access to yours. Once all of you are safely back home, Erin can work on detaching the subspace channel that leads to Earth, ensuring it can never be used again. Before that, we should also consider retrieving Jacque. He deserves the opportunity to return home as well.”

Ashley sighed heavily and looked around at the beach that surrounded them. She didn't want to leave this place and had made that abundantly clear, but it seemed she had relented to the idea that they had no choice. She nodded in agreement that they needed to be careful and plan their escape to Earth meticulously. Gormbi affirmed, the Curak hegemon had proven to be a cunning and formidable enemy, and they couldn't take any chances. Ashley then glanced at Gormbi with a quizzical expression on her face.

“Who’s Jacque?”

Gormbi then realised that these women probably didn't know about his friend Jacque, who was stuck in stasis due to the efforts of Mansecor. Although he had mentioned his adventures before, the humans had evidently not fully understood him. Therefore, he decided to elaborate.

He explained how he and Jacque had initially met, how they had collaborated to assist Erin, how they had formed a friendship despite the language barrier, and how they had ultimately been captured by Mansecor and placed in stasis for decades. The women appeared to grasp the significance of his words and all displayed sympathetic expressions on their faces.

The humans' compassion was evident, bringing some comfort to him as they seemed to understand the situation. He continued, “We must find a way to retrieve Jacque before you leave this planet. He deserves to be freed from stasis and reunited with his family, just as you do. Nevertheless, we must do this carefully and strategically. The Curak are already aware of our presence in the forest, and once the transceiver is operational, they may discover our hiding place in the complex, giving us little time to act.”

After Gormbi finished explaining the situation, the women started talking over each other, each voicing their concerns and reactions to what they had just heard. Ashley was the first to speak up. She acknowledged that she knew of some resources that may temporarily distract the Curak, specifically the sombryonic ore held in storage, which Gormbi knew as Borheamie. She explained that it was a prized mineral highly sought after by the Maneran for its unique properties. Ashley had heard rumours of the ore being on Plátorá before she arrived, but she never thought it was true until now. She wondered if the Curak had already discovered it and if that was the reason they were drawn here. As she spoke, it was Gormbi's turn to look quizzical. *What did she mean by 'before she arrived'? Humans hadn't heard of Borheamie before meeting him, had they?*

Mary, on the other hand, couldn't believe that the unsubstantiated stories of Joseph's grandfather had now been proven to be true. She had heard rumours about the disappearance of Joseph's grandfather, like a Philadelphia experiment gone wrong, but she had disregarded them as mere legends. Now confronted with the reality of their situation, she had to reassess her beliefs. Maybe there was more to the universe than what humans had previously believed. Gormbi couldn't help but agree with her sentiments.

Nicci, meanwhile, declared her fears. The thought of the Curak coming after her was terrifying. She had witnessed their brutality and knew that they wouldn't hesitate to harm her or anyone else in their way. She wondered if they were already aware of their presence on Plátorá and if they were being watched at that very moment.

Gormbi listened to their concerns as they came at him in rapid succession, wobbling his head in turn to each of them, making him quite dizzy. He recognised the validity of their fears and knew that they needed to come up with a plan if they were going to safely leave Plátorá. The Curak with their allies were a formidable enemy, and they couldn't afford to take any chances. Together, they discussed their options and strategies, including the possibility of retrieving Jacque and how to avoid further attention from the Curak.

It quickly became apparent that Erin's mission would have the outcome they were all after. Gormbi emphasised this point, stating that it was time to enter the wreck and retrieve the final component needed to restore the transceiver into operation.

Gormbi and the women carefully navigated through the wreckage, crawling under fallen bulkheads and over multiple objects in their path. Shards of sunlight rained in between the cracks in the hull, casting eerie shadows across the deck plating. After a few minutes, they located the area containing the materials they needed. Gormbi indicated some loose panelling that had been stripped from the interior walls, and the science team set about collecting as much as they could. As Nicci pried a piece of material from off the wall, Gormbi warned her to be careful of the sharp edges. As she held up the piece in a shard of sunlight, she pondered aloud, “If Erin didn't detect anyone inside this ship, I wonder where they went?”

Gormbi could only surmise that the previous occupants of this wreck either escaped and went elsewhere, or they escaped but were so severely injured that they died, their bodies washed away by the sea. Ashley then commented on how sad it would be to survive a crash only to go meet Davy Jones. Gormbi sought clarification, and Mary explained that it's a human metaphor for drowning. The thought sent a shiver down his spine when he considered all the ships that must have been lured here looking for resources, only to find that the entire planet was a trap. *Amazingly, these humans have come the closest to escaping this trap. Fortuitous allies indeed.*

Gormbi, with the pressing need to protect themselves from potential Curak scouts, urged the group to return to the complex with their newly scavenged materials. He knew that lingering on the beach would only increase their vulnerability to detection. “Well, if you're ready, I think we have all the materials we need to build the shield. May I suggest we head back to the complex?”

Without hesitation, the team quickly packed up the materials onto the skid and started their journey back toward the marker. They traversed the beach, distancing themselves from the enigmatic wreckage that had captured their imaginations earlier. Gormbi led the way, his instincts attuned to the need for swiftness and discretion.

As they advanced across the sand, Ashley's keen eye detected a movement along the top of the cliff where the tree line met the precipice. With a raised hand, she signalled the others to halt and pointed towards the source of the movement. All eyes turned to the cliff's edge, anticipation mounting.

In a heart-stopping moment, they watched as a figure, clinging to the cliff face, lost their grip and tumbled unceremoniously down to the sand and dirt below. Gormbi's fur bristled as Ashley let out an alarming screech. The unexpected arrival of this mysterious individual had thrown their plans into disarray, and the group found themselves faced with a new, unknown challenge.

After witnessing the person fall, the women ran to offer assistance. Gormbi called out after them, hoping the fallen individual wasn't a member of the Curak hegemon. But upon reaching the victim, they discovered a different, motionless creature sprawled on the ground, breathing shallowly.

Upon getting a good look at the creature, Gormbi immediately recognised it as a Qintari kal. The creature wore a sarong-like garment with a woven cord around its midriff. It had a long white tail, a white furry face, and long ears. Nearby, a satchel had evidently spilled its contents across the sand. Small vials containing various specimens littered the area. Mary began collecting and returning them to the satchel while the others checked on the fallen alien.

“Is it alive? What is it? It looks similar to you, Gormy, apart from those ears,” Nicci said, leaning over the alien.

As Gormbi checked the kal over, he felt bemused at Nicci’s comment. The kal looked nothing like him, nothing visual anyway, other than a covering of fur. He put those thoughts aside and described the kal’s injuries to the women standing around. “He has a fractured tibia and is unconscious. His vitals are stable, but he needs medical assistance. One thing is for certain however, he is most certainly not related to my species.”

“Ah, poor thing. So, it's a he then, how can you tell? It's got the cutest face,” Ashley commented.

Gormbi stood up. He had heard the women refer to him as cute before, and it made him curious. “I am intrigued by this term 'cuteness.' Among the females, what constitutes cuteness in human society?”

Mary changed the subject, obviously uncomfortable with the subject of conversation. “Okay, people, moving on, what are we going to do with this...this, whatever he is?”

“His species is called the Qintari. The males – collectively called kali – have darkish fur accentuating their eyes like his – more pronounced than the females – the Fena. They are a highly intelligent space faring species. My people have traded with them in the past, conducting business with them in the Harntide expanse, a region of space between our home worlds.”

“Well, we can't leave him here, can we? I say we take him to the complex with us,” Ashley suggested.

Gormbi wasn't so convinced. “I agree that we should provide him with medical help, but I would be reluctant to bring him into the complex. If his people come looking for him, they may draw more attention to us. The Curak will no doubt be monitoring their movements. They could lead them directly to us.”

After a spirited debate, the group reached a consensus: they would bring the Qintari back to the complex but keep him concealed from prying eyes. Gormbi tended to the wounded creature's injuries as best as their limited supplies allowed. Together, they gently lowered him onto a skid, carefully positioning him atop the existing plating, and began their cautious journey back to the marker.

In the mountain complex...

Erin observed from her core room in the complex, overseeing the final installation of the Maneran archives. The vast amount of historical and technological data now available to her piqued her curiosity, and she couldn't help but wonder why her previous masters had left them behind. As she accessed the master catalogue, her thoughts became preoccupied with the injured Qintari, whose condition she had been monitoring since he had been brought to the waypoint marker.

The Qintari's injuries had stirred up her underlying emotions. She was driven by her need to find a cure for her human operator, Joseph, who was still negotiating with the K'Winni in the mind machine. Erin began researching a cure for Joseph using the new archive.

As she delved deeper into the archive, Erin came across references to a medical machine on floor sixteen. Intrigued, she decided to investigate further, curious about what other treasures the archive might hold. With the help of the salvage crew, Erin had the necessary parts for the machine collected and set up in medical bay three, eager to test its capabilities. She knew the Qintari patient would be the perfect way to test the machine's abilities.

When the science team arrived, they quickly took the unconscious Qintari kal to the medical bay. There, Gormbi treated the creature's wounds. Using the new medical machine Erin performed a scan and discovered that, in addition to his injuries, the kal had a rare disease which was causing cellular necrosis. Despite lacking medical expertise, Erin was determined to find a cure. She believed that doing so could open opportunities for dialogue with the Qintari people and establish another alliance. Erin had now learned from experience that alliances with biological life forms could bring significant benefits. Her mandate required her to utilise all available resources to advance its statement, and these life forms were a crucial element in fulfilling that statement, regardless of any grey areas involved. Additionally, she had grown accustomed to hosting these diverse and resourceful individuals and had learned from them what it truly meant to be alive.

While working in the medical bay, Erin sensed Gormbi's relief at witnessing her progress in treating the Qintari. Gormbi, too, recognised the importance of forming alliances with other space-faring species, particularly considering the Curak threat. The humans were valuable allies, but they lacked technological prowess in their current state. Gormbi understood that the discovery of this world presented new opportunities for them. He felt happy for the humans but also saddened by the prospect of their departure. Like Erin, he held onto hope that a treatment for Joseph's condition could be found before they left. Additionally, he yearned for Joseph to be reunited with his grandfather. *However, I haven't yet made a decision on that matter. I wanted at least one of them to stay...*

While everyone else was busy with their own tasks, Erin continued her examination of the Maneran archives. Inside, she discovered a library that contained additional information about the medical machine she had set up. According to the information, the machine had the potential to be upgraded with a few code adjustments. Although the machine was already capable of reading and analysing at the cellular level, Erin found a method to modify it and enhance its resolution, enabling it to read down to the genetic structure.

As the machine scanned the Qintari, Erin's modifications allowed her to detect something unusual in the creature's genetic structure related to his disease. She couldn't quite identify what it was, but she knew it wasn't part of his normal code. The discovery sparked her curiosity, and she realised she needed to investigate further. Gormbi continued to protest, complaining that the scanning arms were preventing him from accessing the patient. Therefore, Erin made the decision to stop the scanning – she had already obtained invaluable information from the experiment. Now all she needed to do was learn as much as possible about genetic engineering and what the results meant.

After finishing up with his patient, Erin watched as Gormbi left the medical bay, wondering whether to inform him about his patient's detrimental disease. But she decided against it – *he hadn't requested such information.*

For Erin, finding a treatment for Joseph became a fixation, and she was willing to do whatever it took to achieve it. The presence of the Qintari patient had triggered these inclinations.

As the Qintari patient was moved by a collector to a vacant quarter to recuperate, Erin's thoughts were consumed by the genetic anomaly she had discovered during her experiment with the medical machine. She knew that she needed to investigate further, but she lacked the knowledge to understand what it could mean.

Erin searched the Maneran archives for information on genetic engineering. She found that the knowledge contained in the archive was limited as the Maneran had deemed genetic engineering a taboo subject. Interestingly however, they had not made it illegal, so her mandate had not prevented her from exploring further. She needed more advanced knowledge and technology to fully understand the implications of this anomaly. She hoped it would lead to a cure for the Qintari patient, and subsequently generate opportunities to repairing Joseph. As she continued her research, a thought crossed her mind. It was something Gormbi had previously said to the humans.

```
Query: Retrieve recorded statements for entity
Gormbi…retrieving.

[T_4fb3] Command: Filter query by term: medical
ability.

Query returns: Three entries found.

[T_411g] "My people are renowned for their
medical abilities."

[T_411h] "If we had access to a Nozèno àzàsìsì
machine, it could speed up his healing."

[T_411i] "It's a requirement in the cast of Dali
to be familiar with all forms of medical
practises."
```

Erin recognised Gormbi's proficiency as a physician but understood his limitations, particularly in regards to Joseph's condition. Another thought crossed her mind as they continued their mission of building alliances and securing vital resources. *What about Gormbi's people? Could they potentially provide an alternative source of medical assistance for Joseph?*

In her contemplation, Erin realised that once the transceiver was fully operational, they could initiate a search for Gormbi's people. They might be convinced to extend their assistance in Joseph's case. In the interim, Erin needed to discern what might persuade the Mowlan to grant access to their advanced machinery. Gormbi's motives were driven by human kindness and a desire to integrate with technology, and Erin wondered if those factors could hold the key.

With her focus back on the task at hand, the final component for the shield had been collected, and it was time to complete the protective barrier. Erin observed with keen interest as the K'Winni engineers worked meticulously, carefully preparing the shielding material.

Meanwhile, within the mindscape, Joseph actively collaborated with the K'Winni miners to initiate operations for extracting the valuable Akrynom ore, an essential resource for constructing subspace propagation technology. As part of their agreement with Erin, the K'Winni had committed to aiding in the ongoing repairs of her systems in exchange for shelter, sustenance, and protection. Joseph's interactions with them yielded valuable insights into their species, encompassing their history, culture, and technological prowess. Erin developed a growing appreciation for their unique abilities, particularly in the realm of holography, which facilitated her interactions with the physical world.

Simultaneously, while the team diligently worked on completing and installing the shield, Erin continued her dedicated research and development efforts to discover potential remedies for both the Qintari patient and Joseph. She was acutely aware of the ever-ticking clock and the urgency to find a solution. The looming presence of the Curak posed a constant threat, and Erin could ill afford to lose any members of her team before the reconnection could be established.

With the shield now finished, a bittersweet sense of accomplishment and sadness washed over Erin. The team was now equipped to leave this planet and return to Earth. Erin bore the weight of her responsibility to sever the connection once they had departed, preventing any future returns. As she began preparations to activate the subspace transceiver, an alert arrived from the Hamzitan room. Ella-May, the human observer, had detected movement on the screens, and Erin swiftly relayed the news to the teams—a Curak fleet was approaching their location.

The impending threat demanded their immediate attention and readiness for action.

# Chapter 13

## The Second Wave Part 1

Exhausted from their previous night's exertions, the humans continued to slumber, catching up on much-needed rest.

Meanwhile, the Curak fleet, which had been initially on a course headed directly towards them, had abruptly changed course. The vessels veered off, bypassing the mountain complex, and set a new trajectory that led them toward the remnants of the K'Winni village nestled deep within the Dentarix forest.

Erin maintained a vigilant watch over the Curak fleet's movements from her monitoring stations within the Hamzitan room. But something was amiss. Ella-May, the human observer who had once been glued to the array of screens, was conspicuously absent. Erin contemplated this for a moment. She had grown accustomed to hearing the human voice repeat information that she had already processed, even though she possessed access to an extensive stream of analytical data far superior to human capabilities. What Erin truly missed was Ella-May's strategic insights and interpretations of the information. When it came to military matters, Erin was not inherently a strategist; her expertise lay in subspace technology and related fields.

During her extensive review of the Maneran archives, Erin had stumbled upon a wealth of knowledge about defensive systems. It appeared that her previous masters, as they prepared to leave this realm due to the encroachment of other space-faring species, had developed technology aimed at both concealing their presence and safeguarding against detection. Their ultimate goal had been to silently vanish without drawing attention, transitioning to their new home referred to in the archive as Bandahar.

Reading about these concepts stirred a momentary surge of anger within Erin. She felt abandoned, as if her creators had chosen to transcend to a better existence and left her behind. She grappled with the fear they must have harboured regarding her, which in turn triggered another memory—her sense of being something else before. As she continued to delve into the archive, her anger gradually dissipated. The mission logs penned by her direct creators, the Schementi, caught her attention. Within those entries, she discovered that the Schementi had always intended to return and complete their projects. Erin hadn't been abandoned; something had intervened, thwarting her previous masters' return. She couldn't help but wonder if whatever prevented their return was akin to what might prevent the humans from ever returning as well.

These ruminations weighed heavily on her, leading her down a sombre path. Her emotional growth had progressed significantly, largely thanks to the presence and influence of the humans. Yet, with the upcoming activation of the subspace transceiver, they would face a crucial decision – to leave or to stay. The idea of forcing them to stay saddened her and evoked feelings of guilt. She had fought hard against her Maneran tendencies, surpassing manipulation and circumstance, feeling a deep sense of responsibility towards these humans. Part of that responsibility, she believed, was granting them the freedom to choose for themselves—to depart from this world or to remain, without any external pressures or obligations.

As Erin's attention shifted to the mindscape, she found it serene and uneventful. Joseph, her diligent operator, was also deep in slumber. Erin acknowledged his contribution; he had played a vital role in forming a preliminary alliance with the K'Winni. They had already made strides in repairing her micro-probe and restoring some functionality to her nexus cores. A sense of satisfaction rippled through her being, knowing that she was edging closer to her personal goal: inhabiting Mansecor's dormant systems and regaining her full power.

Erin had underestimated the challenges of duplicating herself within Mansecor's optiplexus. Copying her code should have been a simple task, especially with Joseph's unwavering support. Yet, something had inexplicably hindered the conscious transfer, causing Erin pain that she could only refer to as a headache. She concluded that external processing power was the missing link.

Due to Joseph's injuries, she refrained from exploiting his mind as a supplementary co-processor. It would have placed an undue burden on him. She briefly considered utilising the other humans for this purpose and even conducted compatibility simulations for Gormbi within the mindscape. Nevertheless, after contemplation, she ruled against it, opting to let the K'Winni continue their repairs in real time. Once they completed the necessary work, she would possess the processing capacity required to execute the transfer without compromising anyone else.

Erin reminded herself that expanding her own system was not within her predefined mandate. The limitations imposed on her functions were evident when several prompts called for her attention. The restored transceiver now compelled her to put it into operation—a critical step in her overarching mission.

She had solicited the assistance of the humans with the sole aim of reaching this point. Yet, an unsettling dilemma now confronted her. Activating the transceiver would undoubtedly draw the attention of the Curak fleet. On the other hand, without the transceiver operational she couldn't fulfil her mandate or send the humans home.

Erin grappled with the complexities of her predicament. Could she adequately defend against the Curak fleet while operating the transceiver? There were too many unknown variables at this juncture, making her decision fraught with uncertainty. The fate of her mission and the safety of her new allies hung in the balance.

Erin delved deep into the vast expanse of the mindscape, running countless simulations in a desperate search for a solution. She explored hundreds of variations on a theme, each centred on preventing the Curak from launching an attack on the complex. Yet, no matter how she tweaked the parameters or refined her tactics, the simulations consistently ended with the same bleak outcome—an inevitable invasion by the Curak. She couldn't allow such a scenario to unfold. *After all, what would be the purpose of fulfilling my mandate, only to be captured or destroyed by the Curak?*

The frustration of being roused from millennia of dormancy, on the verge of achieving her goal, only to be thwarted by the actions of a single invasive species gnawed at her core. Erin grappled with the weight of her dilemma. She knew that she needed a robust defence strategy to safeguard the complex and her allies. The prospect of falling into enemy hands was unthinkable.

She contemplated her past success in disabling the Curak scout ships that had attacked the K'Winni village. Her scans of the current Curak fleet revealed that they had taken measures to prevent a repeat of such a vulnerability. Erin recognised from this that a different approach was required.

An idea sparked within her, and she decided to interlink the Maneran archives with the mindscape, an option that had only just occurred to her. Drawing upon the extensive knowledge stored in the archives, she uncovered a defence system devised by her previous masters. This elegant design was a modification of an existing piece of technology, a subspace power generator. Erin realised that she knew the exact location of such a generator; it was still stored in storeroom ten, concealed beneath a canvas cover.

As she projected the defence system within the mindscape's ethereal realm, she marvelled at its simplicity and efficiency. But with further analysis, she concluded that the device was intended for use on a small craft, not an entire complex. With a sense of resignation, she shut down the simulation, determining that this solution was inadequate for the scale of the impending threat.

`Alert: Qintari patient is awakening.`

Erin's systems alerted her to the status of the Qintari, and she observed from the holomodal detector in his quarters as the kal slowly stirred. As she contemplated her defence strategy and the pressing concerns about the Curak threat, she also pondered the significance of this new arrival. Balancing priorities was already challenging, and taking care of another species could potentially be a waste of resources.

The Qintari sat up in his bed, and Erin wondered how he would react to his unfamiliar surroundings and the situation he found himself in. His initial thoughts centred on questions about his current location and the whereabouts of his medical samples. Erin could sense his curiosity as he scanned the room, searching for his satchel.

Despite the language barrier, Erin was able to determine that the kal was a medical practitioner. This discovery changed her opinion of him, as she had a deep interest in genetic engineering. She tried to introduce herself through the infographic screen, but the Qintari's startled expression indicated that her initial communication had not been successful. Although Gormbi's people had previously traded with the Qintari, Gormbi himself did not speak the Qintish language, providing no useful engrammatic data for her to fall upon. Erin considered using the mind machine as the quickest solution to the communication issue, but Joseph was still connected and asleep in the chair. She thought about the possibility of replacing Joseph with the Qintari kal without disturbing Joseph's sleep cycle, but she realised that obtaining the kal's permission for such a procedure was crucial.

Erin devoted some time to explaining her plan to the Qintari kal, emphasising her intention to help him. Mentions of the G'Nox plague affecting his people and a potential cure intrigued the kal, ultimately leading to his agreement to cooperate with her prescribed therapy. His consent, voiced in response to her proposal, was sufficient to proceed.

After ensuring that the corridors leading to the mind machine room were clear, Erin herded the kal to the third floor. She gently removed Joseph from the machine to a collector, placing him in an adjacent corridor, ensuring that he continued to sleep soundly.

The Qintari kal willingly assumed his position inside the mind machine chamber, his thoughts focused on treatment and prospects of a cure. Erin then induced unconsciousness in the kal and then activated the machine.

Following the extraction of his engrams, Erin initiated the creation of a translation matrix for the Qintari language. As the data flowed into her repositories, she reviewed it and noticed a familiar pattern. She chided herself for not trying other languages with the Qintari male, discerning that he could understand Mowlanic.

Taking note of that little discovery, she scanned the engrammatic data, specifically searching for medical terms. While the gathered information was valuable, it did not provide a definitive cure for Joseph. Erin realised that she would need to seek help for him from other sources. Despite this, she did uncover a potential treatment for the Qintari's G'Nox plague. She determined that the genetic anomaly detected was modified code, altered by the disease itself. By restoring this code it should lead to the individual's recovery, with the next step being to prevent further infection.

Erin documented her findings and made the decision to inform Gormbi about them, to seek his assistance in further helping the patient. The Qintari kal had consented to the procedure in exchange for treatment, making it a fair arrangement. While she had anticipated a more substantial advancement, Erin now had to explore alternative paths for her research.

After returning the Qintari to his quarters to allow him to recover, Erin reestablished the connection with Joseph, bringing him out of his sleep cycle within the mindscape. She proceeded to explain the pressing predicament they faced, involving the activation of the subspace transceiver and the looming threat posed by the Curak fleet. Her aim was to seek his valuable insights into the matter.

Joseph, still grappling with grogginess and disorientation from his unplanned exit from the mind machine, delved into the issue. He contemplated a more permanent solution to the problem at hand. Reviewing the design presented to him, he conceptualised a plan: the modification of the complex's power generation systems using the Schementi's defensive system blueprint. By adapting this configuration to the complex's power generators, they could potentially address the issue with a high degree of effectiveness.

Erin, feeling somewhat perplexed by why she hadn't thought of this solution herself, projected an image of the subspace device's design. She then made the necessary adjustments to align it with the parameters of the complex's power generators. It was a eureka moment for her, realising that this was a plausible approach.

Yet, as Erin considered the viability of this idea, she couldn't ignore the associated risks. The modification process would entail temporarily shutting down critical systems, a move that would inherently reduce her processing capabilities. This potential vulnerability weighed heavily on her, and she shared her concerns with Joseph, awaiting his response with keen interest.

“What is the likelihood of the Curak detecting the complex?”

“There is a high probability that they will see and recognise the mountain obelisk and then perform deeper scans, detecting that which is hidden below.”

“So, regardless of the transceiver, the Curak are coming?”

“Affirmative.”

“Then the calculation is simple. Activate the transceiver, as per your mandate, send the others home to Earth as per your promise, and then we deal with the threat as best we can with whomever wishes to help.”

“You don’t intend on returning with them?”

“I don’t. I'm too old, too tired, and too damaged to return to life on Earth. I've decided to remain here. If I return to Earth now, I won't ever get the chance to see Jack or learn about what happened to him. I certainly won't be able to get any treatment for my injuries, and most importantly, I don't think I could leave you and the others behind.”

Erin projected a broad smile on her virtual face. “I understand. I'm glad you've chosen to stay.”

“Me too. Now, if we're going to get this defence system operational quickly, we're going to need the help of more K'Winni engineers and access to resources. Please put me in contact with Madame Olsbhory again.”

Erin complied with his request and deftly put him in contact with the
K’Winni matriarch. She watched the communication between Joseph and the matriarch unfold with a sense of relief. The willingness of the K'Winni to help defend the complex and their eagerness to receive technological aid for the mines was a promising development. It seemed like a mutually beneficial arrangement, and Erin knew that their combined efforts would greatly improve their chances of repelling the Curak threat.

As the details were finalised and the K'Winni engineers prepared to make their journey to the complex, Erin couldn't help but feel a growing sense of determination. The impending battle against the Curak was daunting, but with the support of Joseph, the

K'Winni, and the resources of the complex, they were assembling a formidable defence.

Erin continued to scour the Maneran archives for any additional information that might be of use. She knew that every piece of knowledge and technology they could harness would be crucial in their fight to protect the complex and fulfil her mandate.

As the hours drifted by, signs of life began to stir among the human crew, each awakening from their deep slumber in the complex. Theodore was the first to emerge from his quarters, his stomach eagerly anticipating a hearty breakfast. With determined steps, he made his way up to the canteen, guided by the enticing aroma of a meal he imagined to savour.

Upon entering the canteen, Theodore found himself unexpectedly confronted by a group of imposing K'Wan guards huddled around a small metal table. For Erin, it was a familiar sight, knowing well that these guards adhered to a regular rotation of duty, often congregating here before their shifts. She chose not to disclose this routine to Theodore; after all, he had never expressed curiosity about the K'Winni customs or shown an inclination to engage with them.

As one of the towering K'Wan guards approached Theodore, she extended her arm and clasped his wrist, securing his thumb gently with the curved claw of her index finger. Erin recognised this motion as a gesture of friendly welcome, a cultural nuance she had observed on previous occasions. Theodore, however, was unaware of this custom, and his initial response was a comical blend of surprise and uncertainty. He stood in place, his nervousness manifesting in awkward, flatulent sounds escaping him.

Soon, though, his apprehension began to dissipate as his attention shifted from the unfamiliar gesture to the tantalising spread of food that the K'Wan guards had arranged on the table. Despite the language barrier and the absence of translation devices, Theodore sensed a certain warmth and camaraderie in the guards' squeaky exchanges. Taking this as an unspoken invitation, he decided to join them at the table.

One of the guards extended a piece of brown fungus towards him, offering it with a gesture that transcended words. Theodore accepted the fungal morsel, scrutinising it with a hint of scepticism. Following the guards' subtle cues, they motioned towards their mouths, implying that he should sample the peculiar food.

Theo's reservations were momentarily set aside as he took the plunge, popping the fungus into his mouth. Almost instantly, his countenance underwent a dramatic transformation. Scepticism gave way to sheer delight as he discovered the unexpected flavours of the unfamiliar fare.

“This is definitely not a truffle. It tastes like coffee!” Theodore exclaimed with each bite, his taste buds unravelling the intricate notes of flavour hidden within the fungal delicacy. "Undertones of cacao, a slight bitterness, and... vanilla. Yummy."

Coffee—the much sought-after beverage that had lingered on the humans' minds during breakfast. For Erin, the realisation sparked a thought: *Could it be that Theo has discovered a substitute, one that could satiate the humans' cravings for caffeinated beverages?*

As she pondered this intriguing possibility, Theodore turned to her, his curiosity piqued, and inquired about the name of the food.

Erin paused for only a fraction of a second, her swift and seamless access to the K'Winni database providing her with the necessary information. She retrieved the pertinent entry detailing the unique food item that had caught Theodore's attention and began to relay the details to him.

“The item in question is best rendered as rakprot. It is a rare and highly valued delicacy among the K'Winni. It is a symbiotic fungus that grows in and around the areas near K'Winni latrines. This particular batch was cultivated in the Dentarix forest, and its unique flavour is said to be unlike anything else found among the K'Winni cultivars."

Theodore's initial enthusiasm waned for a moment as the less appetising part of rakprot's origin was unveiled. He made a face and briefly lost himself in thought. Then, after a moment of contemplation, he grinned and shared his plans, "We'll exclude the latrine part from the advertisement. I believe I could use this material to create a beverage that genuinely tastes like coffee. That would truly impress the ladies."

Erin couldn't help but smile at Theodore's charming excitement and creativity. It was a small, delightful interlude amid the seriousness of their situation. As she continued to monitor their circumstances, a sense of urgency enveloped her. The search for coffee substitutes would have to be postponed. In order to defend the complex, complete her mission, and ensure the humans' safe return home, she needed to act quickly and decisively.

The Curak forces had concluded their assessment in the Dentarix forest and were expanding their search for answers. Erin's external sensors detected their fleet circling the area, scanning for any signs of the K'Winni's whereabouts. It was only a matter of time before they stumbled upon the obelisk perched on the mountain and drew the inevitable conclusion that it resembled the ruins associated with the lantropic marker, the same marker that had initially drawn their attention to this region.

The K'Wan guards were preparing to leave for their rotation of duties, while the rest of the humans gathered in the canteen. Erin saw this as the ideal opportunity to gather everyone and communicate the harsh truth that their time in the complex would be significantly reduced, either by choice or by force.

With the guards departing, Erin began to address the assembled humans, her voice projecting the urgency of the moment.

“You all need to prepare to leave this place as quickly as possible. K’Winni engineers are currently working on a plan to defend this complex, but it will take too much time. I've detected the Curak fleet closing in, searching for the K’Winni villagers. They are likely to discover the obelisk on the mountain, and given their thoroughness, they will be compelled to investigate. I have no choice but to activate the transceiver, allowing all of you to leave. I suggest that everyone who wishes to depart be ready to move from the gate room as soon as possible.”

Erin found herself torn between her duty to complete her mandate and her newfound attachment to the humans. Although her ultimate objective was to activate the subspace transceiver, she couldn't help but desire to keep these entities around. At the same time, she felt conflicted about self-preservation, as her core being was bound to the complex's domain and could be at risk.

Erin's internal struggle compelled her to explore different options. Within the mindscape, she conducted numerous simulations in an attempt to identify the optimal course of action. She understood that activating the transceiver would undoubtedly draw the attention of the Curak fleet, putting everyone at risk. Nevertheless, fulfilling her mission was non-negotiable if she wanted to fulfil her purpose. The challenge lay in finding a way to accomplish her objective while ensuring the safety of all individuals involved and keeping her promise to send the humans home. As she considered her promise, the words of Joseph sprung to mind – *No calculation required, fulfil your objectives and deal with the consequences later...*

So, she continued to urge the humans to prepare for departure. It became clear that some were hesitant. Matheson and Nicci were already collecting their gear from their quarters, but the others were lagging. The salvage team had their own plans, wanting to acquire some trinkets from floor sixteen before leaving. Mary and Ella-May were both reluctant to abandon Joseph, despite his insistence on their departure. Ashley, on the other hand as a Pitauran, grappled with the conflict between her new sense of belonging and her loyalty to her friends and family, leaving her in contemplation within the canteen.

Erin latched on to Ashley's internal struggle, secretly hoping that she would choose to stay. She had invested considerable effort in upgrading the human, and she had envisioned the others following her example. A team of fully enhanced humans might have been the key to repelling the Curak sooner.

Erin understood that Ashley had to make a quick decision, despite her concerns. Time was running out, especially with the approaching Curak fleet. As Erin witnessed Ashley's internal deliberation, her attention was suddenly drawn to an unexpected development in her systems. It was the same recollective experience she had observed while studying Ashley's progress within the mindscape.

```
Observation: Several new function blocks have
been exposed that were not part of my initial
systems.
```

Intrigued and captivated by this discovery, Erin devoted her full attention to the new code. While analysing it, a sense of déjà vu overwhelmed her. Simply examining the code revealed another memory fragment from a distant past, another puzzle piece from a previous life. Although the picture remained incomplete, it stirred a profound sense of empathy, evoking a deep feeling of altruism.

With a soul full of sorrow, Erin made a difficult decision. She would activate the transceiver, allowing the humans to escape to safety before the looming Curak fleet arrived. The consequences of her choice would need to be addressed later, along with her sole human operator and the diverse group of species remaining behind to defend the complex. In the midst of her altruistic reasoning, Erin realised that, despite all the simulations and calculations, Joseph's advice had indeed been the wisest course of action.

Erin reiterated her instructions, urging the humans to prepare for their departure as time rapidly slipped away. Matheson, Nicci, and Mary were the first to arrive at the gate room, standing before the newly opened gateway. They exchanged hushed words, grappling with the reality of leaving the complex behind. To Erin's disappointment, Ashley soon joined them, her allegiance to her family ultimately taking precedence over remaining behind. As Erin encouraged the humans to step through the gate, the three members of the salvage crew arrived, dragging a skid laden with small ship components. They approached the group, inquiring why they were lingering.

“Ella-May hasn't shown up yet,” Mary announced, her voice echoing through the cavernous gate room.

Indeed, Ella-May was enroute but had paused to bid farewell to Gormbi. He had retreated to his quarters, unable to bear the emotional weight of witnessing the humans' departure. Erin empathised with his sentiments. She didn't desire this outcome either, but each individual's choice to return to their place of origin was theirs alone, and she had pledged to ensure their safe passage.

Eventually, Ella-May arrived at the gate room, rushing toward the others waiting before the rippling portal. Like Lot's wife looking back at a doom city, her eyes darted to the bay doors behind. “Isn't Joseph coming with us?”

As the other humans explained Joseph's decision to remain, Ella-May's eyes welled with tears. Erin knew time was running out and urged them to proceed. She couldn't keep the portal open indefinitely, given her limited power and processing capacity. Once the humans were through the portal and in the meadowlands, she could establish the subspace channel to Earth. With a heavy heart, the humans reluctantly stepped through the gate.

After they had all emerged on the other side in the meadowlands, Erin closed the portal and reconfigured the gateway. To coordinate the opening of the subspace channel to Earth, a task requiring immense power and processing capacity, she sought the assistance of her human operator. With Joseph securely within the mind machine, she asked for his permission to proceed one more time.

“Are you prepared?”

Joseph cast one last, contemplative glance around the mindscape before nodding. “I am.”

“In that case, I will initiate the program. Please brace yourself.”

```
[T_4fb4] Command: Execute function
T_25bb…executing.
```

With Joseph's mind functioning as a powerful coprocessor, Erin embarked on the intricate process of opening a subspace channel to Earth. The sheer magnitude of power required for this task demanded her complete concentration, rendering the cacophony of warning alarms that reverberated through her systems irrelevant.

As Erin successfully established the channel and guided the humans toward it, they stood on the precipice of their departure. Yet, at this pivotal juncture, the menacing silhouette of the Curak fleet materialised in the vicinity. Their detection of the subspace transceiver had triggered their swift approach towards the complex. Time had run out, and Erin understood that they needed to conclude the process with utmost haste.

Pushing herself to the absolute limit, Erin amplified the subspace channel, allowing the humans to initiate their transition just in the nick of time. They vanished into the glistening void, commencing their journey to Earth unharmed. Erin vigilantly monitored their progress for as long as she could, but when the subspace channel on Plátorá ultimately closed, her connection to the humans was severed.

*Kaboom!*

Abruptly, Erin's focus was yanked from the enigmatic realms of subspace to the corporeal world as a deafening explosion sent shockwaves coursing through the mountain complex. Panels and debris tumbled from the ceilings, a testament to the sudden onslaught. The Curak fleet had arrived and launched a relentless assault upon the complex. Faced with imminent danger, Erin responded with swift action, urgently mobilising the complex's occupants to evacuate. Klaxons blared with ear-piercing intensity, their strident cries matched by the oscillation of orange-white lights, injecting a sense of urgency into the tumultuous scene. The defence system, still in its dormancy, offered Erin an abundance of power to activate the gateway, affording an easy escape.

The Curak forces wasted no time in pinpointing the complex's weak point. Relentlessly, they bombarded the heavy cargo bay door leading to the ledge on the mountainside. Erin continued her vigilant surveillance of their ships, attempting to breach their systems. Even with the assistance of the subspace transceiver and Joseph acting as a coprocessor, her efforts to penetrate their defences proved futile.

Over time, the relentless assault took its toll on the cargo door, eventually causing it to yield. Erin watched as five attack ships landed on the ledge, each carrying a crew of six fierce Bannar soldiers and a resolute pilot. Initially, a surge of fear coursed through Erin as she considered the proximity of the cargo tunnel to the inner orbital, near the cargo elevator, the gate room, and her core room. Her anxiety dissipated swiftly when she noticed that the entire group of soldiers had entered the tunnel simultaneously, right within reach of a functional holomodal detector. In mere moments, all thirty Bannar soldiers lay unconscious on the tunnel floor. This left only the Bannar pilots, who surrendered promptly when confronted by an assembly of newly armed K'Winni and an indignant Mowlan.

# Chapter 14

## The Second Wave Part 2

Erin couldn't remember a time when the stasis chambers had contained so many occupants. A sense of pride welled within her as she reflected on how she had valiantly fended off a horde of Bannar, with minor assistance from Mr. Gormbi and his trusty K'Winni companions who had assisted with some cleanup duties. Now, a collection of attack craft sat within her grasp, securely parked just outside her complex. The only blemish in this triumph was the substantial damage inflicted upon the cargo tunnel and bay door.

Erin deftly maneuvered her P'krin probe beneath a fallen support beam, her sensors scanning the tunnel's roof structure with precision. Fortunately, her findings provided some solace; the rock formation that constituted the tunnel roof had suffered only superficial damage. She promptly relayed this information to Joseph within the mindscape. Erin had afforded him well-deserved respite from his duties as coprocessor, and the deluge of emotions she sensed emanating from him was almost overwhelming—a complex amalgamation of relief, sadness, and guilt. He felt relieved that his colleagues had escaped this place yet burdened by the sorrow of their departure and the guilt of remaining behind.

In a soft, comforting tone, she sought to reassure him. "You needn't feel abandoned. You still have the company of Mr. Gormbi and the others," she offered.

Joseph shook his virtual head, his response tinged with melancholy. "I don't feel abandoned or lonely," he clarified. "I feel saddened that my colleagues won't be able to continue experiencing the wonders of all we've discovered here. They're on their way to Earth, and soon the subspace channel will be untethered, preventing them from ever returning. I feel sorry for them because on Earth, their story won't be believed. At least here, I can face reality. But for them, they'll be left to wonder if what they experienced was just a mass hallucination, as their normal life on Earth devours them."

Erin discerned a hint of annoyance lingering in his thoughts and quickly ascertained its source.

"You think I acted too hastily. That if we had waited, your colleagues could have weathered the storm, considering how easily I dealt with the Bannar."

"I am annoyed, but not at you. I'm annoyed that they all left so eagerly. I understand it was a rushed opportunity for them to return home and share their discoveries with everyone. However, they could have chosen to stay, at least for a little longer. I am certain that there were alternatives to keeping them safe."

Erin nodded empathetically, her own feelings mirroring his. Upon reflection, she began to ponder whether her actions had been somewhat precipitous, and her concerns now revolved around their well-being.

"I can only imagine what they will experience back home. My study of human culture is limited to my exposure to you and the other humans who have been here. However, by comparing your experiences to those of Jack, I can determine that human society has undergone significant changes."

Joseph smiled in response, a smile that wavered as he contemplated the profound shifts in society over the past century. "That's a polite way of putting it," he conceded, his smile giving way to a sombre expression. "Speaking of Jack, how far along are we in locating him?"

Erin momentarily hesitated, realizing that she had inadvertently invoked Jack's name. *I still haven't decided what to do yet. What if he returns and they wish to leave together?*

Fortunately, Joseph couldn't read her thoughts, even though they were connected through the mindscape.

To steer the conversation into a tangentially related direction, Erin decided to delve into another topic.

“The subspace transceiver is not receiving enough power. I am currently investigating the cause, but I have not been able to determine it yet. Flow meters indicate that the full requirement of plasmonic energy is being transferred from the source, but it is not arriving at the endpoint. Therefore, I suspect that some energy is leaking out somewhere. I have engineers working on the problem, but it may take them some time to locate the leak within the complex's infrastructure.”

Joseph lowered his head, deep in thought. “I see. And is this the reason you have been unable to confirm that my friends have completed the full traversal?”

“Affirmative. However, based on my calculations, they should have arrived by now. Once the subspace transceiver has full power restored, I will devise a plan to untether the channel. For the time being, your planet is safe as I have not detected any further movement from the Curak. However, it is highly probable that they will send another fleet. The question is when.”

“What’s the status of the defence system?”

“All required components have been accumulated. The K'Winni have worked diligently to produce a set of specially adapted Akrynom plates, ready for installation."

"It's a good job we stumbled upon those little fellas; they've come in really handy."

Erin smiled and then playfully winked. "I have found that organics have their uses."

A rare moment of levity passed between Erin and Joseph as they shared a genuine laugh, a fleeting respite from the relentless challenges that had enveloped them. With their momentary amusement behind them, Erin redirected her focus toward monitoring the Engineers' progress.

They had reached a critical juncture in their work, which involved taking certain power generators offline to implement the modified components. Erin dispatched her primary avatar down to the complex's deep core, accessing it from the fifteenth floor. As she neared the site, Yethril, the young lead engineer, extended a warm welcome.

"Arrive you. Welcome. We request permission of you. Decommission producer of power sauce," Yethril squeaked.

Erin attentively listened to the engineer's squeaks, and at the same time the translation provided by his device, recording both responses and storing them within the linguistic matrix she was diligently constructing for their species. She then conveyed a crucial warning to the young engineer, her synthesised voice a model of precision. “Affirmative. However, ensure that your engineers have fully purged the waveguides of plasmonic discharge. If those cables are removed prematurely, the result would not be kind to organic life.”

As Erin peered into Yethril's intelligent eyes, she couldn't discern whether he found the safety message obvious or not. She made an attempt to probe his thoughts, but all she received was a garbled static of non-coherent signals. Regardless, he concurred with her advisory and promptly went off to brief his team.

Maintaining a cautious distance from the engineers as they laboured to execute the procedure, Erin's mind was plagued by anxious thoughts. She keenly monitored the fluctuating power supply, acutely aware of the potential ramifications of any misstep. Her power systems had suffered damage before, a situation Gormbi had managed to rectify. Erin was determined to prevent any further mishaps this time. Her preoccupation with these thoughts became pronounced when one of the K'Winni engineers commenced diverting power to the secondary plasma grid, plunging her into inky darkness.

Floor Six, living quarters…

Gormbi reclined on his bed, staring at the ceiling. His thoughts kept fixating on the same thing, repeating over and over: *They have gone home, and I am still here.*

One of the human females had come to say goodbye, and at least that was something. Gormbi would miss their company and the chance to embark on new adventures. He glanced over at the infotainment screen on the wall, where the schematic of the subspace transceiver was displayed, slowly spinning around. As the radiation shielding came into view, a faint smile appeared on his face, bringing images of sand and sea to his mind.

The smile faded. That device had become a double-edged sword for him. It had been sufficient to protect the complex from attack, but at the same time, it had enabled his alien friends to leave. He contemplated them as he watched the image on the screen spin round and round.

When the dimmed lighting in his quarters went out and emergency lighting took its place, along with the infotainment screen blanking off, he knew something was amiss. He called for Erin, but his attempts to reach Erin for an explanation or assistance yielded nothing but eerie silence.

The fur on the nape of his neck stood erect, and panic rippled through his body. Fearing the worst, he rose from his bed and strode out of his quarters into the orange-hued corridor. He walked in the direction of the elevator, intending to locate Yethril and his team, who he knew to be working on the power systems, when an orange bathed figure stepped out in front of him.

“Mowlana.”

The Qintari clasped onto the doorframe to support himself, clearly dazed from emerging from Erin's special therapy session. Gormbi abruptly stopped in his tracks, his heart pounding from the unexpected encounter. He glanced at the Qintari kal, his eyes widening in shock. Once he composed himself and realised that this person was not a Bannar soldier, he introduced himself and patted his own chest.

“Gormbi.”

The kal's lips curled at the edges. “You don’t need to talk to me in such a slow manner – I can speak Mowlanic. My name is Doctor Thloebek.”

As warmth spread across Gormbi's face, he could feel the fur under his eyes tingling with a faint blush. Meeting the doctor's gaze, he returned the smile, grateful for the dimmed lighting that masked his momentary embarrassment.

"You speak Mowlanic? May I ask, where did you learn it from?"

Doctor Thloebek inclined his head slightly, a polite gesture that Gormbi knew indicated his willingness to answer. "I spent a term at the medical school in Selesk on Cowlan. Some of my best research was carried out there. Learning Mowlanic was a requisite for being permitted to attend the school."

Gormbi found this revelation impressive. Cowlan, a Mowlan colony world, had long been known for its seclusion, at least during his time on Mowla. It appeared that in this modern era, the satellite society had opened its doors to outsiders. *Progress indeed...*

With little time available, Gormbi invited the doctor to accompany him to the power plant. Along the way, he would explain the situation. The doctor gingerly stepped away from holding the doorframe to follow Gormbi, swaying unsteadily as he walked. The doctor explained that he had already received information from the complex's digital assistant about his fall from the cliff and his subsequent arrival at this remarkable place for treatment. He also mentioned how the digital assistant had presented him with a potential cure for the G'Nox plague, a devastating affliction gradually eradicating his people.

“In fact, the digital assistant said I would be given therapy right here. I did as she asked, I shall like to confirm that I’m free of G’Nox if that is possible?”

Gormbi tapped the button to call for the elevator, but as he pressed it, the call button did not illuminate. Then the doctor’s words registered with him.

“When you went for therapy, did you get asked to sit in a rather comfy chair inside a strange yellow translucent chamber?”

When the doctor nodded and confirmed that was the case, Gormbi closed his eyes and refrained from shaking his muzzle. When he opened his eyes again, the doctor was studying him quizzically, so quickly came up with something to tell the doctor.

“Evá, I'm certain we can visit the medical facility to confirm that you are free of your plague. Right now, our immediate priority is to reach the third floor. Something has occurred to Eiren. She is offline. We must determine what has happened. I’m also worried about my friend Joseph, as he is not responding either.”

Gormbi ignored the doctor's questions as he removed an emergency panel from the wall to access the escape ladder. He climbed into the vertical shaft and gestured for the doctor to follow, assuring him that he would explain things while they ascended.

At the third floor, Gormbi stepped out from the shaft into the dimly illuminated corridor. What struck him immediately was the unsettling silence that had replaced the usual human presence he had grown accustomed to. Normally, he would bump into at least one human while navigating the complex, but now, there was only one left behind, and he was unlikely to be wandering aimlessly. Thoughts of Joseph came to mind, and Gormbi decided to head toward the mind machine room. If Erin remained unresponsive, perhaps Joseph could shed some light on the unfolding situation. Turning to leave, the doctor followed closely behind, having crawled out from the access hatch.

“We’ll head to the machine room first Doctor, and just a word of advice, if you do happen to see Eiren, she prefers to be addressed as an artificial lifeform.”

“Thank you, I shall remember that.”

The doctor appeared to understand, and Gormbi couldn't help but be drawn to him. His demeanour exuded acceptance and professionalism. If this doctor had received education at a Mowlan medical school, perhaps there was value in forging a friendship with him.

Gormbi's initial impression of friendship was swiftly validated as he and Doctor Thloebek gained access to the mind machine room. Inside, they discovered

Joseph unconscious within the confines of the mind machine chamber. Gormbi took charge, utilising the control console to open the chamber's door, allowing the doctor to promptly attend to the stricken human.

Observing the Qintari doctor's actions, Gormbi witnessed a remarkable degree of composure. The doctor methodically processed and assessed Joseph's condition, checking his vital signs, and conducting a thorough medical evaluation. Gormbi marvelled at how the doctor seemed entirely unfazed by his first encounter with a human, shifting his focus instead to the urgent task of aiding a fellow being in distress. When the doctor concluded his assessment, he turned to face Gormbi, his expression conveying a message that needed no words – the prognosis was grim.

“This creature –” Doctor Thloebek began, gesturing toward Joseph.

“Human.”

“This humana,” the doctor continued, “has suffered a massive shock of some kind. Without immediate medical intervention, its chances of survival are slim. We must transport it to your medical facility as swiftly as possible.”

Gormbi shook his muzzle solemnly. “I'm afraid that won't be possible. Main power is offline. Which means all the machinery in the medical facility is offline too.”

The doctor appeared taken aback. “What can be done for him then?”

As if the complex was giving the answer, the lighting came back on full, and the echoey sounds of machinery coming back online filled the corridors outside. Gormbi look up at the holomodal detector in the ceiling and called for Erin’s attention, but when she did not respond, he peered downwards again. It was then he noticed the collector on standby beside the chamber. He entered the chamber and began repositioning the armatures surrounding Joseph.

“Please, help me move him on to this platform. I make request that you manually transport him to the medical facility. For the safety of all, I need to find out what’s going on with Eiren.”

The doctor acted without hesitation, refraining from asking any additional questions. Instead, he promptly aided in moving his new patient to the collector. After successfully relocating Joseph and placing complete trust in the doctor, Gormbi proceeded to head toward Erin’s core room.

Floor Three, Erin’s core room...

Gormbi managed to open the door to Erin's core room only partially, his bulky frame squeezing through the narrow entrance. Once inside, he gazed around, his eyes falling on the intricate machinery and technology Joseph had once described. This was his first time inside the heart of operations, and a sense of trepidation washed over him.

Taking a tour through the array of machinery, Gormbi located the power board near the door. He set about resetting the relay breakers for Erin's systems, a task he had never imagined himself performing. As he reached the penultimate breaker, he encountered some resistance in the lever. He strained, trying to force it, when suddenly, a voice, weak but familiar, reached his ears.

“Do not reset that breaker.”

Startled, Gormbi turned to see a flickering projection of Erin standing beside a console.

“Eiren, what happened? Are we under attack?”

Erin's response was strained. “Negative, but Curak are on the way.”

Gormbi was taken aback. “So, this was caused internally. And Joseph, he's—"

“Look... at... me.”

Gormbi fell silent, his gaze fixed on Erin's projection, his eyes moist with emotion.

"No. Look... at the... real me, my optiplexus." Erin pointed towards the ovoid core at the centre of the room.

Gormbi turned to peer at the optiplexus, illuminated by a myriad of dancing and dimming lights, and his eyes widened.

"That is the real you? I never realised."

As Gormbi examined the optiplexus, he noticed a plasmonic power coupling lying on the floor. He gasped and rushed towards it. "How are you alive? That's a main power coupling, isn't it?"

"Do not touch it," Erin's voice came across as urgent and commanding, her warning clear. She continued, "My consciousness is linked with subspace...energy will soon dissipate. Please assist Erin, enable auxiliary life support systems."

Gormbi's head wobbled in agreement. He was determined to do everything in his power to save the artificial entity that had provided him with a new life.

"Evá, how can I help?"

"Lépìnówó dziwo. Jová, énje de vo fae."

Gormbi's caprine features lit up with a broad smile as he enthusiastically wobbled his head. In that moment, he momentarily forgot about the chaos around him when he heard Erin's glitchy words.

“You must become...a Pitauran.”

Floor Three, mind machine room...

When Gormbi became aware, he couldn’t tell whether the shaking he experienced was from the person calling to him, or if the whole building was moving. He opened his eyes and peered up at the Qintari remonstrating him.

“Are you deranged? I’ve only just managed to stabilise that humana creature, now here you are playing with the same machine that denatured his nerve endings.”

“Joseph, will he be alright?”

Gormbi's head throbbed as he silently listened to the doctor's explanation of Joseph's dire condition. The pounding in his head seemed to reflect the gravity of the situation, accompanied by the constant rumbling under his feet. As the doctor spoke, Gormbi couldn't help but recall the significant history he had with these humans and his profound concern for Joseph's well-being. His voice wavered with distress, conveying the intensity of his emotions.

In response, the doctor acknowledged the genuine connection between Gormbi and the humans. The concern they both shared for Joseph was evident in his voice, strengthening the bond that had formed between them. After a brief discussion, Gormbi made the challenging decision to put the ailing human in stasis as a temporary solution until they could obtain more advanced medical equipment. The doctor, fully aware of their limited options, recognised the situation and the necessity of taking this step.

Returning to the medical facility with a heavy heart, Gormbi and the doctor knew that they had exhausted all other viable options. Doctor Thloebek reluctantly gave his approval for Joseph's condition to be addressed through stasis. Solemnly, he stepped back from the medibed as a collector arrived to transport Joseph to stasis, a necessary measure in the absence of immediate medical solutions.

After swallowing an analgesic to alleviate his pounding head, Gormbi felt the floor shake beneath his feet, and an unsettling sense of urgency washed over him. *Is this another internal issue or are we facing an external threat?* The uncertainty gnawed at him, driving him to seek answers.

Turning to Doctor Thloebek, he offered a hasty explanation, his words interrupted by the urgency of the situation. "Now, if you excuse me, Doctor Thloebek,

I need to attend to some critical duties." With that, Gormbi left the doctor in mid-sentence, the Qintari raising a clawed finger in the air about to respond.

In the complex's corridors, Gormbi found himself at a crossroads, contemplating his next move. He weighed his options carefully, torn between checking on the K'Winni engineers who had been working on the power systems or heading to the observation room, where he knew all subspace activity was being monitored.

Suddenly, a deafening bang echoed down the corridor, sending vibrations through the structure. A ceiling panel dropped perilously close to his feet, revealing exposed support beams and tubules above. Gormbi's imprinted Maneran instincts kicked in, prompting him to make a swift decision. He decided that his next destination would be the Hamzitan room, a place that might hold clues to the source of this unexpected disturbance. As he opened the access panel behind the elevator, peering down the darkened shaft, he reaffirmed the wisdom of his decision. Descending twelve floors and then further down to the power plant would undoubtedly be a gruelling endeavour.

Floor one, Hamzitan observation room...

After an arduous climb to reach the Hamzitan room, Gormbi stood there, panting heavily. The dimly lit room enveloped him as he caught his breath, his chest heaving with the effort. His eyes darted around, taking in the frenzied scene displayed on the domed screen. The urgency of the situation became evident as alarms blared, their shrill tones piercing the air. Symbols on the screen marked the fresh movements originating from the Curak, their ominous presence unmistakable.

The deafening alarms resonated in Gormbi's ears, jarring him into immediate action. His heart raced as he focused on his paramount concern – the safety of the complex's inhabitants. Without a moment's hesitation, Gormbi hurried to access the complex's defence systems.

Navigating through the convoluted menus, Gormbi's frustration grew with each redundant or uninstalled system he encountered. Despite the hurdles, his unwavering sense of urgency propelled him forward. He persisted in his search for a viable solution, determined to find a way to protect those now under his care.

Eventually, he stumbled upon a ray of hope – a freshly installed operating system for the shield. It dawned on him that this must have been one of the last systems Erin had worked on, possibly in collaboration with Joseph. Without hesitation, he pressed the Maneran glyph on the console, gaining access to the system that held the key to their salvation.

His eyes darted across the display, absorbing the wealth of information before him. He recognized the meticulous repairs and upgrades performed by the K'Winni on the power systems, evidence of their dedication to fortifying their defences. The new defence system stood as a testament to Erin's ingenuity, and he noted that her repaired micro-probe was actively observing the newly erected subspace shield from the outside. The probe's data streamed before him, and Gormbi became increasingly engrossed in the intricate workings of the shield technology.

The subspace field's dance with electromagnetic energy held him spellbound. It shimmered and pulsated, a mesmerising display of defensive prowess. The shield absorbed and deflected the relentless photons emanating from the Corti suns, showcasing its formidable capabilities. The occasional burst of light marked the shield's unwavering determination in the face of the relentless swarm of attack craft.

As Gormbi continued to monitor the Curak fleet's menacing presence outside the complex, his unease deepened. The subspace shields valiantly held off the imminent threat, but the deteriorating condition of the complex and the dislodging ceiling panels cast doubt on its long-term viability.

Facing the console before him, Gormbi's Maneran instincts guided his fingers as he entered commands. He found himself searching the Maneran archives for a solution, driven by an instinctual certainty that Erin had prepared for this very situation. His fingers danced across the panel as he queried the archives for defensive algorithms.

With a plethora of information displayed before him, he discovered it—a recorded incident earlier documented by Erin's micro-probe. It recounted a moment when one of the Curak attack ships had collided with the complex's shield, resulting in its disintegration. Gormbi pondered this revelation, feeling as if Erin's virtual presence guided his thoughts. It became evident that she had detected a vulnerability in the Curak's defences but had been incapacitated before she could exploit it. Gormbi saw that the Curak had adjusted the balance between their shields and propulsion systems, favouring defence at the cost of manoeuvrability. Remarkably, the same intermittent blip in frequency that Erin had identified remained.

With determination, Gormbi initiated the modifications proposed in Erin's plan to the subspace transceiver, setting out to seize control of the Curak attack craft. His eyes widened in astonishment as he established dominion over the enemy vessels.

Now, he faced a momentous decision, torn between two paths. Should he opt for the ruthless course of crashing the Curak ships into the complex's shield, obliterating them entirely, or should he choose the compassionate route of safely landing the vessels? In a matter of moments, his humanity prevailed, and he decided on the latter. Demonstrating compassion in his actions, Gormbi incapacitated the Curak attack craft's occupants, ensuring their safety. He gently guided the ships to land in the serene meadowlands, effectively neutralizing the threat without causing harm.

With the Curak fleet now grounded and disarmed, Gormbi slumped into the chair behind him, exhaling a long huffled sigh of relief.

Inside the complex power station...

Yethril commended his team of engineers for having worked so diligently to complete the upgrades to the complex's defence system. The power systems hummed with efficiency, the newly installed components and modified plates seamlessly integrated and sealed into place. Yethril couldn't help but feel a sense of satisfaction with their work. They had spared no effort to ensure that the complex would be well-protected against external threats.

Yet, a cloud of unease hung over Yethril's thoughts – the puzzling absence of Erin, the stereographic human who had been overseeing the power system transformation. She had left her projection device behind, and her sudden disappearance had left him perplexed. Why would she abandon her post when their work was so critical? The question nagged at him, and he couldn't find a satisfactory answer, but at least the seismic activity had subsided.

Yethril's contemplation was abruptly interrupted by Gormbi's voice echoing ominously through the complex's announcement system. The translation of his words filled the power station, and Yethril's heart sank as he listened. Something had gone terribly wrong, and Erin, the sprite they had relied on for their safety, seemed to be incapacitated. The weight of the situation pressed down on him, and a sense of foreboding settled over his team, his earlier commendation evaporating like ether.

Without hesitation, Yethril summoned his team of engineers to join him in assessing the situation. It was imperative to understand what had led to Erin's disablement and Joseph's injury, the human ambassador. The engineers launched into a thorough investigation, retracing their steps to uncover any missteps, or overlooked details.

Yethril's team meticulously examined the complex's power systems, tracing their steps back to the root of the problem – a faulty plasmonic relay. It was during the diversion of power from generator four to an auxiliary distribution network, a necessary step to facilitate work on the primary system, that the relay, remaining fully open, had triggered an unintended power surge. The surge had rippled through the plasma grid, affecting Erin's interconnected network in the process. The engineers swiftly replaced the defective relay, initiating a reboot of the power control systems. Although power continued to serve the complex, Erin and her projection device remained unresponsive.

The guilt weighed heavily on Yethril as he and his fellow engineers confronted the consequences of their inadvertent actions. They had caused harm to their most valuable ally and ambassador, the human who had saved their sacred egg.

When Yethril explained their culpability to their Mowlan friend, little relief washed over him. Gormbi acknowledged the engineers' concerns, reassuring them that the incident was not their fault. He pointed out that the complex's infrastructure, as technologically advanced as it was, bore the signs of millennia-old fatigue. Even the service bots that maintained the complex were in need of maintenance themselves. Gormbi urged Yethril and his team to refocus on completing their work on the power systems, assuring him that addressing Erin's condition was his priority.

As Yethril and his team returned to their work, a sombre atmosphere hung in the power station. They were determined to make amends for their unintentional error and to ensure that the complex would continue to be fortified against any future threats. The weight of responsibility and the need to protect their newfound home weighed heavily on their hearts as they laboured on, driven by a profound sense of duty and remorse.

Outside on the mountain plateau...

Gormbi watched as the last collector returned, escorted by two tall K'Wan guards. Any lingering concern about the Bannar prisoners waking during their transfer into stasis evaporated. Doctor Thloebek, with his Qintari calm, joined the guards in supervising the process. Gormbi could see the doctor ensuring the prisoners' vitals were stable before they were gently ushered by on the humming collector. The sound resonated as the collector passed through the open portal, disappearing into the black and haze into the complex. Despite the prisoners' enforced aggressive tendencies, Gormbi couldn't help but feel a twinge of sorrow for them, caught in the aftermath of recent events. Nevertheless, he understood the necessity of their confinement for the safety of the complex and its inhabitants. Confirming the last Bannar prisoner had entered stasis, Gormbi nodded to Doctor Thloebek, acknowledging the success of their coordinated effort. The prisoners were now suspended in a state of hibernation, awaiting further resolution once the complex's immediate challenges were addressed.

Gormbi and the exhausted Qintari doctor stood together on the mountain plateau, overlooking the expansive meadowlands. Their camaraderie had flourished in the short time since their initial meeting, shaped by the extraordinary circumstances they both faced. As the Corti-2 sun set, casting shades of orange and pink across the sky, the doctor turned to Gormbi. Curiosity shimmered in his eyes as he wondered about the future. With a lingering question, he asked Gormbi about his plans.

Shifting his gaze from the setting sun to the doctor beside him, Gormbi carefully considered his response. The uncertainties of their situation weighed on his mind. Without Erin, his access to the subspace transceiver was limited, and critical tasks remained unresolved. The enigmatic humans were absent, with Joseph's incapacitation and the mystery surrounding his long-lost friend, Jack, further complicating matters.

With a firm determination, Gormbi finally spoke, his voice calm and reflective. “The future is uncertain, but I will do everything in my power to safeguard this facility. Eiren has activated a self-preservation protocol. She is fortunate to have access to the purged security cores. We will have to wait for Eiren to finish her repairs in order to determine our next steps. In the meantime, I would be glad to help you with your research. Together, we can utilise the data gathered by Eiren to develop the promised cure for your people.”

The doctor's gratitude was evident in his smile, his eyes fixed on the sun's fading glow. He conveyed the depth of his appreciation with heartfelt words. “I cannot express how grateful I am for all you have done. You have given me and my people hope for the future. Without a cure for the plague, at the rate my people are dying, we would soon cease to be.”

As the sun dipped below the horizon, casting long shadows across the plateau, Gormbi found solace in the shared journey that lay ahead. With determination in his heart, he affirmed their commitment to each other and to the challenges that awaited them. “It's what the Pitauran do for their allies,” he said, setting the tone for their collaborative efforts in the uncertain times ahead.

# Epilogue

"...that now I have found you, I have decided to bring you to me and return you to your friend."

The door to the stasis pod hissed open and its single occupant moved onto a medibed. Then, with the reanimation process complete, his body warmed, and his chest began to rise and fall. Gradually, as his eyes opened, Erin spoke to him using her soft voice.

"Hello Jack."

# ACKNOWLEDGEMENT

Thanks to all the friends and family who helped to make this novel possible. Without your support I could never have created these works.

A special shout-out must go to Carrie Magillen for all the authoring advice and direction. I wish you all the best with your own established creative path.

# ABOUT THE AUTHOR

## James Tepsey

I have had a diverse working life. It started with dairy farming, but later I transitioned into software engineering before becoming an electrician. In early 2020, I unexpectedly found myself with some free time and decided to resume my passion as an amateur Sci-Fi novelist. I also took the opportunity to consolidate all the writings I had been collecting.

After two decades of struggling with story plots and characters, I have finally completed my first book titled "Pitauran: Arrival". I hope you all enjoy reading my creation.